Nicholas Blincoe lives in London where he works as a freelance journalist. He is a regular contributor to *The Guardian*, Radio 4's *Afternoon Shift* and *The Big Issue*. His first novel, *Acid Casuals*, was published by Serpent's Tail.

Other Mask Noir titles

Alex Abella	*The Killing of the Saints*
Susan Wittig Albert	*Thyme of Death*
Gopal Baratham	*Moonrise, Sunset*
Pieke Biermann	*Violetta*
Nicholas Blincoe	*Acid Casuals*
Ken Bruen	*Rilke on Black*
Agnes Bushell	*The Enumerator*
Charlotte Carter	*Rhode Island Red*
Jerome Charyn	*Maria's Girls*
Didier Daeninckx	*Murder in Memoriam*
	A Very Profitable War
John Dale	*Dark Angel*
Stella Duffy	*Calendar Girl*
	Wavewalker
Graeme Gordon	*Bayswater Bodycount*
Gar Anthony Haywood	*You Can Die Trying*
Maxim Jakubowski (ed)	*London Noir*
Russell James	*Count Me Out*
Elsa Lewin	*I, Anna*
Walter Mosley	*Black Betty*
	Devil in a Blue Dress
	A Little Yellow Dog
	A Red Death
	White Butterfly
George P. Pelecanos	*Down by the River Where the Dead Men Go*
	A Firing Offense
Julian Rathbone	*Accidents Will Happen*
	Sand Blind
Derek Raymond	*The Crust on Its Uppers*
	A State of Denmark
Sam Reaves	*Fear Will Do It*
	A Long Cold Fall
Manuel Vazquez Montalban	*The Angst-Ridden Executive*
	Murder in the Central Committee
	Off Side
	An Olympic Death
	Southern Seas
David Veronese	*Jana*
Oscar Zarate (ed)	*It's Dark in London*

JELLO SALAD

Nicholas Blincoe

"Avenues and Alleyways": Words and music by Mitch Murray and
Peter Callender © Copyright 1973 ATV Music, London WC2. Used
by permission of Music Sales Limited. All rights reserved.
International copyright secured.
"Fume": Words and music by Beck. © Copyright 1994 Cyanide
Breathmint Music, USA. BMG Music Publishing Limited, 69–79
Fulham High Street, London SW6. This arrangement © Copyright
1996 BMG Music Publishing Limited. Used by permission of Music
Sales Limited. All rights reserved. International copyright secured.
"Moondance": Words and music by Van Morrison. © Copyright 1970
Caledonia Soul Music, Warner-Tamerlane Publishing Corp., USA
Warner/Chappell Music Publishing Ltd., London W1Y 3FA.
Reproduced by permission of International Music Publications Ltd.

Library of Congress Catalog Card Number: 96–71371

A complete catalogue record for this book can be
obtained from the British Library on request.

The right of Nicholas Blincoe to be identified as the
author of this work has been asserted by him in accordance
with the Copyright, Designs and Patents Act 1988

First published in 1997 by Serpent's Tail,
4 Blackstock Mews, London N4, website: www.serpentstail.com; and
180 Varick Street, 10th floor, New York, NY 10014

Phototypeset in 10pt ITC Century Book by
Intype London Ltd.
Printed in Great Britain by
Cox & Wyman Ltd., Reading, Berkshire.

To Robert Blincoe

PROLOGUE

Hogie stood at the edge of the floor, looking out on the technicians, the cameras, feeling his brains steam-bake inside his chef's wimple. Monitors, left and right, cranked through the running order. The fake kitchen was unlit but ready, the herbs and cuts all laid out in bowls, only waiting for the mikes and lights to swing low. He turned to the researcher and she reconfirmed the cooking spot was fifth on the schedule. The audience was still taking their seats, no one would need him for at least thirty minutes. If he'd forgotten his way back to the hospitality room, she could show him. Hogie nodded. He was just doing preparation, you know—trying to rise to the occasion. He had to say, neither palpitations nor tremors gave the flavour. This was general hysteria, Krakatoa of the skull.

The researcher led him out of the studio and into a corridor panelled with television screens. For the past few hours, she had waited on him hand and foot, mouth and nose. As she walked along, she reminded him—*whatever he needed, he only had to ask.* She told him he should just relax, get to know the other guests in hospitality.

He said, "Did you hear what happened to me on that morning show in Liverpool?"

She nodded. "Don't worry about that. That was daytime, we're past the watershed now. No one's going to notice if you're a bit over-excited."

"Yeah?" She couldn't blame him for worrying though. He'd done so badly that time, he never expected to get a second chance at television glory. His dream of being a top TV chef over because of a wigged-out misunderstanding.

They were just passing the dressing rooms when he heard the theme tune to the on-the-hour News. The TV sets along the corridor flashed blue as the channel logo spun across the screen, followed by a dissolve to the news anchor. It was just past midnight and the programme was leading with a screamer—the fifth in a series of weird killings. Hogie stopped—this was something he needed to watch.

There was a camera crew at the scene but the reporter was soft-pedalling on the colour, sticking to basic details like the place, a rough time of death—giving no real description of the murder. The corpse had surfaced downstream of Bow Creek in the East End, floating in a bubble of plastic sheeting. On-screen, a police officer was refusing to confirm that the victim had been disembowelled but the key word was *ritualistic*. As in all the week's murders, speculation centered on religion, on crime and on drugs—either in combination or separately. Hogie didn't even want to think about any new twist. This time, he was sure, it was Cheb's body they'd found. The researcher tried to grab hold of his arm but he pulled free and set off running.

"Leave me alone."

He didn't even realise he was heading back to the studio floor. He just needed time and space to think. They eventually brought him down at the edge of the seating bank, rugby-tackled by the floor manager and two other technicians. No one was taking any chances on a berserk cooker-boy, fuelled by drugs and regret. The news had finished, their programme was about to begin.

The cameras started to circle a media-friendly psychoanalyst, squirming on the low slung, late-nite sofa. As the opening theme faded, the man began to argue that there was no connection between any of the week's killings—just an unconscious societal wish to turn death into a spectacle. The interviewer said, "What, like a circus?"

The analyst slapped the coffee table with his new book, "Exactly, a circus or a carnival." Pause for close-up on the title—*The Killer Carnival*.

Hogie tore off his hat. No way he could fillet anything, not after listening to a lunatic headshrinker chant *Carnival/ Carnivore, do you see? It's the way of all flesh?* while the woman interviewer just nodded. He wasn't going to cause a scene. He was just going to walk away.

The producer met him at the exit. She was there to remind him he was under contract, if he refused to do his cooking spot she would sue.

"So? Fucking sue me."

The researcher slipped around his outside. With one hand jamming the door and the other on his arm, she told him no other channel would touch him after he'd turned up stoned the last time he appeared on television. He wasn't the only over-hyped, boy-wonder chef in the country but after what happened in Liverpool, he was already an industry-wide liability. This was his last chance and he only had one thing to sell—intimate and personal knowledge of the killer's victims. *Use it or lose it.* Then she whispered that the producer was so keen to keep him in the studio, on-air, the woman was ready to sign over her car, her personal credit card, anything Hogie wanted.

He knew, if he agreed, it was some kind of betrayal—to the memories of the dead, to his friends and their mothers. Going down that route, he could expect serious payback. Cheb had taught him the rules of karma, so he knew what to expect. This huge, fuck-off tragedy was airborne, launched from the swamp lands of his past sex sins. He only had himself to blame.

He said, "One second. Let me go freshen up. I'll be there."

Whatever else happened, it was some way to crown a
bad week...

PART ONE

upforit

ONE

Even standing at the far side of the bar, Gloria Manning could hear every word Hogie said.

"We didn't know why we were losing so much money. We checked the form before every race. We looked to see how they'd been running and how they were fancied. We worked out the combinations: reverse forecasts, always trios. Cheb had some kind of spacey system he wanted to play but I couldn't figure the geometry. In the end, we bet on the favourite every time."

He was sat at the other end of the room telling everyone about his trip to the dogs at Belle Vue. Gloria didn't have to strain to listen but she hung on for the punchline. Paused between a pillar and the bar, she was absolutely ringside.

Hogie never stopped talking. "Not one of our dogs came in. Not one. Cheb was stuffing his pockets with torn-up slips. I was slapping the form sheet on his bald head and screaming they were a tissue of falsehoods. We were looking for greyhounds, all we got was fucking bassets. Then we realised what had happened. We were so stoned, we were always one race ahead of the track. We didn't know it but we'd cashed out on the wrong fucking races."

He scanned around the table, milking the scene. Wide blue eyes and arms outstretched: *Can you believe it?* Half his friends were spluttering, the boy they called the Sandman choked on a round-lipped "God no". Only Jools didn't get it. She held on almost to the end with a misfit look on her cry-baby face but if Hogie wanted to take her with him he was going to have to go much, much more slowly.

Gloria knew all his friends by name, the real ones or the ones they'd made-up. She saw most of them, from time to time, whenever they surfaced in their home corner. Only Hogie and Cheb had ever found a reason to leave Manchester completely: they were both gone before they turned eighteen. This was nothing more than a one-night overnight stop-over. Still, they seemed to fit right back in place. Hogie with all the stories and most of the elbow room, cramped at a table with ten of his friends. Cheb at the bar, failing to buy the drinks. He'd been standing there for fifteen minutes and was still arguing with the barmaid. He had three credit cards fanned out in front of her face, asking her what kind of place refused AmEx fuck-me Platinum.

Back at Hogie's table, Jools was still chasing the dog story, saying: "How could you be ahead of the track? Didn't you know which dogs you'd picked?"

Gloria knew, Hogie was a special kind of idiot but the mistake was easier to make than she realised. Apart from the fact that the dogs all looked the same, you only ever bet on the number of the lane and never on the dog's name.

Hogie said, "No. We'd got no idea which dog we picked, we just checked for the favourite and slapped down the bet. But instead of getting the star dog, we got the one using the same lane in the earlier race. We lost over two hundred quid before we realised."

One of them, a kid called Roly, gagged on a mouthful of peanut splinters. "Shit no. Two hundred pounds!"

"*Oh my God shit yes*. It's what I was saying, Cheb had this system. We had to multiply everything we lost by the odds on the next favourite. Or vice versa. To be honest, it wasn't like I gave a shit at that point."

The Sandman asked how they realised the truth.

Hogie said, "You know at Belle Vue, they have this huge fuck-off scoreboard over the track, where they flash the times of the races? Well, we were watching it all night so we should have known what was wrong, but we didn't. We were laughing, pointing up at the board and saying it was so slow, it was always a race behind. Cheb was ready to complain to the management. He was saying he couldn't fucking believe it, the man keying-in the data had to be tripping, he was so fucking tardy with the results. If they thought this was any way to run a dog track, they were out of the fucking loop. He was ready to run up there and sort it out himself."

Jools again, slurred but still decipherable: "Did he do it?"

Hogie shook his head, No. "We decided to skin up one more time instead and went looking for somewhere quiet. We were halfway across the carpark when Cheb said 'Do you reckon the board was right and we were in the wrong?' It just hit me. Of course we were wrong. We were so monged, we'd forgotten just how fucking stupid we are."

Hogie slapped his forehead for effect.

Pause.

"So then we caught a cab down to Chinatown and won the whole wad back at roulette."

Jools, one last time: "What, everything?"

Hogie nodded as he looked calmly around the table. He'd grown his blond hair long and together with his moustache-beard combination he managed to approximate a Christ-like simplicity. Until he exploded. "No fucking way. We were seriously creamed. We didn't have a prayer."

That was the punchline. This was their school reunion.

Hogie was also friends with Gloria's son, Mannie, who should have been there but was probably too stoned to make it. Her daughter Jools just tagged along. All night, Gloria had watched as the girl screamed or whined and failed to hold Hogie's attention. She was now so drunk she couldn't do anything but shout whenever she needed a fresh rum and coke. Her head barely level with the empty glasses, emptied too fast for the barstaff to collect. The only ones among them that weren't drunk had to be doped-up, speeding or worse, Gloria knew.

Cheb was still hanging on to the bar but the situation was getting ridiculous. Now he was trying to pass off a Diners Club card and expecting them to accept it. Finally he gave up, waiting for the bargirl to turn her back before slipping off the stool and heading for the door. He was an arm's length from Gloria when he passed her but he didn't look up and he didn't see her. The boy had never grown above five foot two. The only things that five years away had changed were his hair and skin. He left Manchester shaggy and sun-free. Now he was tanned to the dome with his head shaved to the bone. When he signalled to Hogie it was nothing more than a nod but his head caught the light.

Hogie saw it, anyway. He skirted round Jools and met Cheb at the exit. Standing next to each other, they looked the same as they had as kids. Hogie was stooped, just a little but there would have been a foot between them if he straightened up. They had always stayed close. And they always had something to say that they didn't want anyone else to hear. Gloria moved along the bar. She caught Hogie's voice first. From the tone, she could tell he was repeating himself.

"They wouldn't take the card?"

Cheb flashed him a *"Don't Ask"*.

"What name were you using?"

"Francis Woo."

"You were using a Chinese name? You look nothing like a Chink."

"I told her I was a Vietnam boat-child but she wouldn't have it. She was saying, *'No you're not: You're Jason Beddoes, I went to school with you.'* I tell you, if she calls the cops we're fucked. We got to shoot."

Hogie looked back over to the table. "Okay. I got Jools's car keys. What do you reckon, we dump her?"

"Fuck yes."

They turned at the same time and found themselves staring straight at Gloria. At least Hogie had the sensitivity to blush. True, Cheb looked anxious, his eyes side-winding around the room, but it wasn't embarrassment. Seeing Gloria standing there, he was probably just worried he might see his own mum, lurking at the next corner.

Hogie said, "We're just off to find your Mannie, Mrs Manning." He tried to make it sound like a goodwill mission but he still hadn't lost his blush.

"Yeah? Well don't get him into trouble."

Cheb turned to look at her, saying: "Not us, Mrs Manning. We couldn't do it if we tried." His face deadpan, as though he expected her to believe him.

Over at the bar, the girl who'd refused to serve him was now talking to the manager. As she spoke she pointed in their direction. Hogie caught the gesture. He had his hand on Cheb's arm, saying, "We'd better be going," as he shuffled on the spot. Only Cheb didn't seem to be in much of a hurry anymore. Once he'd satisfied himself that he wasn't going to see his mother, he seemed happy to stand around and make everyone else uncomfortable. Now he was asking Gloria about her daughter.

"I heard she's doing alright. She's some kind of star, isn't she?"

Hogie had to explain: "Cheb's been travelling for a couple of years, Mrs Manning. He's only just heard about Jools."

Gloria looked back over her shoulder. Jools was still at the table, near to collapse with her hair spooling into the dregs around the glasses. The girl was no star. She was a bit-part actress in a soap and the way she looked now, she'd reached her limit.

Behind her, Hogie said, "Yeah, well we'd better go. Bye, Mrs Manning."

Gloria kept her eyes on her daughter and her mouth closed.

Jools's car was parked in a loop of road, diverted from the main road to give parking room at a kosher butchers. Cheb couldn't believe a TV actress would have such a terrible car.

Hogie said, "What's wrong with it?"

It was some kind of boxy Subaru but Cheb's main problem was the stereo. He claimed it was ju-ju'ed, it had his tape stuck in its mouth but it wasn't swallowing. He jabbed it in and out of the slot a couple of times then gave up.

"So what's this programme she's starring in anyway?"

It was the planet's weakest soap. Hogie said, "It's called *Pony Trek* but she's not the star. She's been on it less than a year and they already want to kill her off."

Cheb said, "Yeah I forgot. You're the only wannabe TV star in the area." He was feeling through his pockets now— when his fingers came out they held a small square of paper, a folded wrap. When he emptied it onto the Subaru's dashboard there was maybe a half line each left of the coke they'd bought the night before.

"Hey Hogie. You want to open the sunroof? Let's do this thing right, underneath the stars."

Hogie reached up for the dinky handle and wound the cover back. It was a drizzle-free evening but it wasn't exactly full moon over Koh Phang Nga beach—or any of the other places Cheb had described. With a million street lights, the sky over Manchester never got entirely dark. The stars were barely visible through the city's amber canopy.

Cheb started work on the coke with a rolled fifty, hoovering away in a wild circular motion that somehow strayed over his line and onto the next. When he passed the note to Hogie, there was nothing but left-over crumbs.

"Yeah, sorry about that Hoges. I guess I got more than

my share. You sure we're going to be able to get more down town?"

Hogie said, "Yeah. I told you, Mannie's a professional pusher, now. Anything we want, that's what he told us."

Cheb nodded and relaxed. "So what about his mam, then? You reckon she was giving you the eye."

"Fuck off Cheb. She was sympathising because I have to put up with so much of Jools's shit."

Hogie turned the ignition. The stereo came on, starting at the first chord to a Beck track—a country kind of a beat with lyrics about driving round in a pick-up truck with a canister of nitrous oxide. Cheb picked it up at the chorus: *There's fumes in the truck and we don't know if we're dead or what.* Hogie joined in as soon as he'd coughed back the sour plug that the cocaine had left in his throat.

They were still singing when Jools came screaming out of the pub and across the dual carriageway towards them. She had her fists up, flailing as she weaved across the central reservation, pure dementia on her face.

Cheb said, "Looks like her mother grassed us up."

Hogie only wound down the side window because she threatened to punch it through. He tried to spin her a line but in the end he had no choice. He lifted the door stud and let her take the backseat, shrugging over to Cheb. "It's her car."

T W O

Shards of a broken brandy glass flecked the tiles. The bottle lay another four drunk paces on in a sticky pool of sun-dried alcohol. Susan Ball stepped sweetly around the debris, her slingbacks slapping at the back of her foot, her high-heels clicking on the tiles. She remembered a joke. Why do women have legs? The punch-line ran: Have you seen the mess slugs make?—but it was Frankie who always came back legless. His slug-trail of brandy, vomit, coke dust and broken glass stretched from the door, out towards the pool and back through the slide doors to the foot of the stairs which was where he'd probably slept. He was gone now but she could trace his movements.

She would have to clear it up. So long as the villa was clean, he wouldn't notice she was gone. It might be another twenty-four hours before he realised their marriage was over. But first she needed coffee. She couldn't face his mess while she was fresh awake, still in her bathrobe and only just out of the shower. She hadn't even had a first cigarette.

The kitchen radio was tuned to the local station, every song clicking away at three Spanish beats to the bar. Susan was naturally a backbeat girl but she tried a few steps, high-tailing it round the kitchen with her robe swinging behind her and her heels stamping out the time. She rounded the movement off with a high-kick before she risked losing the beat. It set her giggling. A cigarette in one hand and the other on the door of a fridge, she danced like a tart in a cheap TV sketch.

Before the coffee boiled she dialled her son. All she got was the answering machine, a snatch of happy techno, fol-lowed by Callum's short stoned message—*Speak up, Hang up or Chill out*—and a run of beeps. There were maybe three or four messages stacked ahead of her. She hooked the phone back on the wall and checked the kitchen clock. He could be out but was more likely to be asleep. Like her, he was a late riser. Twelve years on the Costa and neither of them had got used to the hours. Instead of sleeping around the hottest parts of the day, they woke at noon and got the full glare on their strawberry blond skin. He better wake soon, he was supposed to be buying their tickets home.

It took her another three cigarettes and at least that amount of coffee before she felt like rolling up her sleeves.

The mop and bucket were in the hall closet with Frankie's firearm collection. He'd fitted a rack to the wall for his two shotguns but kept the automatics in an Arsenal bag behind the barbecue briquettes. Only one of the shotguns was in place. The sawn-off was missing, so Frankie had probably gone out shooting things. It explained why she hadn't found him asleep at the end of his slug-trail. He had to be the only person who ever went hunting with a sawn-off shotgun. He claimed it was more accurate and she never argued. Anyway, he was a rotten shot and always had been. He was only accurate over a range of twelve inches but at that distance he was devasting. He even had the press clippings to prove it: a photograph of a bank guard with half his head blown away and an article saying the police wanted to interview Frank "Ballistic" Ball. That would have been in '67, the year she first met him. The case was dismissed and they were married soon after his release.

She looked in the sportsbag, the machine gun was gone too. Susan pitied anyone stupid enough to go hunting with her husband. He'd be wearing glasses by now if he ever visited an optician. Although what good glasses would do against his everyday hangover, she did not know.

He'd have taken her jeep. He always left the Mercedes when he went hunting but she hated driving the big car through the town's narrow streets. Today was even worse, if she dumped his car at the airport he'd soon know she was gone. She'd have to wait until evening to exchange keys. Maybe six o'clock, he'd reach the pub. It was cutting it fine but she needed her own car and if she saw him with a pack of his friends she would at least remember why she was leaving. The other wives put up with the pub, the sing-songs, the Saturday night knees-ups and all the weeping nostalgia that kept their husbands sweet. She didn't bother. Frankie was so whacked out, nothing made much difference. Spain and boredom had done it for him.

It took half an hour to sluice the tiles around the villa, inside and out. Later, she thought about taking a swim but the sun was too strong. She blamed the heat whenever she was on edge, she only ever reached equilibrium when the sun was on its way down. It probably had nothing to do with the temperature. She'd been just the same back in England: a night-time girl. It was why she'd worked as a hostess after she moved down to London. She was nineteen when she left Manchester and had enough talent to have made it on TV, a dancer on *Saturday Night at the London Palladium* or something, but working the clubs had suited her rhythm. Her rhythm and the taste she had for criminals. At the time, she thought there was nothing sexier than a young crook with too much money and too much zinc in his blood.

The third night she met Frankie, she hauled him into the dressing room while the other girls were on stage. Inside two minutes, she had his pants undone and his Y-front briefs pulled sideways around his erection. After she finished, she used the three fivers he'd given her to wipe her hands and his cock then handed them back saying he'd better give her new ones, these were spoilt. Frankie zipped up, took a roll out of his suit and peeled off another couple. He looked so cool. No doubt though, she'd worn better than him. For years she hadn't been able to look at a five pound note with a straight face. Nowadays, she was reminded of him every time she cleaned the fungus off the swimming pool filter and that never raised a smile.

Back in the kitchen, the radio was still pumping its tricky Spanish beats. She re-tuned. The station for ex-pats was playing "If You Go Away" by Scott Walker. When it came to it, you couldn't beat true British pop.

She tried calling Callum another three times but only got the answering machine. Her phone started ringing halfway through Glen Campbell's version of "By The Time I Get To Phoenix". She stopped laughing-along and grabbed for the receiver, hoping it was her son. It wasn't—the voice at the other end was unmistakeable.

She said, "Hi George. How's the accountancy?"

George Carmichael always sounded like he was gargling engine coolant, "Fine. So what about you, are you all set for your return?"

She told him the tickets and her suitcases were ready and waiting for her at Callum's apartment.

"So what are you wearing now?"

She had a wardrobe full of clothes besides the caseful she'd smuggled to her son's the night before. But she admitted she was still in her dressing gown.

He said, "Goodness, if Frankie knew you were talking to me semi-undressed . . ."

Susan said, "He knows you're a puff."

"Is he mellowing with age?"

"He's marinated. Just the same as he ever was only none of it's particularly appetising any more. He's bored and he's stewing in his boredom. So, no, he's not mellowed. I've got to get out, I don't want Callum turning into something like him."

When she told him that she couldn't find Callum, George said, "Maybe he's stolen your clothes and run off to join a cabaret."

It was some kind of puff humour, assuming everyone else was bent. He didn't push the joke or the subtext—that she'd prefer any kind of mummy's boy to a replica of Frankie. He didn't talk business either. Instead, he told her he had a story about a dancer. He'd been saving it for her.

She smiled.

George said, "It seems this boy's main employment was telly commercials. He'd been a high-kicking carrot for a frozen food company, a bank clerk who changed into Fred Astaire for an insurance company, all kinds of gigs like that. The work paid well, but no one could call it regular and he had to find a new way to make money. In the end, he decided to become a male prostitute. He had a soft heart, at one time he thought about becoming a nurse, so he was sure the work would suit him."

George had to explain, the dancer knew a man who ran an escort agency but the agency specialised in octagenarians, cripples and anyone generally unsound in limb. Hence the materiality of the dancer's near-vocation for nursing. Was Susan following? George apologised for getting the whole story fanny-first.

Susan said, "No. I'm following it." It didn't matter which way George told a story. Anytime she heard his gravel-purr voice, she just relaxed into it.

"The dancer visited one particular character who was paraplegic; he'd been in a car crash or something and suffered massive spinal damage. When the dancer first met him, he thought 'Christ!' Naturally. What could anyone do for him, he had no control over anything below his shoulders. But the client was very specific, he explained exactly what he wanted and it didn't call for motor skills— just a few elaborate props. In fact, so elaborate that the client suggested they video the whole scene . . ."

A pause while she listened to him drag on his cigarette.

" . . . well, the dancer normally steered clear of home videos but he agreed. They weren't likely to repeat it often and a video would be some kind of testament to the experience. So a week later the dancer arrived with a rented camera and the rest of the necessaries. The star item was a headpiece, a kind of helmet but open at the top. Can you imagine?"

She pictured a cripple, sat in his chariot, wearing something like a chimney pot on his head. She gave George an *uh-huh*, she had the picture.

"The helmet had an elasticated neck piece so it fitted snug and watertight. Once it was in place, the dancer filled it to the rim with five litres of orange jelly and tangerine chunks."

"Christ, wouldn't that scald?"

"I guess he waited for the mix to cool before he poured it into the helmet. The client got off on the feeling of the jelly setting around him, enclosing him in tasty lumps of fruit."

"How did the cripple breathe?"

"I don't know. Maybe he used a snorkel or something, you'll have to use your imagination. Anyway. Apparently it took a while for the jelly to set. The dancer had to rig up an air conditioning unit and sit the cripple right in front of it until the cold air froze his head. But when the helmet was pulled off, he was left with a perfectly round translucent orange jelly on his head."

"What was the gimmick?"

"He wanted to be orally abused with various objects—nothing bad: a banana, an eclair, that kind of thing—while the heat in the house made the jelly melt. The whole scene would end with the dancer getting a gobble as the mask collapsed and slithered down the client's head."

"It couldn't work."

"It worked, believe me. But what the dancer didn't know was, prior to his accident, the cripple had been an artist and he saw the whole scene as performance art. The next thing the dancer knew, the jelly head appeared on posters all over town. He couldn't believe it, the video won an award at some obscure German festival and was showing at an art-house cinema in the West End. Word got around, Jello Head Man became a celebrity and the dancer couldn't get any more work in advertising."

"Is that a true story?"

George shrugged, What else could it be?

"So what's the moral?"

"No matter how perverted someone seems, you'd better watch out they don't have a rational explanation."

Susan laughed as she said, "Is that a warning?"

"A promise. Your business is safe in my hands. I've even bought you the restaurant you wanted. I've got the opening party all planned to coincide with your return."

She wanted to know, was jelly on the menu?

George said, "Only if Frankie finds out what we're doing."

They both knew Frankie would find out. She was starting divorce proceedings in the morning but if she wanted alimony, she'd need all of George's help. She asked how the rest of the account was doing, "Is it multiplying?"

"Yes. Secretly, assiduously. The whole operation's so legitimate, if Frankie was extradited tomorrow they wouldn't be able to recover a penny."

Susan hoped he'd give them a little longer than that.

George said, "Did you get the keys to your new flat?"

She had. They'd arrived by FedEx at their bank in Marbella with a short note giving an address in Marylebone. Everything was working out fine. Frankie cared so little about the way his business was run he never visited the bank. It was her job to check the accounts and oversee George's investments. As long as his credit cards and the local cash machine worked, Frankie never asked questions.

George was still fussing about the keys. "You've got them then?"

"Yes. Except they're round at Callum's with the rest of my things."

Packed and ready. George had to say he was surprised. "I never thought you'd return to London."

He'd always said she was a provincial girl at heart, that she couldn't take the big city speed. She told him, "I always said London would be a cool place to live. If all the Londoners would sod off back to Essex where they belong and left the place for everyone else."

George was born in Kentish Town but he didn't bother reminding her. All he said was, "Yeah, well hurry back. You're the star guest at the restaurant's grand opening party."

She'd almost forgot, "You remember Callum wants to DJ on the night?"

"You're the boss."

She was. Or she intended to be. She asked George what the people were like who were running her new restaurant.

He said, "There's two of them, Hogie and Cheb. The cook's really good, he's going to be a star."

"And the other one?"

George said, "He's definitely jello salad. But he's also the chef's best friend so he'll have to do. He's some kind of New Age type, interested in exotic religions and back-packing round the East. That kind of thing."

Susan said, "One of those."

THREE

Behind the cathedral, in the loop of cellars beneath Manchester's Corn Exchange. It was only just past eleven o'clock but the club was already so crammed it was unhealthy. Mannie would have had made the bouncers carry government warnings: *Anyone tending towards claustrophobia take a long wide swerve.* The low ceilings didn't help. The place was scooped out of the building's Victorian foundations and styled along some kind of crypt theme with a maze of roughcast fibreglass corridors. Mannie stood with his back to the plastic grotto wall, waiting. This was the absolute worst hour of the night, when a club was hot and crowded but hadn't started kicking. He'd prefer to skip this stage, fuck the sense of anticipation and power up to the next level. Then he saw Cheb and Hogie.

He recognised Cheb despite the serious head-shave. The high scalp emphasised the demon in him. What he'd heard, Cheb had spent the last couple of years frying his brains in Thailand beach bars, listening to old acid tracks and trance and watching Vietnam war films. Whatever, it hadn't slowed him down. He came jolting down the steps like a superball. Hogie's progress was slinkier, tossing his blondilocks. He'd even managed to grow a beard without looking like a prick but he was born lucky and nothing dented his pure aura. Mannie would have called out but he saw his sister in time. Maybe Hogie wasn't so lucky, Jools had followed him around since school. Mannie knew how painful it was having Jools anywhere close so he stayed hidden.

Cheb shuffled himself out of the group before they hit the dancefloor, leaving Hogie and Jools to find a corner seat. He was carrying the wad, so he headed for the bar. On the drive into town he'd made Hogie stop at every bank they passed while he raided the cash machines. This was supposed to be a pleasure trip and he didn't want any more embarrassing face-offs with his credit cards. They might be fakes but they nearly all worked. He collected more than five hundred quid just coming down Cheetham Hill.

He never saw Mannie. A couple of yards shy of the bar, an arm snaked out and pulled him sideways. He found himself standing in a dim alcove, being shouted at by some mournful-looking geek.

"Mannie, is that you mate? Why are you hiding?"

Mannie nodded back across the dancefloor towards his sister. Cheb turned. He had to say, she was looking almost sober after the excitement of the drive.

"Yeah, sorry mate. But she's totally fucking adhesive."

Mannie didn't have to be told. "Forget it, mate. It's good to see you. So what's with the coiffure?"

Cheb ran a hand across his scalp. "Smooth eh? What about you, though? You were supposed to meet us at the pub, you no-show bastard."

At least he looked apologetic. "Yeah, I'm sorry. The truth is, I been feeling a bit schizzy the last few days but I'm hoping to mellow out when the drugs start working."

This was what Cheb wanted to hear. "Yeah? Hogie said you're dealing now."

He shook his head. "That's one of my problems. I had a run of evil luck and quit the business. I won't be able to help you."

Cheb should have known. Whatever Mannie touched, pretty soon it began smelling like it died. He said, "What about our party next week. Hogie said you'd see us right."

"This grand restaurant opening thing? I might be able to sort something out, I don't know. But you're on your own tonight."

There was a boy leaning against the cigarette machine, with a Charlie Manson stare and a pierced tongue. Mannie pointed towards him: "Tell him I sent you. I'll catch you later, when you lose Jools."

Cheb okayed. He was about to go when Mannie called him back.

"Hey, what's with you and the restaurant. I know Hogie's going to be the chef but what are you going to do?"

"I'm the maitre d', maintaining the vibes and bonhomie and shit."

"So why'd they choose you?"

Cheb flashed a fat smile. "Someone's got to make mankind feel good before its eventual destruction."

He carried on smiling, walking backwards into the crowd until it closed around him. He didn't know but maybe he'd got a smile off Mannie for a second. Call him Mr Glum.

Over at the cigarette machine, he asked for eight grams of speed and ten tabs of acid. The guy told him there were no discounts on bulk purchases. That was fine, Cheb never expected to get a good price with Mannie's recommendation. He counted the notes off his roll—£170.

When he got back to Hogie and Jools, there was already quite a crowd. Hogie was entertaining a bunch of strangers with the story of the barmaid and her racist refusal to accept any credit card issued by the Hong Kong and Shanghai Bank.

Someone asked, "How many cards you got?"

"Around ten. Visa, American Express and one Diners Club."

"Ten? All stolen?"

"No, none are stolen. They're copies. Me and Cheb are going to set ourselves up in business making more."

Cheb came up on his blind side, slapping him across the head and slipping a gram of whizz into his hand as he spun around.

"Here, I got some trips as well. Better than an E, we won't end up with Alzheimers."

Hogie stared at the tiny squares of acid, squinting at the picture in the centre of each tab. "Purple dragons? Nice one, Cheb. What do I owe you?"

"On the house, courtesy of the Cheb credit plan." Then whispering, "Just don't tell everyone about the fucking cards."

"You getting antsy, mate."

"I'm fine."

"No mate, you're anxious." Hogie gave him the full comic Oprah, holding out his arms. "Do you want to share?"

Cheb took a step back to look him up and down. "You're fucking beautiful, you know that?"

"Yeah? Then come on felch me you donkey dick bastard."

Cheb was laughing but he dried up as soon as Jools came pushing through. She'd caught a sniff of the drugs and was whining for her share. He passed her a wrap and a trip. Off to his side, he saw Hogie slope off but before he could follow she had him cornered. She told him she wanted to know about Buddhism. She had this idea it might help with her television career.

The sound system had cranked up a notch, still on over-ture mode but beginning to throw out dark hints: slow, deep House veined through with trippy beeps. Hogie swam into it, leaving Cheb to set Jools straight on Buddhist law. Cheb loved explaining that stuff. Only it seemed to Hogie he never quite repeated the principles the exact same way every time. Still, it was Jools's call. So long as it kept her busy.

Hogie kept moving, managing to hit every fault line as he threaded his way along. If the crowd wouldn't part for him, he turned himself into Elastic Man and slipped through anyhow. Eventually, he found the toilets at the foot of a dead-end flight of stairs. The stalls were full but the cubicle was free. Locked inside, he laid his speed out on the top of the cistern box. The painted metal was flaking and rusting but he found a flattish patch and snorted off that.

When the speed kicked in a half hour later he was still wandering, trying to get his bearings while he scouted out Mannie. The way the club was laid out, it was easy to get lost. Far easier to just keep moving and wait for events to arise. Just now, it was time to take his Purple Dragon. As the acid touched the back of his throat, he felt the twang of electricity play across the nape of his neck and shoot down his spine. His solar plexus tightened and relaxed. It would be three-quarters of an hour before the sideshow began but the whole of his body was already in serious chemicular anticipation. By the time he came face-to-face with his boy on the steps down to the ambient room he had forgotten he was even looking for him. He ended up throwing him a hug, saying: Yeah, I Love You Mannie Mate.

"Your eyes, Hoges."

Hogie opened wide. "They looking good?"

"Like fucking saucers. Scary. Wrap your smile around this."

He handed over a loose-packed spliff. Hogie drew hard on the extra-long roach, holding the smoke tight to his gullet as he passed it back with a throaty thanks.

Mannie said, "You seen my sister?"

"Not lately."

"Well I've seen Cheb and he says she's looking for us both. Apparently she's complaining the speed was dud so the bastard said either me or you would give her more."

"Oh shit."

Mannie crossed himself, "Come on, we're dancing. If we move fast enough, she won't be able to catch us."

He led Hogie through a rubberised tunnel, ending in a low room, pumped with dry-ice. The heat from the dancers had turned into vapour, reeking of poppers and Vicks chest rub. Mannie was handed a bottle of amyl and he passed it onto Hogie. The fumes opened out inside his lungs. He just had time to re-cap the bottle before his head went upside in a blast of red noise. The music was punching up into a mindless frenzy. He loved it. As he danced he made silent Woo-Woo train noises with his mouth, sucking at the air in shallow gulps. His arms jacked out in front of him like a mad drill.

Mannie nudged him and passed a cigarette over. He took it without noticing it wasn't a spliff. As he dragged at the filter, something boiled over inside him, kicking a thermo-dynamic charge straight to his heart. The cigarette had been soaked in amyl. Fuck, Hogie thought. I fucking love this.

Woo Woo. He propelled himself backwards, into the pulp core of dancers hoping the crush of bodies would form a protective circle. Across the room, he thought he heard Jools shout his name but she didn't come after him. Soon he was flailing through new waves of dry-ice, losing himself in the lighting patterns, the sequencers, the bpm's. A girl stroked down his spine with her fingernail and when he turned his smile onto her, she smiled back. Her eyes were round and framed in shadows of blueish grey. Her lips were pulled thin by her smile and her hair lay flat and wet against her skull. She might have been nineteen. She bore an imprint of what she might look like in thirty years time. Later days. Later days. Hogie would come back to her if he could. He flung his arms up in the air and span away. Mannie rose up ahead of him, taking the pace up a gear, his six skinny arms waving like Shiva. Hogie kept the faith. He could not believe how fast his legs were moving, they were a blur below him. They bicycled around like the legs of the Roadrunner when he hurtles past Wile E Coyote. Woo Woo.

Jools dragged him off the dancefloor by his elbows. He stood, melting in sweat, trying to catch his wet breath as she talked up at him. The hot drops of water sliding across his face picked up salt from his hair and stung his eyes. Mannie had disappeared. He couldn't concentrate on Jools or the words tumbling out of her widening plastic mouth.

She was saying she had a fear of celebrity stalkers. Whenever she went to the bar, she could feel every sleaze in the place trying to close in on her. Wherever she went, they started crowding in and asking what would happen in the next episode of *Pony Trek*. Could he imagine what that felt like?

Jools had the most unseductive whine. She pleaded with him as she stroked the back of his head. "Let me come and stay with you in London."

Hogie could have choked. "No way. I mean, don't you have to work?"

"Didn't you hear? I've been killed-off. A drunk driver swerves across the road and I'm crushed. So can I come and stay with you?"

Hogie scrolled through a stack of excuses. His flat was a slum clearance project, halfway to a fucking barrio, especially since Cheb had flown in with no home of his own. And if she wanted to hear about work, that was another impossibility. Since he'd landed the new job, he had a mass of preparation to think through. He had no space, he had no time, he couldn't help her and that was the truth. She looked like she had something to say but Hogie started running. He knew if he stayed talking any longer, he'd end by mentioning the opening night party.

Straight up two flights of stairs, he found himself in a pizza queue. The smell of bad food had always made him nauseous. After a full gram of sulphate, the nausea was worse than ever. He staggered round until he found a back staircase and leapt out, touching down in the chill-out room where a warm-oil show was playing across the ceiling and the floor was layered deep in mattresses. The music here was ambient, meaninglessly trippy, but aside from a zippy chick in a tinfoil dress the room was empty. Hogie leapt across her and nose-dived into the mattresses, she followed him with her eyes.

"Hey, you're the *Top Chef* guy, right?"

He looked up, surprised, trying to focus. "Yeah, did you see me on television that one time?"

"No. There was a bald guy in here, he described you. What's a gerontophile?"

Hogie didn't know.

"He said you were one and that you'd fucked his mother."

Hogie flicked to alert. "Jesus no. Was he freaking?"

"Oh yeah, totally." The girl seemed happy about it. "He

was off the fucking wall, screaming the Viet Cong were coming to kill him. You should have seen him."

Hogie tried to get up but his feet had collapsed into the mattress. He was being sucked down.

Way, way above him, he heard Mannie shouting. "You got to help, mate. Cheb's freaked on us."

FOUR

The carpark at Frankie's local had plenty of empty spaces behind its chainlink gate but Susan drove around until she found somewhere else. Eventually, she parked high above the shopping street on the hill overlooking the shoreline. After central-locking the Mercedes, she hurried downhill on the shadowy side of the street. It was too early in the year for the holiday crowds and the home-grown Andalucians were on siesta. Susan hardly saw anyone all the way to the Plaza San Sebastian. Callum lived in a flat above an office selling time-shares. She took the steps round the back of the block and hung on his doorbell until she was sure no one would answer. She let herself in. She hadn't seen his Mazda Miata out on the street but she still half expected him to be home.

Usually, the only place Callum went during the day was El Tozo's record shop. He spent most of his day listening to the latest releases, mostly imports. Later on, he would stop by a few bars before heading off to the club where he worked as a DJ. Four pm was usually a good time to catch him before he disappeared for the night but he'd always been difficult to keep track of.

There was a half-eaten sausage on a plate on the breakfast

bar but she didn't know if it was left from that morning or the evening before. The floor was scattered with torn cigarettes and the air was rank with the smell of stale dope. She opened a window but that hardly helped. While she walked around, she called out his name but there was no reply. His bed was empty except for a pile of dirty washing and, on top, the contents of the leather satchel she'd intended to take as hand luggage. She found the bag dumped at the bottom of his wardrobe but there was no sign of her suitcase.

She began looking for the airline tickets and the keys to their London flat, at first briskly and then more thoroughly. They weren't among the loose change and papers she scooped back into her satchel. Looking around the rest of the flat she found a few things she recognised as hers: a couple of LPs she'd bought when she was dating a Canvey Island soul boy in the early seventies, during one of Frankie's longer prison sentences. She didn't know why Callum had taken them, unless he planned on starting a revival. She put them in her bag and started flicking through the rest of his collection to see what else he'd stolen. Inside a blank CD case she found a poorly re-folded wrap holding more than a gram of a chunky powder, maybe cocaine but more probably speed. Callum had left his photo album lying on the coffee table and its vinyl cover was criss-crossed with the dust trails of old lines. A semi-unfurled fifty peseta note lay nearby. She dropped the wrap into her bag with her records. She left the photo album where it was.

Susan knew all about his photo collection and thought it was disgusting. Every picture showed a girl wearing Callum's dressing gown, sat on Callum's sofa. A different girl in every photo. Susan could imagine the line Callum would use in the mornings: "*Here, put this on and I'll make us a Spanish breakfast. Hey, why don't I take a photo of you? Is that okay? Oh, yeah. You look beautiful.*" There were at least fifty photographs in the album, the last time she looked. Every one with the same lighting and arrangement, right down to the props. Even the girls' expressions were similar. At least Callum didn't collect their underwear. Still, it was disgusting. Even if she had ended up laughing the first time she told George Carmichael about her boy's trophy album. George would occasionally ask how the collection was pro-gressing. She told him, briskly. George would say: One day I'll surprise you, you'll take a peek and see me staring back at you.

Another of his jokes. Even aside from the fact that Callum was straight and George had never liked young boys. The real joke, whenever George fantasised about a guest appear-ance on the Sofa Of Shame, was that it was Susan who was more likely to be tempted by a shallow, stupid kid.

"It could be you, on a different sofa, in another town."

"No. I refuse their dressing gowns and I never pose."

"Not even on video."

"No," Susan had said. "Well, once. But I stole the tape and destroyed it."

She had once asked Callum about his collection. He had shrugged. He was tall, she would say rangey. His red-blond hair whitened further by bleach or by the sun. His arms hung lean and brown out of the T-shirts he always wore. He caught his tan coming home from nightclubs after dawn. Apart from the tan, she'd always believed he looked more like her than his father. He was soft, though. The wide space between his eyes made him look innocent but he was innocent anyway. And his eyes were not simply spaced apart, they were spaced-out. She asked him what he thought he'd be doing in ten years time, "Still shagging tourists and working as a DJ?"

He said, "Dunno." They left England when Callum was ten but he still had a London accent—like his father, like all his father's friends. "Some guys I met over in Ibiza, they reckon they could use me at their all-nighters."

"In Ibiza?"

"Nah. In London, they run a sound-system back home."

She'd said, "What would they want you for, your talent?" It came out sharp and as she said it, she already regretted it. But there were so many DJs around, why would anyone look at Callum and think: Yes, he's just the top talent we need. If they'd invited him to join them, he had to be bringing something extra along—like, maybe, finance. The whole idea was stupid and she ended up telling him so.

But, then, sometime later, she began to think it over herself and the idea stuck. The two of them could go back to London together, and do it on her terms. She didn't want to see him mixed up with any dodgy London sound-system but if he wanted to be a DJ, then why not? Maybe he did have talent. Maybe she could buy a club or something and have him run it . . .

During the planning stages, the long distance phone calls between her and George, the idea of a nightclub was scaled down to a restaurant—it was just a case of being practical. Then, once everything was settled, she finally got around to telling Callum. Which is when she discovered that he'd kept in touch with the people he'd met in Ibiza and had already made his own plans. She nearly got into another shouting match, then, but thought better of it. When they got back to London she'd find a way to run things to her liking. That's the way she had rationalised it—but she didn't know where the hell he'd got to now. She looked at the clock flashing on his VCR. Their flight was in less than four hours.

There was one other photo in the flat, a new one, blutacked to the alcove around the breakfast bar. A group shot taken at the marina, it showed Frankie and his drinking pals clowning on the deck of *My Lady Suzie*. The whole crew were striking Jack-the-Lad poses that they were too old to justify. Susan pulled the picture down and began looking around for a bin when she caught sight of Callum. Off-centre, by the aerial mast, he was definitely out of place but trying his best to fit in: his lips were curled into a Gooner's sneer and he held a foaming bottle of San Miguel to his crotch. She paused then dropped the picture in her bag, alongside everything else she was going to make the boy apologise for.

Before she left she thought to check his answering machine. The first message was from a girl with a Welsh accent, speaking through tears as she said she loved him and promising to write everyday. The time code put the message at 8.00pm so Callum hadn't been home all night. The second message was from a friend he DJ-ed with at a nightclub further down the coast, asking him not to forget the whizz when he came over that night. Susan thought, he'll be lucky, now she had the speed bagged away.

The third message was from Frankie and was for her:

"He's gone you stupid tart."

There was a short burst of laughter before the phone clicked. The time code said twelve noon.

Susan ran uphill to the Mercedes, holding the car keys ahead of her and beeping wildly at the car. The central locking flashed off and on twice. Then she couldn't get the keys in the lock. She slammed her flat palm on the roof. She had to calm down.

When the engine turned over, she pulled away slowly and crept down the hill towards the pub. The carpark was much fuller but the chainlink fence had been removed. At least she didn't have to get in and out of the car before entering. She wasn't sure she was steady enough to stand again and she didn't want to slip before her showdown with Frankie. As she parked, she twisted the a/c dial to deep freeze and stayed seated in the car until she was chilled. Her jeep was sat across the way, Frankie was back from a day killing animals in the mountains. If he'd ever gone in the first place.

She looked round slowly when she caught the tapping at the passenger side window. It was Cardiff, Frankie's sleaziest sidekick. Another North London boy, fat and greying, wheezing so loudly she could hear it over the air conditioning and through the glass. He had one short fat finger out and was miming circles in the air so she'd unwind the window. She pressed the button and the glass slid down.

"Alright, love? How's it going? Fighting fucking fit, I bet."

Susan said, "I'm fine."

"That's the fucking ticket. You coming in for a drink, girl?"

She got out of the car and walked over to the entrance with Cardiff wheezing beside her, his fat legs pummelling the blacktop. The evening breeze had sprung up early today. Susan felt its faint breath against the backs of her legs. Above her head, the pub sign swung an inch to the left, an inch to the right. The colours of the Union Jack glowed in the still bright sunshine, the sun now level with the top of the highest roofs. She passed into the dark pub.

Frankie was sat on the green velvet plush of the bench seat that ran around the main lounge. His ex-pat gang gathered around him, taking turns to get the beers in. Their pint glasses frothed over onto the polished wooden tops of the cast-iron tables. Their meaty hands hovered carelessly over the circular ceramic Courage ashtray. Cigarette ash surrounded them like scales.

Cardiff said, "I'll get them in, girl. Watchyavin'?"

She told him, spritzer. Cardiff waddled over to the bar with its ornate, Brit Vic lathe-turned pillars while she turned towards her husband. Frankie caught sight of her before she sat down.

"Alright, gal. I been telling the lads about my hunting trip. You know that cunt Pedro what runs the marina, he took me out to his cousin's spread. They got wolves up there, a fucking pack of them. Those cunts in Madrid want to make them a protected fucking species but Pedro says they been having it away with the livestock—chickens and fuck knows what else. We got up there, chased the cunts all over the show. Pedro was the wheels, I was riding shotgun—stuck out the fucking sun-roof giving it a bit with me Thompson. Tore the fuckers to pieces. Fucking magic."

"Where is he?"

Frankie made like he hadn't heard, "One in the fucking eye for the Greenpissers. Those wolves are well-fucking-endangered now."

His boys started laughing, one beat behind him.

Susan kept her voice at the same level. "Where is he?"

Frankie looked round the table. "She's asking about the boy." Turning to her, he said, "The boy's come good. Cut the fucking apron strings, know what I mean."

"What have you got him doing?"

"Not me love. The boy come up with a business proposition. I just give him the capital. Set him up in a trade, didn't I."

"What have you done, Frankie. He's doing armed robbery?"

Frankie started laughing again. "That'd be something: chip off the old block. Can't see that soft git with a shotgun, though. No, love. Don't you worry, he's gone into the import/export game."

Susan gagged. "Drugs? You got him running drugs, you bastard."

Frankie turned on her. "Less of the fucking lip, less you want a slap. You spoil him like a cunt, smother him till everyone thinks he's a fucking fairy. Well it's over. He's going into business with his old man. I should have done it years back. Good for him, good for me." He looked round his table and said, "I'm too fucking young to retire, ain't that right."

They all nodded. Susan didn't know what they were thinking. Frankie's last job had left him a multi-millionaire but they were all happier sponging off him than following his example. And now they just sat there nodding, as though they missed the life as much as he did.

Cardiff came wheezing over with her drink and tried to hand it to her.

She said, "Forget it. I'm leaving." Turning to Frankie, she said, "Give me my car keys."

He handed the jeep keys over. "I'll be back later. So get your twat warmed up, alright."

He slapped her backside as she stood.

Back in the parking lot, the air seemed all the sweeter. The sun was blinding. London couldn't still be how they all imagined it, sat in their fake boozer and reminiscing about Frankie's great days. The real place must have changed in the past twelve years.

Frankie had left the Tommy gun in the back of the jeep, covered by the Barbour jacket he hardly ever wore. Susan picked up a fresh drum. As she climbed out of the jeep, she tried to remember how much Frankie had paid for his Mercedes. It was always cash up-front whenever he bought anything big and it was her job to withdraw the money from the bank. No, the figure had gone. She took a long calm look at the car before she started firing. The bullets raked off in all directions, some splintering off the metal and blowing open the windows of the cars to its side. The windscreen exploded, the seats ripped to shreds. When the gun started clicking on an empty chamber, she tossed it into the back of the jeep. Frankie came running out of the pub shouting: "Jesus, Jesus, What The Fuck—My fucking car. What happened?"

"I think it was ETA terrorists, love."

She drove off to the airport.

FIVE

It took Hogie and Mannie more than an hour to coax Cheb out of the toilet cubicle where he was locked, shouting comic book descriptions of what Hogie had done to his mother through the gap under the door. The boy wanted the world to know, his mam had been wild for it, she couldn't get enough of Hogie. She was a front-loading momma and he was her crazy teen machine.

They got him out onto the street with the help of two bouncers. Even then, he wouldn't take a step until Hogie covered his head with a jacket, like a child rapist turning up for a first court appearance. But at least he'd quietened down.

In the cab on the way to Rusholme, Hogie said he might be getting hungry. He wasn't sure. "What do you think? Maybe food will help bring Cheb out of orbit."

Mannie immediately began moaning. "Who says I got any food in the house? I don't keep food in my house."

Hogie wondered how he'd missed his vocation, he could have been a care assistant. Cheb had been easier to handle since he lapsed into something between autism and a coma but still his problems weren't over. Now he had to start nursemaiding a neurotic depressive like Mannie. He played it even and neutral: "Easy, mate. We'll go buy something at an all-night garage and I'll cook up one of my redneck convenience deals."

Even then, Mannie gave him grief. "You know you're paying. I don't have any money."

Hogie had plenty of money on him but decided this treat was on Cheb. He frisked him until he touched plastic. "How about we use this?"

They got the cabbie to stop at the Shell station by Saint Xav's and left him to babysit Cheb on metered time. They spent twenty minutes making the attendant run around behind his security screen, fetching every item one by one: six tangerine yoghurts, Yorkie bars, gingernuts, cigs, skins and anything with vitamin C. When they finally decided they had everything and it came time to pay, there was another problem. Hogie had to step out into the forecourt light before he could read the signature on the credit card.

As the cab pulled back out into Wilmslow Road, Mannie said, "Do you think the guy was suspicious?"

"Fuck no. I was too fucking suave."

"Only, he knows me. That's where I do all my shopping."

"I was like ice. You see how steady my hand was when I signed?"

"And they got those video cameras."

Hogie said, "Will you please just shut it."

He couldn't believe it, Mannie was so hyped to see the black side of everything. It wasn't even funny.

Back at Mannie's, they put Cheb to bed on a pile of cushions in the front room. Hogie thought it was better to keep him close, they'd hear him if he started ranting again. They sat in the back parlour, Hogie on the carpet, shaking a finished joint by its loose end, Mannie on the couch trying to choose the perfect calibre of cardboard for the roach. The yoggo-choc cake Hogie had made sat between them on a mangled copy of *Eight Ball* comic. It was Mannie's plan to keep smoking the dope. Once the munchies had cancelled the effects of the amphetamine, they'd be able to eat the cake. Later they might even fall sleep. They hadn't heard a sound out of Cheb in hours. They were more worried about them-selves now.

Mannie saw the cake as a turning point. Once it was eaten they could resume earth-time. The past few hours had swung violently, never settling on a rhythm, punctuated by flashbacks, creeping or racing. There had been moments when the cake seemed a real possibility. But the moment had spun away, collapsed, reassembled at another point. It would have been unnerving, if he wasn't so used to it. He had spent the past fifty minutes searching for a video of Hogie's first and last television appearance. Now he'd found it, just in time for them to enjoy over the newest joint.

Hogie squinted at the screen, watching his TV image lope forward in full chef's drag.

Mannie said, "With the white suit and the goatee, it looks like the only thing you're gonna cook is the Colonel's Chicken."

On-screen, Hogie shouted kung fu-style and embedded a cleaver a full two inches into a butcher's block.

Hogie grinned, "Check that out. How's that for a serious fucking in-your-face intro."

Mannie had watched the tape a hundred times. He had never understood why Hogie only got to do the one show, anyone could see the boy was a star. "I see all these other chefs and none of them have got your screen presence."

Hogie knew it. "The problem is, I got kind of a bad reputation following that show. I turned up to the studio a little wrecked and I think I managed to neurotize the bosses."

"What happened?"

"It was after the cooking spot. They'd set up this fashion piece and brought out a bunch of models in evening wear. Only, after about five minutes, the presenters ran out of things to say so they improvised by asking the other guests what they thought of the clothes. The model closest to me was wearing velvet trousers, so I thought, you know, it'd be good TV if I reached out to stroke them. The thing was, it felt so good, I couldn't let go. In the end, they practically had to prise me off her leg."

Mannie remembered the show got a bit weird later on in

the programme but he'd assumed it was all rehearsed. He'd thought it worked, Hogie looked natural.

Hogie said "I might have another chance, though. I've got a chance to appear on a new late-night show and I'm going to be more professional. I'm definitely steering clear of psychedelics."

"Good luck, bud."

Hogie reckoned he'd need it. "So far, I've got one fucking appearance while your sister's on every other day. Not that I watch her. I might tape the episode when she get hits by a runaway truck, that sounds like one for the archives."

Mannie said, "I tell you, I wouldn't mind seeing that. I'd pay to see that. Are you hungry enough to eat the cake, yet?"

Hogie couldn't decide. Maybe if they had one more joint. While he smoothed out the Rizlas, Mannie asked about the credit card scam. Hogie tried to get the facts straight. The truth was, Cheb was better at explaining that kind of shit.

"It's some kind of Far East thing. Cheb's got this decoder that plugs straight into the till. You zip a card through the machine and it reads everything off the magnetic strip. Right down to the owner's PIN number."

Mannie thought it sounded smooth. "So you can copy anyone's credit card, and they don't get a whisper until their statement arrives."

Hogie nodded. That was it.

"So you can make as many cards as you want, and never get caught?"

"Foolproof. Except we can't make the cards."

"You said you could."

"No. We can copy information onto a replica card but we can't make the cards. Cheb says you need a serious plastics factory for that, especially with all the new holograms and shit."

"Then the decoder's useless."

"No, he's got a stack of blank cards he bought with the decoder. He wants to install it at the new restaurant. I got him a job there so we can run the scam on the quiet."

Mannie admired the plot, but had doubts: "Are there no risks? I mean stealing off your own customers, doesn't it make you more likely to be caught?"

"No," said Hogie. "Cheb says there's no risk. The man who owns the restaurant, he's never there." Hogie was giggling, it was so sweet. "It'll just be me and Cheb, the head cook and his bottle washer. Why don't you come down. I'll find some sort of menial shit for you. You can act as my ponce and personal runner."

"Yeah. I'll be your ponce. I'll go and kidnap grannies off the street to satisfy your unnatural desires."

Hogie said, "Enough of that granny shit. Cheb was fucking raving."

"So you didn't fuck his mother?"

"No. Okay? . . . Okay?"

Mannie said, "Okay. So now we've got that straight, is it time we cut the cake or what?"

It was an idea. But Mannie's only knives were leant against the gas-fire grille with their blades charred from repeated over-heatings. Before they started rolling the spliffs, they'd smoked the dope using hot knives. That was around dawn, after Mannie had forgotten where he'd left the Rizlas and before Hogie remembered he'd brought new ones at the Shell shop.

Hogie had another look at the knives but he was a professional and refused to use them in that condition. He went through to the kitchen at the back of the house to find a couple of spoons. They could pass the cake between them, taking mouthfuls in turn.

The only spoons were encrusted with dried cereal. Hogie stood at the sink, looking out to the backyard as he scraped away the hardened crap. It was after twelve already. He had

an evening flight booked to London but his bags were at a
B&B near Heaton Park. He still had Jools's car keys in his
pocket, the car must be somewhere in town—wherever he
had parked it. He was lucky it was Saturday—no parking
restrictions. If it hadn't been stolen, it would still be there.
As long as Cheb surfaced in time to remember where they
dumped it, they could get their bags and still make the plane.

The line of thought was overtaken by a solid banging at
the front door.

He shouted back, "Sounds as though Jools has caught up
with us."

All he got back was Mannie hissing, "Shut it, Hoges."

The hammering never stopped and whatever else Mannie
had to say, Hogie couldn't make out a word. There was
something wrong with the guy's voice, strangled and dripping anxiety. He would have gone to see if he was alright
but there was someone coming up through the backyard. A
tall Pakistani, walking with a swing past the outdoor toilet
and giving him a friendly wave, mouthing hello. Hogie waved
back. The man pointed towards the kitchen door, making a
key-turning gesture.

Hogie mouthed through the glass, "Open the door?"

The Paki nodded, smiling, relaxed in the yard with his
hands in his hip pockets.

Hogie slipped the door off the latch. The guy said,
"Thanks mate" and walked through the kitchen. Hogie was
left standing, feeling dumb.

He followed on, still wondering if he'd done the wrong
thing, and watched as the guy passed through the room and
out towards the front door. Mannie was sat on the floor,
green and trembling, but the Paki had never said a word to
him. Hogie could hear him now, turning the latch on the
front door. As he opened it, the hammering stopped.

Before Hogie had a chance to ask Mannie anything, the
guy returned. There was another, smaller, Asian with him.

The only thing Mannie said was "Naz."

The man had the slowest voice Hogie had ever heard. "What's wrong, Mannie. You didn't hear Omar knocking at the fucking door, or what?" The words spewed out in a long flat drone, the sentence never seemed to end.

Mannie tried to apologise but only managed to stutter.

Hogie saw the bulge in Naz's jacket. He couldn't believe someone could smash into someone else's house carrying a gun. When Naz slipped out of his padded leather jacket, Hogie saw what he thought was a gun was nothing but a mobile, worn in a shoulder holster.

Naz said, "Fucking stinks in here. What is it? Cheap shitty dope or the smell of fear? What I want to know, Mannie, is when are you going to pay me my six hundred quid."

Mannie got to his feet, keeping his shoulders hunched as he answered. As though he hoped the genuflection would work some kind of magic. He couldn't keep his hands from fidgetting, from pulling at the sleeves of his sweater, as he whispered, "I haven't got it. You know I'm not going to run out on you but I haven't got it. I wouldn't rip you off Naz. I mean, I'm trying to get the cash together."

"Six hundred quid or three hundred tabs of acid. Payment due last week. You know what I reckon, I should charge interest." Naz turned to his partner. "What kind of interest should I charge, Omar?"

"Take it out his fucking flesh, Naz."

Mannie kept his eyes on Naz, pleading openly.

"You been trying to avoid me, Mannie. I don't understand what the fuck kind of problem you've got, but I reckon Omar's right. I should write you off as a bad debt and just fucking blow you away."

Naz reached round the back of his trousers. He had a gun after all, stuck into the back of his belt. As he pulled it out, Mannie made a noise different to anything Hogie had heard before.

Naz spoke on, slow and nasal, his lips barely moving. "Hey, Mannie. You don't wanna fucking wet yourself. It's not loaded."

He held the gun in his left hand, flat on his palm. Taking a rectangular piece of metal from his pocket, he slotted it into the handgrip. There was a click as the magazine connected inside the gun. Naz switched hands on the gun, racking back a bar that ran across the top of the barrel. As it snapped back into place, he said: "Now it's loaded."

Mannie swam backwards, dissolving out of focus. He collapsed. There was no percentage in him moving again.

Naz and Omar looked down on Mannie from one side, Hogie looked down from the other. As he glanced up, Hogie caught Naz's eye. He lifted his hands and began to back away into a corner.

Naz said, "What's your fucking problem, bud?"

Hogie kept his hands above his head, feeling them shake up there, somewhere close to the ceiling above him. He didn't have anything to say. He didn't need to. Over by the door, he heard a familiar voice saying, "It's okay. We're just friends of Mannie's."

It was Cheb. Back on this planet and not looking at all bad. In fact, relaxed, standing posed in the doorway with a sweet smile on his face and his hands open in front of him. A pacifying gesture to go with the easy calm of his voice. "Why's everyone so anxious?"

Naz turned on him, the gun still in his hand but somehow less threatening. He had lowered it a touch and Cheb acted as if it wasn't there at all. Now he was asking if anyone wanted to put the kettle on.

"Hey, Hogie. You're a chef, why don't you go brew up."

Hogie had to go out for milk. There was none in Mannie's kitchen. He crossed to the shop on the corner where a crowd of kids begged sweet money. Inside were a bunch of men out to watch City play, buying chocolates and crisps before the match. All of the streets around Santiago Street were crammed with cars, some double-parked, although the game was not due to start for another hour and a quarter.

Stuck in a mad press of City fans, Hogie had to wait to be served. He spent the time wondering if there was anything he could buy Mannie. Wasn't there some kind of sweet that was good for shock?

When he left the house, Mannie seemed to be coming round. He was still on the floor, left just as he had fallen, but he'd begun to sob quietly. Cheb and the Pakistanis were getting on fine. There seemed to be no danger that anyone would be shot. Hogie didn't know if Cheb had helped calm the situation, whether he'd chosen to calm things deliberately or if it had happened naturally and he'd just swung with the flow. He also wondered if Cheb was as straight as he'd looked. In general, he didn't wonder about Cheb as often as he should.

He paid for two pints of milk, a dozen eggs and a plastic pack of boil-in-the-bag hotdogs he uncovered in the fridge unit. He knew he was hungry now. The tension that had begun to twist across his chest and neck for the last three hours had unwound across his body, setting his nerves bristling. After Naz put his gun away, the tension turned into a kind of jagged emptiness. If he could eat, quickly, Hogie hoped that he could regain some kind of psychic balance.

On the way out of the shop, he began to regret the dogs. He couldn't offer a couple of Pakis sausage meat. Whenever pork was on the school dinners menu, they were always given a sad pile of grated cheese.

Back in the house, he found Cheb and Naz sitting on the sofa. Naz was showing Cheb how the gun loaded and how to rack the first bullet into the chamber. Mannie was sat on a chair by the fire. Hogie came in waving the carton of milk in the air, saying "I'll brew up, then."

Naz said, "Omar's done it. All you got to do is pour it out."

Cheb said, "Hey, Hogie. You want to know what Mannie did? Naz gave him three hundred trips to sell, he took five to test the quality and hid the rest. Except, he was so stoned he forgot where he put them. He's spent the last week searching the house for them."

Hogie said, "Why don't we pay?"

"Yeah, that's an idea," said Cheb. "We'll give you the money, Naz."

"You're going to carry this fucker's debts?"

Cheb shrugged, Sure.

Hogie pulled a wad out of his pocket, "I've got a couple of hundred."

"Here's the other four," Cheb handed over a fold of fifties.

"Sweet." Naz took the notes and turned to Hogie. "Hey, Blondie, this guy says you're a chef, right? I'm a chef, as well. Or I was, before I started up in business for myself. Now I let Omar handle the recipes. Mixing speed with baby milk or soaking the blotters."

Omar nodded, taking his dues.

"Try some of Hogie's cake." Cheb lifted the plate off the floor.

Naz scowled at the cake.

"We were going to eat it, but all the knives are fucked." Hogie pointed at the knives lying in the grate.

Naz called Omar over. Reaching behind his outsize shirt, Omar produced a huge knife and cut the yoggo-choc cake into sixths. Slipping one segment onto the upturned blade, he handed it over to Naz.

"What do you think?" asked Cheb.

Naz took a bite. "It's alright. For a fucking kiddies party, it's alright. Is this all you do?"

Hogie said, "No. I was wrecked last night, I just made something simple."

"Well, it's simple. I'd say it was fucking infantile." Naz paused while he finished the cake. "You're a chef? Where do you work? In town?"

"In London. I just got my own restaurant. Cheb's the head waiter."

"Sweet. He looks like a fucking head waiter. What you should do, give Mannie a job, as well. Because, I tell you, he's not cut out to be a fucking drug dealer."

Mannie didn't look as though he was cut out for anything much. He was still tugging at the sleeves of his sweater, hunched into his fireside chair. Mannie had been the only one to stay on at school while everyone else went to the tech and got a trade. Mannie had even gone to poly, the only one of them with any hope of getting in. Although he never finished the course. Behavioural Psychology, who needed that? Still, Mannie wasn't the only one who had never worked in his life. It was fucked up but as far as Hogie knew, he and Jools were the only ones who counted as an any kind of success.

Naz was nodding his head, saying, "Yeah, I used to be a chef. I started in the kitchen at my uncle's place when I was twelve. I spent six years at that, until I found my vocation. I'm a natural born gangsta."

Cheb nodded: a total fucking natural. "But you should have stayed with cooking, you could have been the Gangsta Chef—got your own telly show, book deal and everything. Going down the shops and choosing the best joints at gun point. Toasting peppers with a flame thrower."

"Sounds sweet."

"You should think about it man. Look at the crap they put on the telly. Like Hogie, for instance."

Naz turned to Hogie, Yeah? "You been on the television?"

Hogie nodded. "Once." He was about to point out the video but Cheb started speaking again.

"Everyone's on the telly these days. Even Mannie's mad sister, even she's been let on the telly."

"What does she do?"

"What does she do?" asked Cheb.

Hogie shrugged, waiting for Mannie to tell them. When he realised everyone was staring at him, Mannie mumbled: "She plays Derek Taverner's step niece from his second marriage."

"On *Pony Trek*! I watch that. She's Charlie Brompton, yeah? She's alright." Naz nodded, sucking slowly through his front teeth. "I tell you, I wouldn't mind a bit of that."

Cheb and Hogie stared at each other. Cheb spoke first: "She'd probably like you. I'll fix you up if you want. Why don't you give me your number."

SIX

Monday morning, back in London. Hogie had been awake an hour when he heard Cheb's radio. Steadying his bowl of Ready Brek in one hand, he pushed open the door and walked in. The room was a nine by ten box Hogie used as a junk room. He couldn't recognise the place now. Cheb had lined the walls in tin foil, rippling the entire height of the room. Left-over strips dangled from the ceiling, catching the light and sending it fingering across the bare wood floor. And right at the centre: Cheb. The metal guru in his tin foil yurt. Sat cross-legged on the mattress, studying a blanket-sized map of England.

Hogie said, "You're awake."

"Yeah." As it happened, Cheb hadn't even needed his radio-alarm. He was still wired to East Asian time and was out of bed before his tape of the last sermon of the Reverend Jim Jones got to the interesting part. "What do you reckon to this?"

Hogie followed the gesture, a hand sweep around the room. He said, "Nice one."

"It's a feng shui thing. You wanna live right, you got to maximise the potential of your living space."

"What happened to the carpet?"

"That had to go, it was doing my head in. You know, I hadn't realised what a wrench coming back home would be. After losing my box in Manchester, I got to thinking. I need to re-acclimatise." He jabbed at the outspread map with his finger. "Co-ordinate. You know what I mean?"

"Sure." Whatever. Hogie stood spooning his breakfast mush with no discernible appetite, knowing he didn't look half as sweet as Cheb. Manchester had worked opposite spells on them both, giving Hogie a short lift and a sour comedown and Cheb a full-spin but setting him down revitalised, re-modelled even. His motor neurones all in a line and motoring in one direction.

Hogie said, "Listen, I'm throwing a sickie. I don't need to be there until opening day tomorrow. The staff don't arrive till then anyway so as long as I'm in early I can't see a problem." He hoped that by tomorrow evening he'd have some kind of culinary experience worked out.

Cheb said, "What about food?"

Hogie had pencilled a short list of basics for Cheb to fax through to his suppliers. He said he'd get the rest himself, early in the morning at the markets.

"How early?"

Hogie came up with a number, "Around five, that should do it."

"When did you ever get up for five?"

"I'll score some whizz. It's standard practice when you do the market."

Cheb picked up the mail at the door, flagged a cab and ripped through the envelopes before he reached work. There was nothing but a tax demand, a wad of promo literature from different foodie companies and a clutch of Good Luck cards from other chefs. Cheb stuffed the lot into his case. He spent the rest of the journey checking the sights, counting the streets to Soho, the centre of his new city.

The restaurant was well-placed on a side road, only a short step from Dean Street. From what he'd seen on his other few visits, this was the gay area of town. The restaurant was called *La George*, which fitted right into the general ambience. The name was flourished across the window like a huge queen-ish autograph but behind the glass the interior gave off a haughtier, look-don't-touch, vibe. So much cooler than the street in the middle of this early summer heat wave. Cheb unlocked the door and double-clicked the catch behind him. The dining room was heavy with damp gloss fumes, the white wood floor threw out an unscuffed sheen. No doubt, the place looked ready for business but Cheb could still think of a couple of discreet decor ideas.

He shimmied the length of the room, sloped under the bar and flipped his case onto the counter next to the answering machine. The red message light was flashing. Cheb triggered the recall button and listened through: half of them replies to the party invites, the rest shameless begging for an invitation. It was like no one in London could pass up on a free meal. He had better things to do than take the numbers.

He opened his case. Just the touch of it made him feel Secret Service suave. He'd bought it during the three hour stop-over in Qatar, en route from Bangkok. It was duty-free and irresistible, built from toughened plastic and in-laid with foam, costing $400 complete with a set of multi-head screwdrivers and a cordless drill. He had no use for a toolkit but, once he'd emptied it, it was a perfect size for his credit card machine. This was Far East criminal technology, the gear demanded respect. You couldn't keep it rattling round an old Adidas bag, sandwiched between Timothy Leary's *Tibetan Book Of The Dead* and other in-flight classics.

Standing on the bartop, the machine was a piece of work: black and square with a groove across the top, just wide enough for a credit card. The groove already looked like it was gagging for a bite of someone's credit. Cheb got down under the counter and found a free plug socket. The whole thing was sweeter than sweet, over tout de suite. With the machine stashed under the cash till, he could copy someone's card in seconds—do it right in front of their face without them even noticing. It was so easy, he hardly deserved a free shot from one of the bottles on the shelf behind him. It wasn't going to stop him though.

He counted labels until he saw the one that caught his mood, a top-shelf armangac. Once he'd fetched a chair and reached for the bottle, he poured himself a solid double. It tasted not-quite smooth, playfully venomous with a delayed punch. He would have mixed it with coke but knew there wasn't any. He took it straight and chaseless and hoped he'd remember to phone the suppliers.

The bottle went back on the shelf. A quick rinse and the tumbler could go back on the rack. Cheb pushed through the swing doors at the back of the restaurant and slid into the kitchen. The place looked undisturbed but something put him on edge long before he picked up the smell of cold cuts.

He found the corpse sat on top of the stove. The head was veiled inside the steel hood of the extractor fan but he could see the guy was dead long before he got close. Whoever sat him on the stove had pulled down his trousers to get better contact between the rings and the buttocks. The gas was off now but Cheb could see the damage between the man's spread legs. The summer's first flies were whispering around the torture scene.

The body smelled of burnt hair, giving a faint acrid tinge to the soft smell of his meat. Cheb pulled hard at the skinny arms and swung the body out from the hood. The head clapped against the steel sides before crumpling onto the kitchen top. The guy had been young. Cheb thought, just about his age. The bruises across his face had ruined his looks but left him recognisable. Not that he recognised him. If the guy looked like anyone, it was Hogie.

There were gobs of burnt flesh stuck to the gas rings. Cheb reached out, absent-minded as he prised a lump free with his thumb nail. In front of him the body lay slumped and twisted, the gas rings branded as a five point crown across the upturned cheeks. Cheb stood looking as he cleaned a gluey speck of grease from under his nail with one of his dog-tooth incisors. He yanked his finger out of his mouth the second he realised what he'd done. He once read somewhere that the ancient Aztecs ate the loins of their victims. He could see the logic but he was no cannibal. He was a by-stander.

Cheb frisked through the dead guy's pockets and found a few twisted Rizla skins but nothing that could pass as ID: no cards, driving licence, video membership. He had no idea how to play this kind of situation. Maybe if he spent the day figuring the possibilities, he'd see the move. He began a circuit round the kitchen, then another. After five turns he was spinning in anxiety, his left cortex fused and his right cortex in linear paralysis, fixed on a satellite stroll around the floor tiles while his nerves soft-wired his body.

What he decided to do, was clean up.

There was a shoulder-high wheelie bin in the corner of the kitchen, one of a pair. It took some time to man-handle the corpse to the edge and topple it inside. The guy was at least a foot taller than him and was nothing but arms and legs but he managed, sealing the job with the bin lid.

Afterwards he washed his hands and walked back through the swing doors into the dining room. He had his eyes on the floor but looked up when he heard the squeal of a taxi brake. Out in the real world, Jools was stepping out of a black cab onto the kerb. She was hefting a world-trip size suitcase and rummaging for her fare. Cheb thought about locking the door on her but in those few seconds she paid the driver and turned around. She was in clear view, beyond the plate glass, pulling a sour face. He was in clear view, pinned inside the restaurant.

She came banging through the doors case first and red-faced before he even had time to move. She let the case drop as she collapsed onto a chair, "*La George*? What's that mean?"

Cheb said, "It's named after the owner. What are you doing here?"

All she said was "Where's Hogie?"

"He's not working today—what are you doing here?"

"Leave it Cheb. I'm dead on my feet. I need either a blast of coke or a stiff drink, and then I'll be out of your way. All I need is the keys to Hogie's flat."

"What?"

She pulled in her breath, and let it slip out the bottom of her clenched teeth "Don't give me any shit, Cheb. You know Hogie asked me to come stay with him. I've had a nightmare fucking journey. I got hassled loads on the train. Now, I need a line or a drink, and then I need to put my feet up. So get with it."

Cheb went to the bar and fetched her a brandy—not the stuff he'd been drinking but something that might keep her quiet. If she thought she'd had a bad day, she should try his for size.

Jools was telling him about her headache, brought on by

the fumes in her train. She said the whole of her carriage stunk of amyl. Two sleazes from Liverpool were sniffing poppers, rolling spliffs and hassling her loads—all the way to London. When the train reached Euston station, she found out they both worked for British Rail: one driver and one guard, assigned to take the Inter-city back to Lime Street. She swore, next time she was going to fly, like Hogie did. Cheb didn't tell her the plane was his idea, Hogie had wanted to drive.

Jools took time out during a breathing pause to look around the restaurant.

"It's alright."

She was impressed. Her mouth was open and wasn't making any noise. He asked her how she'd found the place.

Jools pulled a copy of *Time Out* from her shoulder bag. "It was in here. I bought it for an article and found a photo of Hogie inside."

Cheb took the magazine. It was crumpled with about a day's worth of wear and tear so she must have bought it before she left Manchester. Flicking onto the contents page, he saw an article headlined "Pony-girl Must Die?" next to a smudged picture of Jools.

"We've both got our photos in the same issue, me and Hogie."

Cheb nodded, Uh huh. It must be written in the stars. He found the article about Hogie and *La George* in the Intro. section—three-hundred words backed with a glossy pic of Hogie, all bright-haired and stoned grin. It read as a brief bio, written in x-plicit prose that made Hogie sound more like a porn-stud rather than an over-hyped caterer.

Cheb flicked on through the magazine, asking Jools if there were any photos of her death that might upset his stomach.

"No. The TV company isn't releasing any stills of my

accident. They plan to keep the exact details secret to add to the dramatic impact."

Cheb said, "You get hit by a truck. Everyone knows. You told most of them."

Jools said, "I got an interview on breakfast television tomorrow, talking about the message we're trying to give."

"How to get rid of a fat actress by wasting her with an articulated truck."

"Fuck you, Cheb. There's some kind of road safety angle. Anyway, the interview gives me a chance to talk about my film career."

He got her moving eventually. Out on the street, he pointed down the road and told her Piccadilly was that way. She would find a key-cutting stall inside the tube station. He told her he was fucked if he was letting her walk off with his only set.

Jools said, "I'm too hassled for this shit. Just give me yours. I'll be in the flat when you get back, so you won't need them."

Cheb hung onto his keys. Jools screamed, "Give them to me."

"No way."

"Okay. I'll cut a new set. Where's Piccadilly?"

Cheb pointed out again. Down this street, over Old Compton Street and right at the bottom. She couldn't miss it.

Jools nodded, Okay . . . Okay . . . Okay.

Cheb said, "And leave the suitcase."

Jools had tight hold of her case. He knew she had no intention of getting the keys cut. The second she was out of sight, she'd grab a taxi and that would be it. Now he was faced with a massive embarrassment of a stand-off, right out front of the restaurant. The two of them wrestling for possession like street muggers. It would only take the police to walk up now—that would crown his day.

Jools had a new thought, "You get the keys cut. I'll stay here."

No No No. "Leave you in the restaurant? Fuck that. I'm irresponsible, I'm not a jerk."

Jools put her case down, "Okay. So where's Piccadilly?"

Cheb waved his arms about, exasperation turned to maximum amplification, "I don't fucking believe you. It's down the road. See this road, it's at the other fucking end."

He had his arm out, sticking horizontally in the right direction when Jools swung the sharp edge of her handbag onto his wrist. The keys he'd been holding fell to the floor. He was still shrieking and clutching his wrist as she bent for them but he managed to kick them away before her hand closed around the ring. She didn't even try and chase them. Instead, she gave him a pitying look, like *tut-tut-tut*, and punched his nose in. He was left reeling in the street while she scooped up the keys and started away with her suitcase in her hand.

Cheb screamed after her, "You don't have the address, you stupid cow."

She heard him but kept on running. Cheb was sure she didn't have the address.

Fuck, she must have the address. He started after her, remembering the mail lying in his case, cold on the bartop; all of it addressed direct to Hogie's home. She must have lifted it, though Christ alone knew how or when. The girl was pure deviant; she'd be incapable of even walking straight, even if her fat bum didn't throw her off-kilter.

He caught her as she was hauling on a taxi door. He slammed it shut. She could shout at him all she wanted but he wasn't going to move.

He said, "You've got every key, you moron. The restaurant, my mam's house in Manchester, all my keys for everything."

"You'll get them back."

"I'm taking them back." He pulled her bag off her

shoulder, the keys weren't in her hand so they had to be in there. Dodging away to the kerb side, he opened the clasp and found them stuffed between the stolen wad of letters.

"Look at these. Look at them." He fanned the letters out, waving them at her. "What else did you find?"

"What?"

He could feel it boiling. "I said, what else did you find? Where else did you go looking?"

She couldn't have gone into the kitchen, he was sure. But not too sure.

"Nothing else? What are you talking about, Cheb?"

"The kitchen?" He said it. "Did you go in the kitchen?"

"What is this, Cheb?"

The blood was shunting about his brain. His scalp was drum-tight, too thin to cope with all the pressure. He sank down to the pavement, head in hands, trying to hold the throbbing in place.

"No. I didn't go in the kitchen. What is your fucking problem?"

The taxi pulled away. There was nothing she could do about it so she joined him, sat at the kerb. It looked like she had finished fighting but Cheb hardly cared. He was down to a cracked whisper when he said, "I don't need this grief. I don't even know why you bother."

She said, "Come on, Cheb."

He was ready to tell her. He didn't want another scene, but he was ready to tell her the truth. "Hogie's a freak. You know you're wasting your time but you still show up."

That was it. She flared like a rocket: "Fuck off Cheb. Just because Hogie's screwed your mother."

He looked her in the eye: "Yours too, Jools. Yours too."

She screamed as she let fly but she was running against the facts. He told her, "I'll show you the polaroids if you don't believe me."

SEVEN

Susan was being followed. She sensed it soon after leaving the taxi. Trying to settle the fare on the street outside Harrods had been painful. She'd dumped her loose change in among her pesetas which meant every coin had to be individually sorted. Throughout this orgy, a figure skulked to her right. She assumed it was someone vulturing on her cab but once inside the store, she became aware of an uneven tempo threading its way among the anonymous crowd of shoppers. Something eager, something out of place.

She idled through menswear and bolted when she reached the tobacconists. Spinning through Harrods like a twisted wheel, she hoped to force her tail out into the open. Nothing happened except the feeling grew stronger. Standing in the delicatessan department, the fragrance of moist cheese never numbed her suspicions. She slipped past the cooked meats and circled a stack of jarred and pickled vegetables. She knew from experience that pickled baby eggplant was not worth eating. She only picked up the family-sized jar as a ruse and scanned the whole of the food department through the purple juice.

Someone was sniffing out there but the dog was staying hidden. There were some seriously maladjusted hairstyles, there were three brassy hassidic wigs to her left, but nothing that could be classed as sinister. If the feeling hadn't been so strong, she would have blamed her edginess on post-flight jags. After booking a flight from Malaga to Manchester, she'd driven four hundred miles to Madrid and caught a different flight to London. The whole manoeuvre had been choreographed over the phone by George Carmichael; it was a safety play, based on the assumption that her husband would follow her. George rang off with a *bon voyage* and a promise to hide a spare key to her new flat under the doormat: all ready for her to bed down. In the end, and thanks to an air traffic controllers' strike, she didn't reach central London until nine in the morning and by then she was too wired to sleep. She asked the cab driver to drop her off outside Harrods. Until Callum surfaced with her suitcase, she had no clothes. So she might as well shop.

The brassy wigs were a three generation family unit, the family that the family-sized eggplants had been waiting for. Susan handed them the jar and left them debating olives in the central aisle. She thought she would get a kick from doing her shopping in Knightsbridge. It would be a kind of welcome-back-London gig. But the feeling of being followed took all the kink out of the food hall.

She dumped her wire basket on the glass-topped fish counter and headed for the clothes department. Forget food, she had no appetite and no intention of buying anything anyway. Aside from the damage that the complimentary airline cocktails had done to her stomach, she had snuffled through all of Callum's speed on the drive to Madrid. She was on the lam, it was a night flight—screw it, she could take a share of her son's sulphate if she wanted.

The business-like amphetamine aura stayed with her as she marched through the perfume hall, waving away anyone who wanted to infect her with free samples. She strode ahead of her discomfort, keeping long shiny stretches of floorspace between herself and her suspicions. Leaving cosmetics, she was ready to blame her paranoia on the Spanish amphetamine. Like Callum said, the speed in Spain is mostly good for clearing drains. But then she caught sight of a reflection, skipping across the panels of the elevator doors. The other shoppers faded out of focus, she had her man.

The doors slid open. Susan waited her turn to step inside. She pushed to the back, through the pair of Arabs, the plumped-up Japanese girl, the old drunk in the Burberry hat. The doors were ready to close when the last person stepped across the grooves. Susan turned to the mirrored walls, ready to look him over. She saw a tall boy with shoulder-length blond hair. A well-groomed moustache above an uncertain smile. A trimmed beard beneath his slight pout.

The car stopped at one, two and three. The overall balance barely changed: a mother and daughter combination replaced the two Arabs, the drunk was traded for a dried-out crone, then two veiled Saudis stepped inside as the mother and daughter left at three. Susan nudged her way to the front. Her man took the bait, assumed she was set to leave and stepped out of the car ahead of her.

She left him on the third floor. All it took, the scent of indecision, a moment humming over the department menu, then she shook her head and shrunk back behind the closing doors.

Hogie could have cried. He banged the buttons on all the remaining elevators and when none of them opened looked about for a staircase. The store signs pointed him away from the elevator hall, too far to run to. The swish of a descending elevator raised his hopes, but he had to wait another half minute before he caught one travelling his way. He had lost her, for sure.

The fourth floor was almost entirely given over to women's fashion. Standing on the landing, Hogie had to make a decision. From what he had seen of her, from the taxi onwards, he believed he could guess her tastes. But now he didn't have a clue which direction to take.

After blowing out the restaurant that morning, he decided to spend a cool day cruising department stores. The sight of the red-headed woman, the reach of her inside leg as she stepped out of the taxi, was just what he'd been waiting for, a live throbbing goddess. The way she swayed through the ground floor was unbelievable. Her square-shaped bottom rubbing at the material of her linen suit-like dress. He could sense a superior kind of underwear beneath the fabric. When she reached the food hall, he believed that he'd have his chance. All she had done, though, was stare at a jar of pickles. How was he supposed to spin an interesting line from a chance meeting over an aubergine?

He caught an elevator to the most boring floor, the one that catered for the bland unisex stretch of chicks and pricks aged fifteen to twenty-plus. Hogie slid past the dressing rooms and rails with his dick slackening inside his strides. He tugged at different suits hanging off their rails and messed through the piles of sweaters but couldn't be bothered to pull out any of his credit cards. When he decided the only thing to do was eat he went looking for the furthest, most unfashionable coffee shop. He was going to sit and watch the older women pass by.

The signs took him through hall after hall of women's fashion. Not all of it, strictly, fashion. Hogie saw gold chains, scary buttons, glittermania, none of it to his taste until he thought of the women who might wear them. He was thinking Jewish, maybe Arab. He knew he could get excited about their flesh tones, as long as they were not too short, fat and mama-ish. He liked the early 1960s style bouffants that Jewish women wore, a touch of the Jackie O's but bleached white-through-to-orange rather than true Jackie black. Hogie slowed down as he passed a very particular middle-eastern chick, late-forties, medium-firm . . . giving the assistant a hard time with her foxy white teeth jagging out of ultra-red lipstick.

Into Americana and all the pale country shades: white shirt and slacks. Too simple. But a corn-fed cleavage seen through the lines of buttons on a pressed shirt could be irresistable. Especially if the ensemble was rigged on top of horse-ridden buttocks. But there was nothing remotely like that around today.

Hogie passed on to another French room where he had a more complex reaction to the styles on display. He loved the big freeze feeling of haute couture, the hint of suspense, the still-life shoe displayed on a plinth. On the minus sheet, the styles were favoured by the bonier older women and he had an aversion to them. He could appreciate the wafer-thin silhouettes thrown by ultra-rich ageing chicks, but it was a strictly hands-off experience. Best to leave the better-dressed fully dressed, that was his motto.

What he did find was a collection of dresses styled after lightweight macs. These were a live turn-on because any dress that resembles a coat looks like a coat worn directly over underwear. Which is next door to naked.

The next hall was where they draped the underwear. Hogie almost collapsed. The changing rooms loomed over to his left. He wanted to run in there, punch-out the hag at the entrance and kick down each door. Juiced with sexual fury, he had to find somewhere to sit, smoke and calm himself.

The upper circle café was a late 1960s extravaganza, based on a circular design and never fully re-habbed. The main entrance was a white plaster archway, almost a perfect circle, and the walls were dotted with port holes open to the rest of the store. The main colours were white and green, space-age vinyl white and leather racing green. Although it was reminiscent of either one of Stanley Kubrick's films, the café looked even more like one particular German porn flick. In the film, the white shag carpet in the hero's living room led to a huge circular sofa. The curving walls had round arches carved out of the plaster with a different woman naked in every alcove. The hero walked around sipping champagne, having his willy stroked or his bum tickled as he wandered round. Susan couldn't remember the name of the picture but it was better than most of the obscene dross Frankie used to borrow from his pal with the cine club on Great Windmill Street. She must have seen it around seventy-one or two. They had watched the film together in a Chelsea flat with a big plate of prawn crackers, a crate of pale ale and a bottle of Hennessy's. Chelsea had been swish, although they didn't live there long. They bought the leasehold on the proceeds of a bank job Frankie pulled in Southgate and gave it up when he was arrested two months later. At the time she was pregnant with Callum and the apartment was too small for a family anyway.

It was a while before Susan noticed the blond boy who had been following her. She gave him a puzzled stare, he looked back down at his coffee. He was no professional, but it would have taken a clairvoyant to have followed her today. Wouldn't it? Sulphate only makes you paranoid as you're coming down and she didn't feel at all down.

At last, it came to her. Hogie's sheepish smile, his blush, the way he played with the bangs at the side of his head. She should have guessed earlier.

Susan looked away, not wanting the giggle that was pushing at her lips to be misinterpreted. She lit a cigarette to give her mouth something new to do. She sipped her coffee. She wondered if she was doing too many things at once. She did not want to give the impression she was either embarrassed, perturbed or flattered. She decided to lead him around for a while to test his seriousness. She took her time over her coffee or her cigarette. She gave him a feeling that there was both time and space to play with and waited until he lit a fresh cigarette. Then she collected her bags together and left abruptly. She cast a cool glance over her shoulder as she left and for a second, their eyes locked.

Descending to the lower halls by escalator made it easier

for him to follow. She took her time between the cosmetic stands, using the mirrors to keep watch on the boy.

At the exit, she paused to button her lightweight mac before stepping outside. He was still behind her, reflected in the glass of a display case. She watched him tangle with a crowd of Japanese tourists. He had only the faintest impression of her as she pushed through the doors and turned to her right. She tacked across the swelling pavement, avoiding the busier traffic. When she reached Sloane Street she stepped crazily into the traffic. He was stranded on the opposite pavement, watching as she disappeared through a side door at Harvey Nichols.

Hogie hustled around the back of a bus but was held up by the on-coming traffic from Knightsbridge. He had no hope of catching the woman. He pushed through the doors into another cosmetic hall knowing his only strategy was to take things slowly, floor by floor. Providing she wanted to be tracked down, he would find her. Hogie looped around the separate stalls before taking the escalator.

She wasn't on the first floor. It should have been his safest bet, it carried the kind of labels that she looked to favour. The second floor was a white-out, too. He had no faith in the third floor, the clothes there were either too young or too frowsy. The food hall and restaurant on the fifth would be more likely. Hogie only passed through the third floor for the sake of completeness. Then he saw a flicker of reddish-blond hair at the far side of the floor. He checked the possible exits and circled wide, trying to throw a dragnet across the whole department.

There were no further flashes but he knew that whoever's hair he had seen, they couldn't have got past him. He had narrowed all the possible foxholes to a series of changing rooms and the women's bathroom. He waited.

The red-head woman swinging out the changing room door

was an American called Lauren. When she heard the
pounding of boots across the wooden floor and turned to
see the blond kid charging her way, he was already almost
on top her. He went into a slide, skidding to a stop only
inches from her painted toes. So she said something like:
"Whoa, hold on there."

He didn't hit her. He did surprise the hell out of her.

"I'm sorry, I fucked up. I thought you were somebody
else." Calming himself with a few deep breaths as he picked
himself up and dusted himself down. "I thought you were
this woman I'm after."

He'd made a bad call, what could she say? "Well, I guess
I'm not."

"No."

He dropped back a pace, shifting his feet and imitating
pure teen awkwardness. Though he wasn't a teen, maybe
just a couple of years into his twenties. He had a way of
looking from under his floppy fringe. The fringe had a way
of sucking in the sunlight from all around and making a
fountain in the centre of the room.

He was paying attention to her now, saying, "I'm sorry, I
mean tell me if you mind, but that's a Ben de Lisi dress
you've got there, isn't it?"

It was. Lauren had picked it up in a rush of vacation
shopping frenzy. She said, "Uh-huh, but I figure it's not for
me."

"Did you try it on?"

"This?" She looked back to the dress dangling off its
hanger on the tip of her finger. The thing didn't weigh anything at all, she could forget it was there and just stare at
the boy.

He was smiling, wide open. "Yes, the Ben de Lisi dress."

"No, I didn't try it on. I held it up against myself, but I
didn't try it on. I figured it was too young, you know?"

He began shaking his head, his fringe dancing out in

filament threads of light. Even the beard, which she'd only just noticed, wasn't exactly deplorable. What he was saying was, "Oh no no. No way. I mean, that's a misapprehension. What it is, Ben de Lisi isn't easy to wear. Not a nightmare or anything, but he's a bit tricky. . . . If you want, I could help you out."

"You could? Do you work here."

"I work around the department stores in general. I know women's clothes inside out."

She felt her smile creep out. She guessed she'd let him push it a mite further, see how far he was going to try and play the old gigolo. One eyebrow raised, she said, "So you're, what, a kind of freelance consultant, huh?"

"No. I'm a chef. But if you want to come back into the changing rooms, I should be able to sort you out."

The grin on the boy's face, he knew he had her. But it was the kiddie enthusiasm that won her over, not anything he managed to blurt out. As she turned and walked back to the changing rooms, Lauren felt the vampish swing in her hips, like, *va-va-voom*. There were two changing rooms, the far side of the unattended archway. Lauren took the one to the left, Shampoo Boy was dancing right on her tail. It was his idea to lock the door.

"I'm Hogie," he said, trying to turn in the under-size box.
"Lauren."

When he slid his hand up to take a hold of hers, she swore she could feel the pulse racing in his thumb. She took a half pace forward, knowing there was no room. They brushed together, remaining finger-locked until the back of his knees caught the edge of the corner seat and forced him to sit down. Hogie, the boy wonder, looking up at her like he couldn't believe how far his luck had brought him. Lauren had put on a flower-print dress that morning and was tired of it by lunch-time. She knew it outlined the range of her curves and, in the hot weather, the material got so it was just about ready to bust. Now, standing above him, looking down at the wide boy blue of his eyes, she felt there was no good reason for the dress to hold together any longer.

He said, "Do you need help with the zip?"

"It's at the side here," she lifted an arm. Built into the seam was a six inch zipper, set at waist level.

He pulled on the zipper. And the hell with it, she would have to squirm like crazy to get out of the dress. He moved one of his hot little hands to her hip, ostensibly to hold the material straight, but he was out exploring.

With the zip clear, Lauren pulled the dress upwards and began shrugging her shoulders, lifting her arms as she tried to work the dress over her head. She was pretty much caught, blind, when Hogie reached behind her and took a hold either side of her butt. His grip was firm but not too tight. She stopped wriggling. There was a pause, then she went Hogie's way with a moan. He slipped his fingers beneath her underpants and pulled them down. Somehow, the boy got himself in a position to push his mouth against her inner lips. She staggered and regained her balance. He was breathing shallow hot breaths. Whether it was his excitement or nerves or genuine technique, the damp heat of his breath was making her steam. She opened her legs by buckling her knees. His upturned mouth matched her own pouting lips, size for size. His tongue felt soft and fleshy as it pushed against her most sensitive spots. He spooned warm liquor over her inner ridges, his tongue trailed her everywhere.

As he surfaced, she found a way out of her dress and threw it to the floor. Standing stripped to her bra and summer sandals, her arms pushed out to touch both walls of the dressing room, she felt she dominated that tiny room. Hogie stood to meet her, kissing her as he pushed himself into her curves. She returned his drenched kisses and they slithered together for minutes before Hogie dropped his trousers and told her she had better turn around. There wasn't room for no other way.

She fell forwards with her arms outstretched, palms to the wall mirror and her body bent at the waist. Hogie stood reflected behind her, looking downwards through the floppy bangs of his hair. As she felt him probing forwards, she pushed back and gasped as they swallowed together. Then she closed her eyes. He moved with a rhythmic stirring, matched by the movement of his hands on the soft cheeks of her ass. The air saturated with her perfume, with their double sweat and with the fresh smell of his hair. He had such a good smell and . . . maybe . . . he was a touch chaotic and in too much of a darned rush, but the burbling of his breath and the shout of joy as he came into her and that sweet sweet smell all around him, it made the world of difference.

She had powerful lungs. Hogie was knocked backwards, she was at least twice as loud as any of his friend's mothers.

EIGHT

Cheb's troubles kept him away from the unlocked restaurant for almost an hour. The whole length of Old Compton Street, all the gays treated the Cheb-and-Jools show like it was the day's top entertainment. Unfortunately, they had him tagged as the villain and once Jools started weeping the mood on the street turned ugly. Cheb had no choice, he turned over his keys and helped her to a taxi. He even gave her his cigarettes to smooth the journey. The problem was, they all recognised her. He'd been out of the country too long, he couldn't know she'd got herself elected as some kind of gay icon.

Back at the restaurant, George Carmichael was stood at the bar. Cheb saw him even before he'd opened the door. As he stepped through, the man turned on him with a glare, rasping: "I want a word with you."

His voice was a subcutaneous croak, like Vaseline on sand. Cheb didn't know when he last heard anything so fucked-in-the-throat. He nodded, stopped in the centre of the dining room. The man had the bar-top phone in his monster hand, his fingers part way through a dial code.

"Wait there."

Cheb froze.

There were no 999 calls, no hint of a murder case or even that George knew what was waiting for him in the kitchen. Cheb spent the best part of thirty minutes waiting, keeping quiet surveillance and wishing he hadn't given his cigarettes away so easily. The calls were nothing but low intensity nonsense, drifting around the empty restaurant. What he learnt was that George Carmichael was queer for sure and he was only the frontman for the restaurant. The real owner was some woman, domiciled in España but soon to touch-down in London, England. Carmichael was ringing around to cancel anything that might clash with his appointment to meet her. The voice rumbled on, saying he couldn't make it until late, he had to go through the accounts with this woman ... *blah blah blah.*

Carmichael finally rasped out with a curt, "No, she's an ally. It's the husband who's a problem ... aren't they always." His goodbye words. When he slapped down the phone Cheb was nowhere: staring out into space. Carmichael snapped his fingers.

"So why was this place unlocked?"

Cheb shook his head. "Unlocked? Because you're here." He held up his keys. "I only just arrived."

"What, now?" Carmichael looked at his watch. "What about Hogie?"

"He's not been in either, Mr Carmichael. We been . . ." It had to sound good. " . . . speaking to suppliers. Hogie's still out doing the rounds. It's the party tomorrow."

Carmichael knew it. He picked Cheb's case off the bar, holding it by one handle so it flapped open. "What about this. Isn't it yours?"

Cheb looked at the empty case. "Not mine, Mr Carmichael."

The man shrugged. Then said, "Well go and look round the kitchen. I've already had a glance and nothing seems to be missing but we'd better make sure before we decide whether to call the police or not."

Cheb nodded, "Alright", and pushed through the swing doors.

He didn't know where he should look. Anywhere but the wheelie bin. He opened a drawer, all of it neatly laid out with whisks, ladles, pastry cutters. The next drawer was full of knives.

When he heard the man's footsteps, he turned around. The kitchen doors opened out like wings behind Carmichael as he stood, considering the room. He had hold of a bottle of Otard cognac in one hand, two brandy glasses in the other. The cigarette dangling from his lips was about double the girth of a Marlboro.

"Anything missing?"

Cheb said No. The man turned around and put the glasses on the work top. His greying skinhead rucked into soft folds at the back of his neck as he guessed at a couple of unmeasured shots, weighted in his favour. "Well, there's no reason to bother the police then."

Cheb said No.

Speaking over his shoulder, the man said, "Was it Hogie who told me you were a Buddhist?"

Cheb closed the third drawer—palette knives and a bunch of stainless steel things he couldn't put a name to—and walked over to accept his cognac. "I know a bit about it, Mr Carmichael. But I'm definitely not a Buddhist."

George shrugged, he must have misunderstood. "Hogie told me you studied Buddhism out East."

"Yeah, I studied it. But on my own, I didn't go for instruction."

"So you're not one of these tantric sex gurus I've been reading about in the style magazines?"

Cheb shook his head. No he wasn't one of those.

"You've never had a five hour sex session?"

Cheb thought he would have remembered.

Carmichael looked around for an ashtray. When he couldn't see one he handed the smoking butt over to Cheb and let him run to the sink to douse it. Cheb tried to maintain an efficient look, keeping a lid on his nervous twitches. He dropped the sodden butt in an unused soapdish and handed it to Carmichael. "Will that do?"

"Thanks. So what's your take on Buddhism, kid?"

Cheb took a gulp at his cognac, taking it all in one shot. By the time it reached the back of his throat, he was gagging for air. "What?"

"I was asking what you thought of Buddhism."

Cheb tried to gauge the man's interest. He was lighting another cigarette. It was the only thing that cracked his down-turned mouth, semi-permanently clenched between heavy jowls. With a face like that, Cheb didn't know if the guy cared or not. There were no signs of outright negativity. He was ready to give it a shot. It was better than the horror in the wheelie bin.

"What do I think? I think it's sick." Cheb gave him the equation: "Buddhists live off rice, and rice gives you Beri Beri, which is a wasting disease."

"Is that right?" Carmichael nodded his huge slab of head,

his eyes narrowed in the bulges of his lids. "Is this something I should worry about, as a restauranteur?"

Cheb zeroed the idea. "No. It's pretty rare, now. If you're worried, then stick to brown rice. Do you have a spare cigarette?"

Carmichael handed the packet over: Gitanes. He said, "Yeah, I've heard of people eating brown rice. Me, I prefer to eat white. But I guess some people like both brown and white rice. What do you say?"

The man was playing with him. The offer carried a subtext but it wasn't genuine. Though it was delivered with some style. Cheb said, "I wouldn't know. I never touch either."

"A genuine pervert."

Carmichael lifted his glass and sank the last drop of his brandy. When he stood the glass on the kitchen surface and poured his next measure, Cheb slipped his own glass next to it. Moving so fast, he worried the gesture screamed desperation. Carmichael just looked from glass to kid, then smiled. "Cute." He slopped another few ounces out of the bottle and left the freshened glass for him to pick up.

Cheb could have sucked the whole bottle down in one but he tried to slow the pace. He let his next sip spread over his tongue, feeling it burn into the jelly as he tried to figure a softening tactic.

He went for the full clinical account of Beri Beri.

"I'm not saying all Buddhists have Beri Beri, Mr Carmichael. But a priest who lives on a handful of rice a day is more likely to have it than a peasant who mixes a few vegetables with his meal. What happens, the disease shuts down the central nervous system. Which is why you get these guys pushing spikes through their arms or burying themselves alive. All of those nappy-wearing gimmicks."

Carmichael sipped on his cognac. He seemed to be listening and Cheb wasn't ready to quit.

"The priest gets the peasant's respect because he's totally

indifferent to pain. So, eventually, the kind of life Beri Beri makes possible becomes the blueprint for all the devout. And right at the limits of possibility, you got the promise of nirvana, total inertia: the natural end of a society devoted to malnourishment."

Carmichael thought he might have heard this shit before. Whatever, he was definitely cooling on the conversation. "Is this one of those 'opium for the people' speeches? Buddhism is nothing but a way to bear a sick civilisation."

"There's no such thing as a healthy civilisation. Buddhism doesn't mask the symptoms of a sick society. It *is* one of the symptoms. But it's also the program-code that allows the disease to spread without oriental societies ever quite collapsing."

"You made all this shit up?"

Cheb nodded. "Some of it. You know, from reading and talking, seeing the sights and visiting the shrines."

Carmichael stubbed the dying butt of his last cigarette in the soapdish and gave Cheb the once over. Then, shaking his head, he said, "Listen kid, do the theorising on your own time. This is a straight place. I don't want any freaky psychotic shit disturbing the ambience."

He carried the makeshift ashtray over to the bin, saying: "Just keep the place clean and we'll get on fine."

Cheb couldn't stop him. The man had opened the bin and was looking down.

What Carmichael said, the bin lid in one hand and a brand new expression on his face, was, "We might have a problem."

He had taken his time, staring down into the bin for forty ticking seconds. Cheb just counted them.

Cheb said, "A problem?" He was already backing towards the doors.

"Yes, I would definitely say so." Carmichael stared at him and this time there was nothing to crack the grim line of his mouth. His look coming straight at Cheb through slitted eyes. "Listen kid. You're a sick fuck, wouldn't you say? Well, I've got a paying job for you. I just hope you can handle it."

Cheb nodded, working himself up to showing surprise as Carmichael began outlining exactly what was on his mind.

NINE

Lost in the perfume hall, Susan had managed to sidestep the first girl. The second took her out with a five second burst of perfume at breast level and struck her down. The amphetamine sulphate in her bloodstream vapourised, leaving her defenceless against a raging headache. She reeled to the left and ahead of her the main doors swung open. She reached the street without looking back, forgetting that she was being pursued. Her hand went out blindly, taxiing her to the edge of the pavement.

Her driver asked more than once if she was alright. Huddled on the back seat, she mumbled, she thought she could hold on. She only wished the cab didn't stink so heavily of peach air freshener . . . she felt like she was being smothered under a tart's duvet. They were past Portman Square before she began to regret losing the chase through the department stores. She couldn't expect to see the blonde boy again.

Later, when the entry phone buzzer woke her, Susan had no idea where she was. She took it piece by piece and worked it out: a furnished mansion flat on New Cavendish Street, Marylebone. The taxi driver had got her there thanks to a scrawled address she'd found in her handbag. Once she'd found the hidden key and was safely through the door, she staggered from room to room until she hit a bed, passing out as she flopped down. According to her watch she'd been asleep for almost six hours. The buzzer kept on raging at intervals for as long as it took her to answer it.

There was a four inch monitor screwed to the landing wall. It was lit-up bright white, radiant as a distress flare and shrieking like a bitch. On-screen, George Carmichael came out of nowhere in glorious, looming fish-eye.

Susan said, "George."

Out of the box, the familiar growl: "Susan?"

"Get your finger off the fucking button or I swear, I'll bite it off."

"Susan?"

"Come up George. I'll be in the shower—but make yourself comfortable."

She unlatched the front door and tried to get a sense of where she was. In the kitchen she found a plastic bag holding a pack of English sausages and a dozen eggs. One hundred servings of one-cup tea bags were scattered around the melamine worktop, the grey tissue squares soaking up a pool of spilt orange juice. There was a Food And Wine store on the opposite corner, abreast Marylebone High Street, but she didn't remember buying anything. She noticed the orange juice was produce of Seville: concentrated, hydrated, half-empty.

After a five second cold shower she dried off, shivering: remembering she had no clean clothes. At least someone had hung a bath robe behind the bedroom door, the only welcoming thing in the whole room. Otherwise, it was flowery wallpaper and matching sheets, scattered lace doily's and pine bedroom furniture. In the bathroom, as in the kitchen, the sink had separate taps rather than a mixer faucet. Everything as it was, only slightly skewed. Over time, it seemed she'd grown unaccustomed to English ways.

When she walked into the kitchen, George looked at her and said, "Jesus, which side of the bed did you get out of?"

She looked that bad? All she said was, "How do you work the fucking central heating?" She'd seen a plastic box in the hallway with a flickering digital screen and a row of buttons, but she couldn't make sense of it.

George said, "You're cold? Come on, it's got to be the hottest day of the year."

If it was, she was standing in a heat exclusion zone. She said, "Just fix the heating please George."

He walked off, shouting from the corridor: "What do you want? Heating or water?"

"Both, put them on constant."

She was hungry now. She thanked God or whoever that there was enough food in the flat to cushion her sulphate come-down. She had to eat before she could even begin to think about looking at the accounts. George had set four thick ledgers down on the kitchen table, his cigarettes placed on top.

She was half-way through a plate of fried eggs and sausages before she looked up and said, "You know George. It's good to see you."

"You too, you cranky bitch." He said it with a smile, softened by a cloud of cigarette smoked.

Now she was looking at him, her first impressions were solid. It wasn't just that he was older and greyer; everything about him had gelled. And it wasn't simply that his fat had hardened into bulk. It was something else entirely. He'd got gravity and he carried it off well. Except that he winced every time she put a fresh squirt of sauce on her eggs.

She said, "What is it? You can't stand the sight of ketchup now you're such a big cuisine queen?"

"No, it's not that." He reconsidered, "Well, not just that. I've had one of those days, that's all. There was something of an upset at the restaurant so I guess I've got that on my mind."

"I thought you might be worried about showing me how badly you'd cooked books."

He wouldn't go that far. He knew he had some explaining to do. He said, "You'll never break me, doll."

"No?" She lifted an eyebrow: "There's a Corby trouser press in the bedroom. Don't make me use it."

He put up his hands: "Okay, okay. I'll talk."

They both knew the accounts he'd been sending her these last twelve years were less than accurate, that he was guilty of something close to embezzlement.

She pushed her plate away: "Are you ready?"

He squared up, showing that solidity again. Growing old had done him nothing but favours. True, he needed reading glasses. Whenever he came to explain a line of figures, he would slide the glasses to the end of his nose and follow the columns down with his ring finger. That was an odd gesture, holding his hand so that it fluttered across the account book. But even that suited him, a hint of flash against his usual calm.

George Carmichael called himself a choreographer when she first met him. Even when he began handling Frankie's investments full-time, he was still Dancing George to her, a friend at the other end of a long distance line. Which was why she had never challenged him on any of his reports. Presumably he had his reasons and she trusted him not to jeopardise the whole account. But now it was time for him to get on stage and sing.

She never expected it to be so intricate. After ninety minutes listening to him explain where the money had gone, it was Susan who suggested they take a break. She had left her reading glasses in Spain and borrowing George's stronger pair gave her a headache.

When she offered to make the coffee, he asked if she'd

mind him going through to the front room. For some reason he wanted to watch the local television news.

She was still in the bathrobe. Her only clothes had felt unclean and until she bought more, she had to wash and wear. They were now coming to the end of their spin cycle. She stuffed them in the tumble dryer as she waited for the kettle to boil.

When she took the coffee through, he was watching a local news on-the-spot report from somewhere in Stoke Newington.

She said, "Anything interesting?"

George jumped. He said, "No. Nothing."

He turned back quickly enough, as though he was scared to miss something. She looked over his shoulder and saw a close-up of a nightclub sign. The voice-over claimed the holes punched across its surface had been made by a semi-automatic weapon.

She said, "What is it? Something to do with you?"

It wasn't. George shook his head and laughed. He guessed he must look distracted. He pointed to the screen and said, "No, I was just thinking, that kind of thing never happens at gay clubs."

"What kind of thing?"

"Gun-play. You know, it's got so the police wish everyone in the country was a faggot."

She said, "You've never been so popular."

"I lap it up, believe me."

He took the coffee but only managed one sip. In small ways, at least, he knew it paid to be straight so he told her he never drank instant: "It's like being dragged back to the seventies: instant cash, instant drinks, bad taste."

Susan tasted her own cup. It was terrible, she wouldn't have touched it in Spain. The speed come-down must have short-circuited her judgement. Either that or the apartment had taken advantage of her tiredness to pull a kind of Amity-ville stunt: haunting her with her bad old English habits.

George was right about the instant seventies when every-thing was quick, cheap and disposable. Money came in fat paper rolls, hauled out of tin boxes or paper bags. And because it could never be returned to a bank, it had to be spent quickly. Everyone in the life knew about inflation and the fastest ways to beat it. More than once, Susan had spent an hour in a shop and bought enough furniture for an entire apartment: vinyl sofa, mini bar, fitted melanine wardrobes and smokey glass tables—delivery included, deliver it this afternoon. It didn't matter that she might only live there for a month. Frankie Ball was working every week, either a wages snatch or a building society. The money had to be spent.

George was the closest thing they had to a bank. He was not a quite a money launderer, not quite a loan shark. It sounded strange but even then he was an investment specialist. If Frankie, or any of his friends, was carrying too much, George Carmichael would take it off their hands. They knew they'd get it back whenever they asked. In the meantime, they would have the run of his clubs: a bar tab, a few girls, anything within reason and always in lieu of interest. It was the blagger's bank. A listening bank, because George knew everything. Before Frankie's last job was even organised, George had spoken to Frankie and suggested that he handle the proceeds.

The television had turned to a new story. George had turned back to the screen. Now he was pointing to a figure hurrying across a carpark, flanked by two uniformed men. "Remember him?"

The guy on-screen was trying to hide his face but as he stooped into a police car something made him look up in surprise. The newscaster's voice gave his name and rank, the man was a sergeant with the Stoke Newington police.

Susan said, "He was with the dirty squad in the seventies. What's he done now?"

"He was caught selling crack." As the camera froze, the copper's face was framed in the car window, looking stupid and feral, caught bang to rights. George said, "He was a junior with the dirties when they were busted. I don't know how he kept his job but it must have ruined his chances of promotion."

"I remember him. He came into this club I was working in. He suggested to the manager—Flat Stanley, you remember him—that he'd take a pass on his money, he'd prefer an hour with me. Flat told him it wasn't a good idea. That I was Ballistic Frankie's wife. So the copper changed his mind and shagged another of the girls instead."

"Were you working at the same time you were married?"

"Not at first. But Frank got sent down for a spell in '73, so I went back for about eight months."

George said, "You were a great dancer. The Queen of Soho."

Susan corrected him, "You and me both."

Dancing George and the woman who could have been London's Liza Minelli if she wasn't married to an armed robber. And could sing rather than strip.

George said, "Seeing that ex-Vice cop's brought it all back. I knew they'd be finished one day. Even when they were swarming all over Soho, pissed on free booze, dribbling spunk and stuffing envelopes I knew they'd be thrown out because a square mile in central London couldn't stay a frontier town for ever. It was time for the cowboys in Vice to pack up and mosey along. But there was no reason for the gay scene to disappear with them. It was no longer a crime and was never exactly a part of the sex trade. Just because it thrived in Soho, there was no reason for it to remain semi-shady. It could be gentrified, too."

This was his big idea: "There is no business like gay

business: a huge turnover, absolutely peaceable, and totally wide open because only a queer knows where a queer likes to hang out. And having to be queer was only one of the barriers to entry. There were other disincentives. Places that were theoretically legal after the law changed in '69 were still bribing the police in the late seventies. I bought every dive bar, every hole-in-the-wall club I could get my hands on and paid next-to-nothing. When the Vice Squad were sent down en masse and everything got more relaxed, I knew the time had come. I put all the spare money into redecorating and building huge neon signs saying 'Puffs R Us'. It was beautiful, and only the banks were still too straight to get into bed with me. So, when Frankie's money came along, I took it all and put it to work."

Susan said, "I believe you're a genius but Frankie wouldn't see it that way. He didn't sweat over a hot shotgun just so bumboys could lead a better life."

George snorted: "The only difference between a straight criminal and a queer one is half a bottle of scotch."

Maybe he was right, Britain's first Out celebrity was Ron Kray. But Frankie had got more conservative as he grew older.

She said, "So we own Soho?"

"Most of it, the freeholds at least."

It was worth a toast. They could drink to their chances of keeping hold of it.

She said, "How about it, partners?"

George said, "I can't promise anything over this coffee. Wait a moment, I'll go and buy some gin."

Susan remembered seeing ice cubes stacked in the freezer, left over from the previous tenants and dusted white with age. She did not believe ice went off. There were no lemons.

George said, "I'll get all the ingredients. Five minutes."

She didn't just wave him out, she applauded him. Then she turned to the kitchen and went to check the tumble dryer. Her clothes were dry and wearable but too crumpled for a millionairess property tycoon. She started searching the apartment for an iron. At the end of the corridor was a second bedroom that she hadn't even looked at yet. She gave it a try.

Opposite the bed was a mirror. For some reason, she sat down and stared at herself. Framed there, hands in her lap, looking at herself in the bathrobe, the scene looked so strangely familiar. Then she got it: she looked just like one of Callum's overnight girls, posed in his trophy album. She'd just been too dazed to recognise his bathrobe when she put it on. She stood up, pulled open the doors to the wardrobe and found her suitcase: just one new flight sticker attached and her name printed neatly on the label in Callum's own hand.

She hauled it onto the bed, unzipped the zipper and started pulling out her clothes. There had to be a reason Callum took her bag. When she found the six kilos of cocaine, heat sealed in polythene and wrapped in her party clothes, she felt something surge through her: hate shaking her like a cheap drug. Who did she hate the most: Frankie for letting their boy smuggle the stuff or Callum for using her case to do it? She was still shaking when George came hallo-ing back into the apartment.

TEN

Jools took just one look at him and stormed to the bedroom. Hogie was there, standing in his own flat, feeling like the stranger who turned up to dinner with a cowl on his head and a scythe in his hand. Only the ringing of the phone pulled him out of it.

Mannie on the other end. Hogie said, "Jesus Christ, you're a fucking life-saver man. What the fuck's going on?"

Mannie was hanging on a pay-phone at Euston station. He said, "Don't ask me, I'm just her brother. What I need to know, what's your address?"

"Don't worry about that. I'll pick you up. I've got to get out the flat before Jools turns psycho on me. She's not said a word, just locked herself in Cheb's room, but I can feel the vibes. I got the stereo on full blast and I swear I can hear her pounding round the room and crying."

Mannie said, "She's not said one word?" Maybe it was serious.

"Just wait there, I'll be down in ten minutes."

Hogie hung up. Mannie didn't even get a chance to tell him he wasn't alone. As he spooned the receiver, Naz came up behind and said, "So, we getting a taxi or what?"

"No. Hogie says to wait. He'll pick us up himself."

"Sweet. And your sister's there?"

"Yes. She's there. How did you know?"

Naz smacked his lips and didn't answer. Just said, "Looks like I'm sorted then. Where do you want us to wait?"

Mannie looked round. There was a clump of steel tube chairs, welded into the floor at the centre of the grand hall. It was as good as anywhere. They would be out in plain view so even Hogie should find them. Naz loped off, leaving Mannie to pick up the cases as he followed on.

The whole journey from Manchester to London, Mannie had sat slumped, inert, listening as Naz explained just how bad his situation was. He already knew. Maybe he'd looked a little dazed but that was only because spending any length of time with Naz sent him into spins of hyper-ventilitation.

Naz was still making his point three hours on. As Mannie

struggled over with cases, he looked over and said, "I gotta say, losing one sheet of acid is a fuck-up. Losing two sheets of acid is taking the piss."

Mannie sat down. He knew he'd made about as big a mistake he could ever make. The way business worked: he took Naz's merchandise on trust with a verbal guarantee that he had them on a sale-or-return basis. In practice, nothing was ever returned because there was never a shortage of customers. Come their next sales meeting, if there was anything Mannie hadn't sold, it was only because he'd taken it himself. He'd spent two whole weeks thinking the system was not just fair it was even equitable. But after a month, holding the drugs had fermented so much paranoia and amnesia that he spent half his time devising elaborate hiding places for his stash and the rest forgetting exactly where it was. If there was some special talent to drug dealing, Mannie didn't have it. He'd proved his uselessness for sure. But Naz still had uses for him.

Naz said, "Worrying about you is so much fucking stress, it's no wonder I need a holiday."

Mannie couldn't see how the guy looked stressed, stretched out on the seat, but he nodded anyway. Or tried to. He was in so much pain himself he could barely move his head. Hypertension had turned his neck into a gnarled stump and the tight pain across his heart extended all the way down his left arm. If this was a declared holiday, it was strictly unilateral.

When Hogie came wandering over twenty minutes later, he had to say Mannie looked bad. With a face like that, he could model for the Droopy dog in those Tex Avery cartoons. At one hundred paces, he'd seen the little storm cloud that always hovered over Mannie's head . . . figuratively, but visibly. But then, when he yelled out Mannie's name and saw the Paki look around, he grew his own baby storm cloud too.

"Hiya. Naz." Hogie's arms were hanging by his side. "I didn't expect you."

"No?" Naz didn't see it was his problem, saying: "Cheb asked us down for a bit of R&R. You know. Spend some time relaxing without worrying how I'm going to put the gangster shit on this cunt and the other useless fuckers working for us." He jerked a thumb over at Mannie. "It should be sweet. Just enjoy a bit of a smoke, go to this party you got coming. Maybe later take a pop at Mannie's sister."

Hogie misunderstood. What did he mean, take a pop?

Naz said, "Seduce her."

"Really?"

"Yeah. She looks cool." He turned to Mannie. "You don't mind, bud?"

Mannie said, "Fuck, no. Whatever you want Naz." He shot Hogie a helpless look as Naz started walking for the exit.

"This way, huh?"

Hogie said, "Yes. Straight outside, Naz."

Hogie's estate car was parked at the edge of the taxi ramp, somehow free of parking tickets although it had drawn interest from the local cabbies. Hogie centrally unlocked and they all climbed in, Naz making himself comfortable in the front, Mannie sitting in the back: skinny and weak looking among the torn maps, Lucozade bottles and empty crisp packets. Hogie circled around the front of the station and turned left, taking the smaller road that also led to Camden High Street.

Naz found his armrest and pulled it down. He said, "Expensive car."

Hogie wasn't sure what to say, it was quite expensive.

"So why'd you buy a Volvo?"

"'Cause its safe. It's got side impact stuff and a crumple zone at the front. You know, all the features so you don't get killed."

"Why didn't you get an automatic as well, so you could still drive no matter how wasted you got?"

Hogie nodded. It was the idea. Just sit down, put it in D and as long as he kept an eye on the speed, it would be smooth all the way. He flashed a smile at Naz but Naz didn't seem to be smiling back.

They were approaching the big V in Camden where the underground station jutted out into the junction: its sign shining in the dusk, one side of the station's white walls colouring with the setting sun. Hogie pushed on his indicators, trying to claw his way back to the right-hand lane. He found the space to drift across the junction, moving at the same pace as the scraps of paper and cardboard that dossed across the foot of Kentish Town Road. He ignored the horns around him, keeping it slow until he saw the space that a stopping bus would leave, then ramming for the opening as it appeared. He told them his flat was coming up on the right, the next turning off Camden Road.

When he stopped in the middle of the street, he said: "Do you want to get out now?"

Naz started opening the door. Mannie said, "Why, what's the problem?"

Naz said, "The guy's got to park."

They were outside a flat-roofed Victorian house. There was a buzzer for every storey but only the upper floor button was decorated with a water-transfer of the Silver Surfer. Mannie looked at it, rolled his eyes upwards and pressed. He and Naz waited in the porch, watching Hogie try to edge his big car into its parking space and listening as the sound of footsteps inside the house got louder. The door opened before Hogie was even half way through his manoeuvre. Mannie turned and found himself looking at his sister.

What struck him first: her mascara had run. Looking closer, he could see tears backed-up in her eyes. He thought to ask if she was okay but she didn't look ready to talk, only turned around and started trudging back up the stairs. Naz pushed ahead of him, keeping one pace behind Jools. Mannie stayed at the back, weighed down by the bags.

She left the flat door open but carried on walking, through to a room at the back. Mannie only caught a glimpse of the decor before she slammed the door. He recognised the Chebbish traits like the silver foil taped to the walls. He'd seen a man on TV describe the way the foil would amplify a room's latent energy and deflect it to specific focal points. He'd thought at the time it was an idea Cheb would go for.

Even before Hogie got in, Naz was comfortable on the sofa, licking strips of Rizlas. As he fitted them together, he said, "So, what's wrong with her?"

Mannie shook his head.

"Some woman thing or what?"

He doubted it. When Jools had woman's things, it was always more dramatic. He couldn't remember the last time he'd seen her so mute, so depressed.

By the time Hogie came stumbling through the door, Naz had the joint all fired up. When he asked who was going to make the tea his voice came out in the breathless choke of a man savouring his first blast. Mannie went to the kitchen area and shook the kettle. Hogie followed, ready to help by locating the ingredients.

Naz shouted, "Make a cup for your sister as well. Does she have sugar?"

He was stretched out on the sofa, his head overhanging one arm and his feet the other, relaxed. He didn't seem to mind that Jools was in the middle of some kind of breakdown. Like he was playing a longer, waiting game. Mannie had to ask himself how long this London holiday was going to last.

He and Hogie stayed huddled in the kitchenette until the kettle was boiled and then stood silently over the four mugs as they waited for them to brew. When there was no more hope, Mannie slopped out the bags and carried two mugs over to Naz.

Naz had swallowed up the whole joint and was back on his feet. He grabbed the teas, saying: "Sweet. I'll take them through."

Mannie watched him go. There was a knock at the end of the corridor and the sound of the door opening. That was it.

He and Hogie spent the next few hours watching re-runs of seventies TV on cable. It was getting dark and Mannie was already worried they might begin to hear certain sounds through the wall. Hogie had the same thought, using the remote to keep prodding at the volume until the flashing lights on the VCR panel nudged over to the red. No doubt, the flat was a disaster area.

Just when Mannie knew he couldn't stand it any longer, Hogie was there first.

"We've got to get out, Mannie man." He was ready to buy the drinks just so long as they got out now.

They were walking down Camden Road, back towards the heart of Camden, when Hogie said: "It's down to Cheb, he's got to get rid of them."

Mannie said, "Why do you think he asked Naz down anyway?"

ELEVEN

Cheb couldn't say exactly how he came to take the job but one of the things he insisted on: he couldn't do it on his own.

Carmichael hadn't argued. The boy in the bin was about six foot tall and weighed at least one hundred and fifty pounds. Cheb scaled in closer to one-twenty.

He said, "That's fine. Hire who you want, it's your decision." He held out his hand and Cheb found himself holding it, shaking it. The deal done.

As Carmichael was leaving, Cheb said: "Why aren't we calling the cops?"

He turned back at the door, nothing more than a swift look over his shoulder as he said: "I'm a restauranteur, not a police informant."

Cheb could have spent the rest of the afternoon thinking that one through, if he could have thought about anything.

One of his problems, he hadn't been able to eat since Manchester. The last time he'd tried, the night before, he'd opened the fridge and found a fish pie Hogie had made; ingredients: a tin of Campbell's soup, a tin of tuna and some kind of crumbled biscuit on the top. Cooking for himself, Hogie mostly used crumbled biscuit and either Campbell's soup or yoghurt, depending whether the recipe was sweet or savoury—peach or pineapple slices when it was both. That was the problem of shopping after midnight when only the Paki supermarkets and petrol stations were open. Cheb had taken the pie and given it to the microwave. It came out fine but he still couldn't eat it.

Now, sitting in the kitchen a few yards from the body, he only had enough appetite for the smallest meal: one tab of acid and a gram of sulphate. When he next opened the bin lid and looked down, he felt less overwhelmed, which was good. But he was still short on the inspiration adequate to the undertaking. It wasn't enough to just do a job of work, it had to be done with sympathy and a sense of destiny.

He toppled the bin and dragged the corpse out onto the kitchen floor. The boy seemed whiter than he had that morning, perhaps an effect of the fluorescent lighting, lifting the shadows of daylight and turning the kitchen into a sci-fi sterile morgue. The light brought out the bruises on the boy's face; like freezer bags of purplish stock, frozen borsch sealed in cloudy skin. The worst of the damage around the left side but also encompassing the broken nose. Then, aside from the stove brand across his backside, precious little damage to the rest of the body. Looking at the face, Cheb got the idea of buying a rapist-style mask from one of the Soho sex shops, something with a zipper mouth and sealed eye pieces that would cover the bruises completely. He wasn't sure the strategy answered but he felt like getting out. He justified it: he was putting some distance into his planning. Rather than let the problem play over and over in his mind, he'd lift the needle out of the groove and busk it.

The evening breeze was beginning to sneak under the car fumes and clear the air. As he set out from the restaurant, Cheb felt he was breathing freely for the first time that day. He tried to centre on the tripping buzz in his chest, tune to the pulsing lights of strip joints and bookshops around him. Basically, feel the Brownian motion at the heart of the capital.

A Manchester-born boy, he'd never got around to visiting London before he moved in with Hogie. But towards the end of his time out East, he borrowed a map of Britain and traced the path of each road and rail track. London was the place where the lines warped and collapsed, the twist at the centre of the paper, the un-ironable kink. He pictured the city as a Gothic version of Singapore, or maybe Hong Kong: an international city cut free of any local significance. But unlike the other cities, London came with a history. Take any of the words that tagged with London and you got a wide-screen picture of medieval horror: bloody towers, falling bridges, fog, fire, plague, blitz. The words meshed with the stories he'd first heard as a kid and later caught in bars on the satellite news channels: ferries sinking in the

Thames, the monarchy collapsing in flames and vomit, live-TV pics of ministers stalking mad cows across the lawns of parliament. Above all, he saw a monster fed on global money, tearing chunks out of the digiverse and sucking them down into its hell. London was a blast of the unreal, the last City, the baseline for the entire chaosphere. Landing at Heathrow was like touching down at ground zero. His close reading of the map convinced him. The timelines, the flight arrows, the roads of England and the folds of the map all concentrated on a black spot, a negative space like the shadow on a catastrophe graph where every fact gets flipped onto a new scenario: from cuddly puppy to rabid hound, light sleep to nightmare, pedestrianised strip to riot-zone et cetera and contrapuntally yours, London.

Faced with the corpse, Cheb almost lost the full breadth of this vision and got hooked on the blackness. But now the feeling of dynamic possibility was coming back, stronger than ever. He'd find a way to slip into the folds of the catastrophe, ride the cusp and see how far he could flip. He could feel his synapses twang. He was going to have no problem losing the stiff. Throw it out into the night, let it skip and bounce away to another level.

Passing along Old Compton Street, he mixed with the crowds falling kerbside into the chocka coffee shops, a thousand dilated eyes hovering over café lattes. Cheb kept scooting. He had an agenda, he was on a sex shop prowl. No time to be looking at the fauna hereabouts.

A neon silhouette pinned to the window of an old strip joint showed a woman, outlined in pink with bright blue nipples. As the light flickered she appeared to slink across the glass. A display case by the door was filled with coy photographs but a poster promised *All-Naked All-Nite Strip-Ola*. The neon sign flashed all the way back to the sixties. None of the newer shops he visited had as much style. As he shopped, the assistants tried to interest him in their videos and he watched whatever they showed him. One that kept recurring featured a pale German girl pushing a slippy hand up another girl's bum. As a twist on the camel-through-a-needle gimmick, it still had some appeal. He once read that the Mayans incorporated fisting into a few of their rites. He didn't know who'd revived it: from Meso-America to Mittel Europe, a hand across the millenia. Although Cheb had seen similar stunts in Bangkok.

He spent hours searching the specialist shops on the northside of Soho. He never saw a mask he liked, nothing but frail constructions in cheap vinyl, impulse buys for tourists who would split the welded seams when they grimaced under duress. When he was asked if he wanted to try something on for size, he was too depressed.

The assistant said, "Is it for your partner?"

Dog-tired of looking at racks of plasticky cowls, jocks and restrainers, he said: "Yeah. Have you got anything about Airedale size? I need one with holes so the ears can poke out."

He walked out of the shop and stood at the edge of Dean Street, where Soho was bisected by Shaftesbury Avenue. Ahead of him lay London's Chinatown. He pouted eastwards with amphetamine eyes. The mask idea hadn't panned out but he wasn't beaten yet. He was just waiting for the cavalry.

George Carmichael had a bottle of gin in one hand and a swinging sack of two lemons in the other. He said: "Why are you so sure it's cocaine?"

Susan looked from him to the six bags stood on the kitchen table. She said, "Come on. What else would they be? What else would you smuggle from Spain to England?"

George thought: Picassos, El Grecos, broken down donkeys, bull's cojones and, before skunk weed was invented, black Moroccan. He said, "Okay. It's probably cocaine. Why did Frankie do it?"

"Because the bastard's senile. I'd bet it wasn't even his idea. Callum's been messing around with some nutters of his own lately—they probably sold him on the idea and told him to get his dad to bankroll it. And Frankie would have agreed. He's changed a lot. If you saw him, you'd understand. The soft life doesn't suit him. These days he's nothing but a slobbering psychotic bum, growing maudlin about the old days."

She had a photograph in her hand, her proof. A picture of Frankie and some other men, playing about the deck of a yacht.

George said, "What's this, a holiday snap?"

She shook her head: It was no holiday.

George took the photo and scanned across it, finding Frankie standing just off-centre. He said, "It looks as though he should cut down on cholesterol. Blood pressure might be a future health worry." He took a closer look. "Who are the fuckers around him?"

"Who don't you recognise?"

Squinting now: "That's not Cardiff is it?"

Susan nodded.

"What's he doing in the picture?"

"That's it: Frankie's gang. The people he hangs out with."

George couldn't believe it. "What happened to the guys who pulled the bullion job with him?"

"What do you think?"

George said, "No."

"Frankie said it would make waiting easier if only one person had to be patient instead of six."

"They're all dead?"

She nodded.

"I heard a few whispers but nothing like that. I knew one

of them had died in a drugs deal that went wrong. Who was that, Jimmy Viva?"

"Jimmy was the third to go. Frankie paid for him to be thrown overboard, halfway between Morocco and Gib. They're a lost generation, George. No one noticed they were all dying."

"And now Frankie hangs out with slags like Cardiff?"

"Drinking in a shitty English pub and talking about the old days—when he wouldn't have let a creep like Cardiff carry his pool cue to a beating."

George ticked along the line of faces. He was about to hand the picture back when something about the blond boy at the end made him stop. He said: "I think I need my specs."

Susan picked them off the table and looked over his shoulder as she passed them to him. She followed his finger and said, "My son." And then: "What's wrong George?"

He knew he'd gone pale but as long as she was behind him, she couldn't tell. He managed to shrug.

She said. "Have you seen him?"

He shook his head. "No." Paused. "Maybe." Another pause. "Look I don't want to say anything now. But I promise I'll ask around."

She said, "Yeah, do. Because I'm going to kill the little bastard."

He mixed a couple of gin and tonics and drank them both before Susan finished dressing. After he'd refreshened the glasses, he took them through to the living room. The TV was still on. He flicked through the channels but he wasn't really thinking. It had been so easy to persuade Cheb to get rid of the body. No doubt, the kid was deranged but George had gambled on him being just sane enough to do a good, clean job. If there were any complications, George had been prepared to swear he knew nothing and pray the police swallowed it. He was certain that Susan never would.

Partners. He knocked back his third gin and poured a fourth. All day, he'd been trying to think who'd do that to him—dump him with a dead boy. The only name he came up with was Ballistic Frankie, which was why he'd never dreamed it was his son lying there. Susan's son lying there.

"Partners."

He looked up. Susan was standing there saying: "Wait for me, this is supposed to be a toast."

George picked her glass off the table. She took it with her free hand. Only now, George noticed she was carrying a small mirror, holding it flat like a tea tray. There were two lines ready cut and laid out, their underside reflections making them look as thick as sugar fingers.

He thought: Why not?

It was sometime later, Susan said: "Why don't we kick back the carpet, have a dance here." Then, like a delayed reaction, she was suddenly hot for the idea. "Come on George. I've brought a couple of my old records along with me."

She was scrambling for her satchel, coming up with two records. "I found these in Callum's flat. The bastard had stole them off me."

George shook his head. "The AWB? What's that?"

"The Average White Band. The record came out about 1973. You must know it."

George shook his head. "I didn't buy a single record for pleasure between the death of Judy Garland and the birth of the Village People."

"That's not true. What about the music in your clubs?"

"That was business, it was music to strip to. Songs for swinging titties. I used to buy compilations of James Last, Mandingo and The Dave Pell Singers. Or stuff like TJ Brass, you know, anything that's big on Bossa."

Susan last heard James Last on ex-pat radio, she didn't remember the other names. She skimmed the Average White Band sleeve onto a table and held up her other record. "You remember this, though. Van Morrison."

George squinted at the cover. "Maybe."

She hoped he'd like it. Together, they'd resolved the question of the accounts. It was time he began to lighten up.

She put "Moondance" on the record player and held her arms out. As the piano chords began chiming Susan said, "Are you ready, George?" George stepped up to her and they began a slow, near classical jive.

When he first spun her out, she glided so smoothly to the ends of his outstretched fingers that he almost believed he'd made it happen. It gave him confidence. He hadn't danced like this in years. He remembered a party, at least ten years ago, he'd agreed to dance ballroom for a laugh. It hadn't worked: two forty-year-old men with moustaches and flight jackets, arguing about which of them should lead. In the end, George's partner threw up his hands and flounced off. Then this skinny comic actor, well past pensionable age even then, had said he'd play femme. It had been beautiful, the old man could really dance. But not like Susan—she was a dream, she could be an icon.

Susan let herself be wound in until she was up against George's hard, barrel-shaped chest then took two short, slightly rapid steps, backwards. She knew she was helping him out but he was light-footed and even when he was less than fluid, always managed to carry each step off with style. With subtlety, too. She didn't notice he was wearing eau de cologne until they were cheek-to-cheek. She could hardly believe how well he'd aged, he had slipped into his mid-fifties as though that was exactly where he had always wanted to be: middle-aged, restrained and grey but super-cool. She had wondered, at least for a moment, if he was still overweight but had finally thought to hide it beneath a well-tailored suit. Dancing with him she realised that he had no more than a few pounds of fat anywhere, and all of it was laid over muscle. He was box-shaped and proud, his suit emphasised it.

He broke off before the middle eight. She thought he'd had enough until he brought his hands together and clapped to the beat. Then she knew what he was thinking. She twirled around and started shimmying, letting her hips emphasise the beats and arching her back to make her bottom seem rounder, her waist smaller. She put her hands on her backside and used her fingers to ruck the dress material. Inch by inch she clawed the cotton upwards until the skirt ended only fractionally shy of her cheeks. She only let the material drop back as she turned to face him again. He conducted her with his hands, suggesting movements with short gestures. She followed him, bringing one leg into a slow, circular kick and then, as he reversed the direction, making the same swinging arc kick to her right. Each time her leg soared, the paler skin on the inside of her thighs glowed for a second. As George led her on, she let her hands flutter by the top buttons of her dress, easing the first three open and holding the lapels apart to show the freckled v-bone between the rise of her breasts. She turned away again as she slipped the dress off her shoulders, left then right, before letting it slide to the small of her back. Her fingers only had to touch the clasp of her bra for it to spring open.

George had either recognised the song or already memorised it. He began singing at a verse ending: "*Can I make some more romance with you, my love.*" The mock bass profundity never disguised how well he sang.

Susan turned again as the dress fell all the way to the floor, holding the bra in place with her cupped hands. George had the sense to give up singing before the very last verse, the one where Van got a burbling scat-thing going, and Susan used the few, free, bars to improvise a slinky shuffle. Her face glowing around laughter lines, a giggle parting her sweet red lips. As the music ended, she tossed the bra away . . . da dah! George was already applauding.

She took her bows. George poured the celebratory gin, saying, "We can still work together."

She agreed, standing in her panties, toasting with her glass: "To Soho. We own it."

George said, "Frankie will be pissed off when he finds out."

"And pissed off when he finds out I've left him. So what are we going to do? Could you arrange some sort of spectacular crash so it looks as if all the money has been lost?"

"And then we split it between ourselves? Yeah, I could do that easily. Except that a fund manager isn't supposed to put all the money into one project. He might sue for negligence."

"That isn't Frank's style."

"No, he'll save himself the solicitor's fees."

Twice over. He wouldn't bother with a drawn-out divorce either. Susan said, "I can't believe the bastard once reminded me of Terence Stamp."

George swilled the dregs of his gin around. He knew what Susan wanted him to say. She wasn't even being coy. There was only one thing to do, they both knew it.

He said, "Okay, but what if Frankie kills us first?

TWELVE

Cheb snuffled back to the restaurant, empty handed but for a bottle of poppers he bought along the way. As he pushed

back into the kitchen, he caught the flickering tip of a cigarette, glowing in the restaurant's shadows.

"Who's that?"

A slow drawl answered. "No, mate. Who's that?"

It wasn't a cigarette, Cheb could smell it now. He said,
"Naz, you made it."

Cheb heard a suck, long and smooth enough to burn
through a whole joint in one graceful drag. When Naz eventually spoke, his voice came out in glorious monotone,
playing at thirty-three: "Yeah, well it's time I came down,
took a look at the sights and shit: Big Ben clock and whatdya
call... the bridge with flaps. Maybe try for a holiday
romance with Mannie's kid sister."

"Yeah?"

Only I got a problem. Jools is a bit tense. It seems some
idiot's been saying her mum's a slag.

Cheb said, "That was me. Is she still upset?"

Naz inhaled, bending the sound into an affirmative "Uh-
huh".

"She'll come round, Naz. I don't know if you noticed but
I've got a situation underway that could use a cool head."

Naz said, "It fucking looks like it." He banged on the light
switch.

The body lay where Cheb left it, spread across the floor.
Cheb said, "It's pretty much like I told you on the phone."

Naz nodded over to the corpse. "What happened to his
arse?"

Cheb told him how it had looked, sat up on the stove
top.

Naz walked towards the semi-dressed corpse. It was
slumped face up, its head slightly turned. A young face with
long blond hair. Naz asked Cheb if he knew him.

"No."

"You don't think he looks like your mate, the cook."

Cheb had thought so. All he said was, "Well, he's got yellow hair."

"He's about the same build. You didn't kill him."

Cheb was shocked. "No."

"It's what I'm saying: you didn't kill him. If you had, I wouldn't be helping. As it is, I guess I'll do it."

Good. That was good, it hadn't occurred to Cheb that there could be a problem. He said, "Did you get Hogie's car?"

"Yeah. It's in a multi-storey, near a street with a shit load of Chinese restaurants."

Cheb said. "What's it doing there?"

"You think I'm going to drive for hours looking for a parking space?"

"Well, you're going to have to get it. Bring it down the alley at the back here."

Naz walked over to the fire doors at the far end of the kitchen. He pushed through and looked up and down the alley-way, it was pedestrian only but a car would fit. He nodded. He carried on nodding, thinking Okay. When he stopped, it was to shake his head. Out loud, he said, "This is really fucked up." He turned and left.

Twenty minutes later, Cheb was back at the door, watching two red eyes glowing in the darkness as they drifted towards him: the reverse lights on Hogie's Volvo estate.

Naz held the car steady as he reversed towards the open fire doors. Looking in the rear view mirror, he could see Cheb peering round a huge galvanised bin. He guessed Cheb had put the body back inside but he did not know how long Cheb had been waiting there, just a boy alone on a back street with his dead body. When he'd pulled level to the fire doors, he got out of the car. But he first gave the steering wheel and gear stick a wipe with his sleeve. When he closed the driver's side door behind him, he wiped the handle of that too. He told Cheb that he was going to wait at the end of the alley, near the street.

"Why?"

"As the look-out. Also, if anyone stops to wonder what you're doing with a dead body, I can run off."

"How am I supposed to get the stiff in the trunk on my own?"

"You got it into the bin."

Cheb nodded, okay he would figure something out. Naz handed Cheb the keys before he strolled away, "Drive the car up when you've finished and I'll get in."

He kept half an eye on Cheb from the far end of the alley. No one went down that way but there were enough passers-by walking across its mouth. If none of them noticed anything peculiar, it wasn't Cheb's fault. A metallic crash echoed along the twin walls of the alley; Cheb had pushed over the wheelie bin. A girl out walking, dressed in silver with cute knee socks, turned towards the sound. Naz looked her over, from bare thighs to exposed midriff. She didn't seem bothered by the crash and he watched her walk away, swinging her bum a little. He turned back to Cheb. Reflected light from the kitchen glittered off the bin, lying on its side on the paving stones. Cheb was out of view, probably crouching. Naz heard a grunt, Cheb was hefting the body into the trunk. Naz resumed his look-out gig. There were few enough people around but he took care as he scanned around.

Another crash, Cheb had slammed the fire doors shut. Everything he did, the actions of a brain-addled English boy. Like the night lights of city traffic caught on a slow exposure, a ring of chemical confidence left glowing trails as he moved. Naz watched as he crossed to the driver's side door with gestures swollen large enough to fill the halo around them. Altogether too much front for such a little fucker.

Another crash, Cheb had reversed into the wheelie bin.

The car stalled, refired and leapt a foot forward before stalling again. Naz heard the squeal of synchri-mesh and the car bounced a few yards towards him before jerking to the right. He hadn't thought of this, Cheb couldn't drive. Naz hared back down the alley-way. As the car stalled for the third time, he stuck his head through the open driver's side window saying, "Get over. I'll drive."

Cheb smiled placidly, "If that's what you want."

Now in the driver's seat, Naz saw the wheelie bin roll on its dented side in his rear view mirror. Ahead of them the quiet of the road running around Soho Square. Before they reached the end of the alley, Naz had got the needle up past forty. He took the corner by hauling hard on the handbrake. The car quivered slightly and straightened on the empty street, hardly slowing through the turn. He was going to shoot through, round Soho Square but he had a thought. He went into an emergency stop: "You did cover the body?"

Cheb swore he had. Through all the swerves and wheel spins, Cheb seemed to be getting more and more excited. Like he was enjoying himself. As Naz drove on, he was even bouncing a little in his seat.

It was another hot night. The shifting crowds around the Centrepoint building and the junction of Charing Cross Road were dressed for sun although it was way past midnight. Dust blew along the gutters, fine and bone dry in the dervish gas fumes. Naz pulled ahead of a cab, passed Centrepoint and crossed through the next set of lights.

Cheb said, "Okay, we're going south. Take a right."

Naz swung the Volvo into a bus lane. At the next junction the signals forced him round into another right turn. Soon he was heading back the way he'd come, facing back towards Centrepoint. The building towered above them like a monstrous packet of breakfast cereal.

Naz said, "Does it look familiar?"

Cheb shook his head, "No. I don't really know London."

Naz turned again, completing his round-the-block tour. The next time he looked for a southbound road, he'd wait for a sign to point the way. "Just tell me where you want to end up."

"All we have to do is follow the river. I checked out the A-Z already, it's straightforward."

They were spinning around another building now, weaving through six lanes until Naz threaded towards an underpass. Cheb had no idea: he was rummaging through the glove compartment with manic fingers.

"I thought there was some skins."

Naz said, "You're going to roll a spliff."

"Yes."

"It's an idea. Then if the cops stop us, they do us for drugs as well as carrying a dead body."

Cheb nodded, good point: "And you probably got a gun, too."

Naz turned a slitted eye on Cheb. "Why would I? I only use it for business and this is your business not mine."

Cheb could have said it was no one's business: it was a trip. Instead, he swept his arm out of the open window and felt the wind lick through his fingers. They were on a bridge now, the Thames was fat and sluggish below them. The lights reflected off the river like fried eggs floating sunny-side up. Cheb fumbled on the floor beneath his seat for Hogie's box of CDs, looking for some kind of musical accompaniment to fix the experience. He picked out a disc, sunk it into the hole of the hi-fi machine and watched as the green arrows flashed his decision. In a start, the sound cranked into a high-speed chaotic ticking, a thin wail etched over the noise.

While they waited at a crossroaded roundabout, Cheb said, "Did Jools tell you I'm a Buddhist?"

Naz nodded, he believed Jools had said something about it. He had been trying to get her to speak when all she wanted to do was stay squat and huddled with a duvet wrapped around her, covering her to eye level. Trying to step lightly through her miserable sniffling, he'd waved a hand around the room and asked why there was tin foil hung over the bedroom walls. She had told him it was something Cheb had done: because he's a Buddhist.

Cheb was expanding, " . . . kind of a Buddhist. You know, karma 'n' kismet. I'm into a dissenter's dharma."

Naz said, "Kismet's an Arab word."

"Yeah, right. Are you watching the road signs, we're going west."

Naz took the fork towards Wandsworth. He asked where now and Cheb told him to look out for a nightclub called Comecon. When they saw a queue one hundred yards strong, Naz reckoned they'd found the place.

Cheb said, "Can you pull in behind those coaches."

There were coaches on the left and right sides of the road, bringing in clubbers from the capital's satellite towns. Naz asked, "What now?"

"We'll have to wait for the queue to die down. Cigarette?"

Naz took a smoke from the packet. Cheb flicked on his bic and leant over to give Naz a light. He asked Naz how well he knew Arabic.

Naz said, "Not much. My languages are Gudjurati, Urdu and English. Also a bit of Hindi."

"Yeah? That's some fucking list. What's the Arabic for? Are you a Muslim."

"Yeah, like you're a Buddhist. Only I've been a Muslim like you're a Buddhist for longer than you've been a Buddhist like I'm a Muslim."

Cheb said, "Yeah? I tell you, though. I got no time for these dust bowl religions, me. The Bible-bashers, Hebes or the Towel-heads. No offense."

Naz looked over to the queue outside Comecon. It was still no less than a hundred yards long. Whatever Cheb was planning to do, at least he had the sense to wait for the area to quieten.

Cheb was saying: "My problem is, all three are the same. They've all got this sad respect for senility and they're all based on wheat farming. You've heard of the fertile crescent, right? The birthplace of civilisation? But the only thing it's fertile for is wheat."

He leant over to adjust the volume on the hi-fi, this was something people should know. "And if you look at wheat out in the field, the grains are microscopic and covered in spikes. Even before you grind them down, you could grow old just figuring out how to get any nutritive content out of the cunts. It doesn't make sense."

Naz coughed on a dry toke of cigarette. He'd seen a van selling soft drinks over by the far kerb. He interrupted Cheb, suggesting they score a drink of something. Cheb said, No they should keep low. It was better that way.

Naz said, "So I have to listen to you?"

Cheb didn't have a problem with that, he was only getting started: "Yeah, dig it. I was saying, wheat's got disadvantages. But it's also the healthiest of the staple food crops. Which is why wheat cultures have a surplus of old people. A bunch of crusty old farmers, worn-out but hanging on."

Naz watched as the clubbers disengaged themselves singly from the queue and bought drinks from the van. They carried handfuls of bottles back to their friends who'd stayed to hold their place. At the back of the drinks van, a skinny boy in a hooded top stopped three out of every five shoppers and sold them wraps, probably speed, perhaps E or trips too. Naz saw the money and the drugs change hands and remembered the cash Cheb had promised him over the phone, earlier that day. He couldn't complain about the pay, just the work conditions. Cheb was telling him nothing he needed to know, like what they were doing or why they were here, and everything he didn't need to know. Cheb never stopped. Now he was saying that religion was the social face of food technology.

"You want to know why these religions are always looking for converts? To build trading blocks. You see, there's different types of wheat, hard grained and soft grained, and to make a loaf of bread that's not going to rot after a few days you need to get a balance. So wheat eaters have to trade half of whatever grains they've got for the other type. No farmer can afford to live far from a market. These fucked-up, senile farmers know their crop's travelling all over the world but they're pinned to their farms. They're conscious of an expanding world, but they can't understand it and it terrifies them."

Cheb's voice had grown spacey, or spacier. He used the burning tip of his cigarette to sketch the expanse. Naz had stopped watching the drinks van. Now he watched as Cheb described a rapidly expanding world and the paranoid freaks that it ploughed in its wake.

"The world of wheat neurotizes everything it touches, it's a machine churning out pitiful self-obsessions. The wheat eaters close in on themselves because they're scared of the world and scared of being cheated. They have to trade but trade terrorises them. At the same time, the situation makes them rich. Or at least, it makes the old men rich. So it all ends with a twisted reverence for old age, coupled with constant dreams of patricide. It's a sick way to live but it's the basis of monotheism: God, most of his prophets and all his priests are old men; property is sacred, theft is wrong, killing becomes a crime, greed is condemned as a sin. At the same time, the whole culture promotes greed and encourages murder because the only way to get ahead is to kill the old fuckers and steal their land."

Cheb laughed. Naz gave him a break, let him see that he'd caught at least half his attention. Maybe he'd nearly finished.

"Like the different kinds of wheat, there's a million varieties of the religion but, currently, only three basic species: Islam, Judaism and Christianity. All three are necessarily multi-cultural, whether they admit it or not, all of them constantly sub-divide and every one is at war with the others, despite being practically indistinguishable. They reckon to despise each other but it's only a symptom of the generalised neurotic buzz."

"So there's never ending wars?"

"No. It's over."

Naz saw a crack beginning to open. He said, "What about Bosnia? The Lebanon? Sudan?"

"Freak shows. It's over. No one lives purely on wheat. America and China never have done. It's what I'm saying, we're ready for a new world religion. And the first sacred act is going to be a burial. It's almost time to get the body out of the back."

THIRTEEN

Hogie told Mannie he wasn't going to be responsible for Cheb's actions. Because it was a certainty, the guy would go insane when he found Jools camped out in his room. "You don't know, but he was up all night tracking the room's psychic energy."

Mannie said, "I don't believe rooms have psyches."

"It's some kind of karmic shit. You'd get into it if Cheb explained."

They were stood in the Good Mixer, a market pub off Camden High Street. Later, they were going to move along to the Dublin Castle. Hogie felt he should explain why every pub they'd visited was so disgusting.

"It's not like Manchester. London's really run-down."

"Aren't there any, like, modern bars, or anything?"

Hogie told him, "There's a few, down Soho. But they're so tiny, they're not worth the hassle."

Anyway, they were so drunk now, it wouldn't matter if the next pub turned out as bad as all the others. The Good Mixer was a bare wood and formica place, built around flaked paint and semi-broken tables. The big surprise for Mannie was the place was so crammed, they could barely move. Judging by the decor and the beery whiff, it should have been strictly an old man's place but everyone there was about their age or younger. Most of them pod-mods tapping their feet to old R&B tracks. There was nowhere to sit, there was nothing but plastic leatherette wall seating and it was all taken. A few couples were sat on top of the pool table, which was covered in a plywood sheet, and others were crouched round the floor but most people were standing, bobbing their heads slightly to the Kinks riffs from the jukebox or mouthing the lyrics.

Mannie said, "What about outside?"

Hogie shrugged, "Yeah okay. Maybe after we could try the Spread Eagle. It's cleaner but it's all done in Victoriana-style. You got to understand, a lot of these places haven't been done up since the 1980s."

They took their drinks out and sat on the edge of the kerb. The night was hot and still, with no wind to blow away the daytime market smells. Mannie sniffed about, asking: "What is it?"

Hogie pointed across the road where matchwood crates were piled with unsold vegetables. The smell didn't bother him, what he could do without was the reminder that he had to get to the market in—he checked his watch—maybe five hours. He hadn't told Mannie yet, but he was getting nervous about the party. For the past few hours, his stomach had been churning over. He couldn't even think about food, never mind cook it up. The beer wasn't helping, it was fruity and flat and only made him want to run to the toilet.

Mannie must have picked up on something, his green face or the rumbling in his guts. He said, "What's your problem?"

"Just nerves, about the party and the menu and that."

Mannie didn't believe it. "What, really? I thought you were just up for it, like you didn't give a shit."

Is that what he thought? "No. I'm a touch nervous. Alright. I mean, do you think I'm the kind of dickhead who doesn't worry about anything?"

Mannie thought it over. "Basically, I'd have to say, Yeah. Like, don't have an epi or anything. It's just that you're teflon-coated."

Hogie sat silently for a moment and thought. "Yeah. Well I try to maintain."

Mannie said, "I mean, you always landed on your feet before. Like you only went to cooking college because Cheb made you, but you're the one who's the big success."

It wasn't quite like that. Hogie said, "Give me credit. It was a, what d'you call that shit? A conscious decision."

"I thought, what happened, you and Cheb had just come back from this mental holiday in Ibiza and he persuaded you that you could live like that the whole year if you started working in hotels."

That was part of it. Cheb had enrolled them both on the catering college at the tech, straight after he got them kicked out of school. But that was only the beginning, when they were sixteen. And even then, it turned out Hogie had talent. The real story, though, centred on the art student. Hogie said, "You know how the tech was divided in two, with half of it as an art college and the rest of it for catering. There was no antagonism or anything: we just thought they were morons."

Mannie nodded. He remembered them saying.

"Yeah. We never really mixed until Cheb found out the art students were ready to pay over the odds for drugs. So we started going along to their parties and turning these big profits from complete shit. Anyway, I was talking to this artist one night and I said to him, 'Why do you want to do art, you can't draw.' He came over all aggressive, telling me that wasn't the point. So I started stubbing my finger in his chest saying, 'You just want to be famous but you're living in fucking dreamland, man'. I told him, 'the only way anyone gets famous is either playing football or joining a band.' I can't remember what happened after, we either had a fight or I passed out—one or the other. But the next day I started thinking maybe you could get famous if you were a chef. Or even if you didn't get famous, you could live like you were. So I got Cheb to write me letters round all the best restaurants, got a start in a Michelin one-star place and worked up from there."

"So you're a self-made man. You done good, mate."

"Better than the art student, anyway. One time I went back to Manchester, I saw him trying to juggle in Market Street and he was crap at that as well."

Mannie started laughing, "The sad thing is, I nearly tried that once. And I can't juggle either." He had a shoulder bag slung at his feet and now he began rustling through it, saying, "Maybe I should just get some drinks instead. Calm you down and drown my crapness." He said it like he still meant it as a laugh but it wasn't how the look on his face read.

Hogie stood up, "No, I'll get them."

Mannie carried on digging through the bag, as though he expected to find some money hidden in there. Hogie took a peek at the mess inside and said, "Come on, mate. I said I'd got cash."

"Wait." When Mannie lifted his head, the sad look had

disappeared entirely. Nothing but a wide grin as he flicked a sheet of paper between his fingers and said: "I can't believe I've found it."

"What?"

"A virgin sheet of acid."

Hogie stared at it, an A4 sheet printed every centimetre with a picture of a sun. "Is that the one you lost last week?"

Mannie wasn't sure. He'd lost a lot of stuff, both before and after. But you could say it belonged to Hogie and Cheb, seeing as they'd paid for one sheet.

He already knew the answer but asked anyway, "So what do you reckon we should do with it, Hogie?"

It was late when they returned to the flat. In the dark, in the main room, Hogie and Mannie clung together giggling. They didn't know who else was in the flat. Mannie suggested there might be hundreds by now: little copies of Jools and Naz, bouncing jelly baby devil spawn. Hogie started shaking and yukking again.

Mannie said, "What is it?"

"That Jelly Head, Jesus."

Mannie started giggling too, "You're tripping off your box."

"I swear I saw it, man. On the side of a wall, staring off a poster."

"Yeah, yeah, yeah. A guy with a jelly head."

"That's right. And I tell you something else, I fucking want one for myself."

They fell into each other's arms again, sinking to the floor. When Jools switched the lights on, they were rolling around the carpet together.

Mannie said, "Jools, how're you doing? Where's Naz?"

"He's out." She stared at them, tiny blue eyes sparked with evil. When she spoke, it came venom-coated. "Get away from that fucking pervert."

"You what?"

Jools grabbed hold of Mannie by the back of his jacket and dragged him off Hogie's back. "I'm telling you, get away from that pervert."

Mannie and Hogie never stopped laughing, even though she was crying. It took at least five minutes before either realised she was serious. They tried stroking her arms, Mannie to her right and Hogie to the left. They barely touched her with their outstretched fingers but whispered anything that sounded comforting. They told her, Cheer up. They asked her not to cry.

Jools shrugged away from Hogie, telling him to get his hands off her and bursting into fresh tears.

Mannie said, "What is it Jools? Why are you crying Jools?"

She said, "He's a pervert, he's a pervert."

"Who is? Naz?" Mannie grew cold, wondering if she was going to make him defend her.

"Not Naz. Him." She pointed. "Hogie."

She started coming for him, screaming: "And don't you fucking dare make out that my mother's to blame. Don't even think about trying to worm out of it by saying she abused you."

Hogie backed away until he felt the wall behind him. Suddenly he realised he was going to have a bad trip. He'd never had one before.

Putting it together, later, Mannie had to admit that Hogie never once blamed their mother. At first it was difficult to understand anything through Hogie's gibbering but it seemed he wanted them to believe it was nothing, just a brief affair. When that didn't quieten the situation or stop Jools from beating him, he began to make it worse. He told them he'd been drunk. He told them he'd been drinking Olde English cider at lunchtime. Too wasted to make classes, he had looped over to their house to see if Mannie was home.

Instead, he found their mother, stepping around her bedroom in nothing but a towel.

Jools stopped beating him for a while. But she still looked dangerous: "What happened between the two of you?"

"Gloria's okay. I mean, I always liked the way she looked but you should have seen her that day. Undressed, in nothing but a bath towel."

Mannie made a noise he'd never even heard before. A kind of squeal that he couldn't stop from turning into a giggle. Jools turned her death-look on him. He wanted to say, It's not me, it's the six tabs of acid I took. Instead, he ran to the end of the flat and started sprinting up and down the stairs. By the time he returned, he'd almost managed to persuade himself the whole scene was nothing but a strange Oedipal trip. But when he walked into the living room, he found nothing had changed. Jools was screeching, Hogie was crawling under the sofa telling her he needed time to think: "I'm a bit, you know, I can't focus." His voice was indistinct but Mannie heard him plead, "What am I supposed to say?". His eyes swivelling round as though he didn't recognise anyone. Turning between the two of them, both orphan cold, his left arm clutched upwards, reaching out towards Mannie to tug on the sleeve of his jumper. Begging: "I'm sorry."

For hours, he didn't know how long, he sat and watched Hogie thrash around on the carpet, moving in and out of different attacks of hysteria. He was still there, curled on the floor, and Mannie was sat close by, drinking beer. Some people favour orange juice as the best way to neutralise acid. Mannie knew the only way out of a bad trip was to sit still and drink yourself unconscious. So long as you never moved, no harm could come to you and eventually you'd just slip away. Now the beers were finished, he would have to drink the bottle of Mount Gay Rum he'd seen among the tomato tins in Hogie's cupboard.

Jools wasn't crying any more. When Hogie finally quietened she started making toast, tea and cereal like nothing had happened. She even placed a bowl of Weetabix on the floor for Hogie who couldn't eat but had rubbed his face into the mush instead. There were still a few strands of his long blond hair spooled in the milky gunk.

While she boiled the kettle and worked the toaster, she talked. Talked absolutely non-stop and all of it about Naz. She couldn't finish the list of his good points, physical and intuitive. Mannie could not believe there were so many shades to Naz's personality. That he was both a drug dealing gangster and a pro-active lover, whatever that meant. But he appreciated the change of subject.

Their mother had been shagging Hogie. It was the tie-in, an explanation for all kinds of things that once had no significance but were now monstrous indicators: his mother and Hogie were the only ones doing any conjugating during the last French classes on Wednesday afternoons. She was his detour on the Friday cross-country run. The days when Mannie came home from school and Hogie would be there, ahead of him, saying, "What kept you mate, I been waiting ages."

One other thing was clear, so clear that even Jools had guessed, one day Hogie stopped visiting. No one had said anything since Hogie's mad explosion or the fit of autism that followed but the only reason Jools had begun to describe her perfect lover was because she wanted to prove a point. There were some men who tried to relate. There were others that only precipitated declines.

Just about the time Hogie stopped calling round and began spending more time at Cheb's mother's place, Mannie would come home and find his mother sat at the kitchen table, wrapped in her dressing gown and a tired haze of perfume, three quarters of a bottle of gin in her soft belly

and that same look on her face. The image stayed with him:
a look mixing anger with a fitful daze and slow tears.

FOURTEEN

The queue had dwindled. Naz saw only a couple of dozen
people gathered around the crash barriers at the front of
Comecon. Cheb was already out of the side of the Volvo
and walking towards the hatch back. Naz pulled the keys
out of the ignition and pulled himself out of the car.

Cheb said, "Throw me the keys. You go and find a bus
with its luggage spaces unlocked."

Naz okayed him, throwing the keys in a smooth arc for
Cheb to catch. Over at the club, the drinks van had run out
of customers and the dealer had climbed inside with the
counterman. Naz walked over to the line of coaches.

In most of them, the driver was either sat at the wheel
or sprawled across the front two seats. None of them would
be able to see him. It was dark, he was dressed in black
and the coach windows were high but he still crouched low.
He rattled at the flaps along the sides of the coaches, looking
for one that had been left open. He felt self-consciously
careful. Cheb's religiosity had left him edgey. They had a
body that needed disposal, it wasn't everyday stuff but it
was something he'd expected to happen one day.

The flap on the first coach he tried lifted easily, the
luggage space was empty. Instant access. He straightened
up.

Walking back to the car, Naz saw the trunk lid open, its
square edge framed in a haze of light. Cheb was leaning into
it. The flashlight lit his face from below. Naz had no idea

what he was doing, but it looked sick. It was worse than he could have imagined, Cheb was cutting the buttocks off the corpse with a kitchen knife.

Cheb said, "It looks fucked up, I know."

Naz just stared.

"Come on. Stop looking at me like that. You're making me feel guilty. The shape of the cooker rings are branded into his arse. I'm just cutting the evidence away. I don't want to mess up the body any more than it is."

"I thought it was part of your new religion."

"Not mine. But I was thinking, the more ritualistic it looks the less chance the cops have of solving the case. They'll put it down to some sicko psychotic."

Naz said, "That'll put me in the clear."

Cheb started sawing on the left buttock. He asked Naz what he thought they should do with the discarded parts of rump. Naz didn't know, he didn't even want to think about it.

Among all the other pieces of debris that had wound up in the back of Hogie's car, there was an empty ice cream tub. Cheb said, "I guess we can put his arse in this and throw it away."

He popped the plastic lid over the two slabs of meat and walked to the nearest bin. Came back, slapping his hands and saying okey-dokey. It was time to move the body. Naz took the head and shoulders and most of the weight. Cheb kept the feet from scraping along the pavement. When they reached the designated coach, it was Cheb who opened the flap. Naz swung the body inside the luggage compartment and they pushed it into the shadows together. Once it was stowed inside, they stood back. The body was all but hidden. Cheb thought it would be even better if they pushed the body around so it lay across the width of the coach rather than pointing from the back to the front. He climbed inside the compartment to manouevre the body alone. Once it faced the way he wanted, he rolled it to the very back of the bus, hard against the wall that separated the luggage area from the engine.

Naz said, "It's gonna roll forward when the coach starts moving."

Cheb had thought of that. He was planning to secure the body. He asked Naz if he saw a driver in the coach.

Naz checked back. After a few seconds, he returned saying: "Yeah, there's a guy up front in a uniform, reading the *Sun*."

"I think the best bet, you lure him out."

"How?"

"Tell him you'll suck his dick for a fiver."

"Fuck you."

Cheb grinned out of the shadows, the streetlight shining off his teeth and dome. He said, "I was joking. A better idea: go rob that drinks van. After you've run off, the drivers are bound to get out and look over the scene of the crime."

Cheb was being serious, Naz could not believe he was being serious. "I'm supposed to just run off? Where'm I supposed to fucking run to?"

"Round the block. Meet me back at the car."

Now Naz knew this was all screwed up. Suppose he was chased around the block.

Cheb said, "Who's going to chase you? You've got a gun."

Naz stopped, paused really. He said, "I told you. I don't have a gun."

"I know what you said but you were lying."

Naz could have said, Who're you calling a liar? But when Cheb had suggested he go down on the driver, his hand had flickered over to the left hand side of his belt to where the gun was nestled. Instead he said, "I also told you that the gun was for my business and this is none of my fucking business."

"Make it your business. You saw the trade that dealer

was doing out of the back of the drinks van. You'll probably pick up a couple of grand."

Naz could have taken time and thought it over. But it was one of those nights, kismet and karma running the whole show. He walked off, pulling on a pair of black leather gloves as he went.

He wanted to take in the whole length of the road in long slow strides that would give him time to get his act straight. It would make the deal more of a western, when a man treads that deserted main street. The few stragglers leaning against the wall of Comecon, waiting for the bouncers to relent and let them inside, those few rejects would be the witnesses. The townsfolk who desert the main street for the saloon, or who hide behind the lace curtains of the frontier town parlour window.

The gun was a Browning automatic. The cash-take would have to be heavy to compensate for losing it, if he was forced to lose it. Once he fired a shot, even if no one was actually hit, the gat would have to go into the nearest gutter. It might be the very last time that he touched it. Naz decided to make the most of it. He was within twenty-five yards of the van.

In *Boyz N The Hood*, Ice Cube used the ring finger of his left hand to lift up the edge of his T-shirt. The gat was stuck inside his pants, the grip facing to the right. Combined with the look on Cube's face, that was a good play: it was fucking unstoppable. He didn't even have to touch it, the expression said it all: "Yep, there's the piece. Now it's down to you, do you figure it's a salient fact or not?" Naz would have followed the Ice Cube method if there was a hope of his Browning being seen over the van counter.

In *States of Grace*, Gary Oldman held his pistol at arm's length, the arm tilted forty-five degrees upwards but the gunhand angled downwards. As he fired, he lunged forward into a kind of sword fighter's stance. That was about the weirdest use of a firearm in a feature film. So mishandled that it turned a corner and became effective. There was no doubt, whoever held their piece like that loved firing it, whether they hit anything or not. Another option: Naz had seen more and more films where the gat was held upside down and fired using the little finger or, alternatively, the trigger finger of the opposite hand. The Chow Yun Fat-style, although it was spreading everywhere.

Five yards from the van, Naz decided on a standard gangsta stance, arms crossed. He pulled the Browning out of his trousers. It felt comfortable in his right hand, tucked underneath his left armpit. When he reached the van, he could stand at the counter until they opened the window. They'd go, "Yeah", he'd turn slightly to his right and lift his left elbow. They'd see the Browning, angled towards them, his finger wrapped around the trigger. He reached the van.

The two men were sat inside, smoking together in the dark. Neither of them noticed him on the far side of the sliding counter window. If he looked deeper than his own reflection, Naz could see the Comecon security guys lounging at their doorway. Four of them were stood talking together, a fifth was standing some way off leaning against a parked car and chatting to the driver. Naz refocussed, looking through his reflection to the glowing end of the shared joint. The two men, the drug dealer and the fizzy drink dealer, never looked up. Naz tapped on the sliding window with the middle finger of his left hand, taking care to keep his gun hand out of sight. One of them turned towards him, mouthing "We're closed" through the glass. Naz tapped again, putting on a grin.

The problem with a grin, it might charm them into opening shop but it would be impossible to reassume the flat stare. No one with a dead prison stare also had a shit-eating seductive smile. It was the one or the other: Bruce Lee or Jackie Chan. Naz committed, turning a full smile onto the two men. Only one of them looked up, the same one, the lab-coated drinks vendor. He said, "We're fucking closed." This time he was audible. His partner didn't even look up.

Naz thought, this is going to be a drag. He took the Browning out from the warm hollow under his arm. Holding it by the barrel, he hammered the grip through the window pane. That had them both looking. The one in white with tutti frutti stains spattered over his coat. The one in the hooded black top, the hood pulled back now, showing a hatchet face at least ten years older than Naz had imagined. The pair of them with wide what-the-fuck stares.

Then they ducked, heading below the counter. Naz assumed they were taking cover, that they'd seen the Browning swinging through his hand as he switched his hold from barrel to grip. But as they came up, white-coat was holding a sawn-off shotgun and black-top had a semi-automatic pistol. Naz shot white-coat in the chest, hearing himself say "Name of God" out loud as he fired but not sure in what language. He remembered a pinhole wound exploding in the lab coat, matching the tutti. A one frame still, the entry wound and the raspberry drips, frozen in Naz's eye as he dropped onto the pavement.

Naz panted, sat on the kerbside, his back to the van. He felt the heavy jabbing of bullets hitting metal behind him. Black-top was trying to fire through the bodywork, hoping to punch through and hit him on the far side. Naz thought, this dick really has seen too many films, that trick only worked in the movies.

The bouncers at the door of Comecon were staring, breaking out of their stares and running. A flicker of move-ment made Naz look over to the fifth bouncer and the car parked by the doorway. The trunk had sprung up on its own. The driver must have released the lock from inside the car. Naz knew, without knowing where the thought came from, that the car was an armoury. The men ahead of him and the dealers in the van behind him were all a part of the same crew. It should have been obvious. He'd been stupid. He'd been dreaming like a cowboy and now he was in the middle of one one of those Alamo situations.

Naz looked up. The square barrel of a gun was creeping over the sill of the van, leading a hand. Naz sprang off his haunches, grabbing hold of black-top's wrist as he went. With the wrist in his left hand, he drove his right elbow round, through the remnants of glass until he hit bone. When he turned around, he saw black-top's old sharp features buckled around a broken nose, his gun arm lodged into the glass at the edge of the window. Naz pushed his Browning into the man's face and looked over the counter. White-coat was still alive, his piggy blue eyes staring out of a round face that could have been red but was now drained. The shotgun lay across his lap.

Naz said, "Pass me the shotgun . . . the other way round, dickhead."

White-coat turned the shotgun around, holding it at the end of an outstretched arm. Naz leant over, grabbed the stock and pulled the shotgun across the counter.

In the time it took him to disarm them both, Naz registered two or three shots behind him. Another shot hit the side of the van, four feet to his left. He thought: all these fucking gats, has no one else ever done any target practice? He stuck his Browning back into his belt as he turned. Lifting the shotgun up to his shoulder, he took aim on the bouncer standing by the open car trunk. He had no idea how accurate a sawn-off was, but used it like a standard rifle. It took him two shots, emptying both barrels, before he put the man down.

Naz prised black-top's automatic from out of his bleeding arm. It was a nickel-plated Beretta. A spare magazine lay on the counter. Naz took that too. Using the stock of the shotgun, he swiped at the driver's side window of the van and reached through the broken glass to take the van keys. As he walked towards the door of Comecon, he threw the keys and the spent shotgun onto the ground.

There were four bouncers, somewhere. Five if the driver of the car was counted. Naz could only see two, both of them holding guns they had taken out of the car trunk. One was firing wildly. Even at night and twenty paces away, Naz could see the gun arm bucking and swaying, upwards and downwards. The other was taking slow aim. Naz jumped to his left and started running, swerving and keeping his head low. As he ran, he emptied the Beretta in their general direction. He didn't think he'd hit anything, but he couldn't see anyone either. The men must have taken cover behind the car. Naz pulled his Browning out from his belt and dived down towards the car, skidding on his stomach. When he saw a knee and a white trainer beneath the undercarriage on the far side of the car, he took aim and fired. There was a scream. Naz rolled to his left, towards the rear and the open trunk. When he popped up, the trunk lid partly shielded him. On the other side of the car, a head stuck out and looked around. Naz shot it open. That was horrible, the front of the skull flipped up and disappeared.

There were no more shots. Looking to his right, Naz saw the passenger side door of the car was open but there was no one inside. The driver must have been one of the two men he'd shot which meant there were three others inside the club's doorway. They were probably unarmed. He couldn't see them. He couldn't see anyone. Those few people who'd stood hopelessly in the queue had turned themselves loose as the shooting started.

Naz checked the car to see if its keys were in place. At first he couldn't even see if the steering wheel was in place. The car was a left-hand drive. Better that he found out now rather than later. He walked around to the trunk where a leather sports bag lay open, cradling a glint of the metal.

Naz lifted it out, dropping the empty Beretta and its spare cartridge inside as he started for the club.

As he passed the end of the car, his hearing clicked onto a high-pitched shriek. Behind the car a man lay screaming as he held his leg. Naz kept his Browning on the screamer. He could see the man had no pistol but there was a gun lying skewed across the pavement, a yard from the guy's hand. There may have been others he couldn't see. Naz felt a soft wad of nausea choke at his gullet but coughed it back as he shot the injured man three times in the chest. The man might have crawled to a weapon. It would have been stupid to leave him but straight thinking, simply looking ahead and reasoning things out, had never made him feel so sick before. When he walked into the club, he was stalking on automatic.

The remaining bouncers were pushed up against the walls of the foyer and the cashier was pale inside her box. Naz said, "This is a robbery. Nobody move but the cashier."

A quick look through her window. Naz saw a pile of bags and coats. He said, "Empty out a bag and fill it with money."

She scrambled out of her chair and started looking through the pile.

"Nothing too effeminate. The duffel's fine."

The bouncers were frozen to the walls. The dumb cunts, all of them had gone into "posing relaxed" positions, which meant all of their muscles were rigid and cheesy grins had spread across their faces. They had spent so long following the body builder's code, they didn't know how to be inconspicuous. They were so stiff, if Naz walked up and pushed them over they'd fall one by one like dominoes. When he asked if they did much weight training, they all nodded, their heads quivering in their bull necks.

Naz forced his voice down to a slow crawl. "What do you reckon, you have to pay extra for outsize coffins? Those three guys I just shot, they're going to take some lifting so if you want to play pallbearer at their funerals, you'd better listen. I'll take all the guns away, so you won't have to explain to the cops why you were tooled-up like a fucking commando unit. When I see tomorrow's papers, I want to read that you were hit by a gang of ten men or more, any race, colour or creed other than a Pakistani dude. Got it."

They nodded.

"I fucking hope so. Because it's going to be the easiest thing in the world to come here next week and put a bullet in each of your heads."

The cashier whispered that she'd finish. Naz said, "Bring the bag out here, love."

She let herself out of her office and handed Naz a bag that felt wildly heavy, if it was just full of paper.

"Did you put coins in here?"

She shook her head, only notes. A sign on the cashier window said *Comecon Entry: £15.* Naz had seen at least a thousand people queuing, with maybe that number again already inside by the time he and Cheb had arrived. Naz thought, "Name of God". He shouldered the bag and left.

He decided to take the bouncer's car. He didn't recognise the make but when he slapped down the trunk he saw Oldsmobile spelt out in chrome letters. Starting the car up, he wondered why there were too few pedals and realised it was an automatic. He'd only ever driven geared cars before but shoved the stick to the D and the car began pulling away.

The first car he passed was Hogie's Volvo, jolting around the empty drinks van and bunny-hopping along the line of coaches. As Naz overtook, Cheb smiled and waved. In another fifty yards, Naz reached white-coat and black-top, limping their way up the street. Naz slowed down to their pace and told them to hand him their bag. They passed it over without a word.

Naz said, "If there's less than four grand in here, I'm coming back and shooting you again. Okay."

Black-top pulled a plastic bag out of the muff of his sweat shirt. Naz took that too and thanked them.

He hoped Cheb knew enough about the highway code to recognise a right-hand indicator. Naz signalled nice and early before taking a corner and parking up, waiting for Cheb to hop past. When he did, the first thing Cheb said as he squirmed over to the passenger seat was: "Was that the plan?"

Naz said, "Was what the plan?"

"I'm not complaining, it was fucking great. Once the shooting started, none of the drivers got out of the coaches. They just hit the deck and stayed there. I figured that, with the noise of the shooting, no one was going to notice me stuffing a body into their luggage trunk."

"There wasn't any plan. It was a fuck-up."

"There's always a plan. It looks like an outbreak of madness, but it's just another program. We're wired to the future. Look at the way the world mapped out before we got here, based solidly on paranoia and warped on stability. We're superheroes. We've done nothing that wasn't stupid and dangerous and in one evening we've grabbed about thirty-five thousand pounds."

Naz said, "You already worked out how much you're sitting on?"

Cheb said, "It's yours, I don't give a fuck about money. It's not about getting rich, only how insane you can get wasting it. And I've got so many credit cards, I don't need to worry about my mental health. I'm going to burn."

Naz said, Good. He wasn't thinking of giving Cheb any anyway. But he told him there was several grand's worth of weapons in the sports bag. Cheb said, Cool, he wanted some kind of pistol. He was already spinning around in his seat, grabbing at the bag lying on the back seat. He asked Naz what kind would suit him.

"Have you ever used one before."

"Yeah. Kind of. In arcades and stuff." He had his head down, rifling through the bag. He came up with the Beretta, saying, "It's a lot weightier than I expected."

Towards dawn, Naz and Cheb walked into the flat. Nothing about the whole scene seemed to surprise them. Cheb took in the pitiful shapes: Hogie on the floor surrounded by toast crusts and cereals; Mannie slumped down in a chair surrounded by emptied beer bottles.

He turned to Naz and said, "See, what'd I say? When the end of civilisation comes, it'll be down to too much wheatie goodness."

PART TWO

---

outofit

FIFTEEN

Susan asked George to drop her at Cambridge Circus. She
wanted to walk past the café he'd told her about, the one
where the male prostitutes sat out in the sun, wearing their
mobile phones like jewellery and booking their clients into
fat, desktop diaries. Earlier, she had suggested they book
themselves a home visit. If she had to, she could dress up
in male drag. George had asked, Are you that desperate?
Well yes, honey, she was. What she'd seen of London so far,
only the fags were worth the time.

"Count me out. Those depilated buff puffs do nothing for
me. You get to a certain age, you start looking for character."

Susan wondered how long it would be before she got
there.

They hadn't spent the whole morning talking sex, only
the last few hours. It was a way to take their minds off
other things, like the fact that she had to get out of the
apartment on New Cavendish Street. That was George
getting serious with her, telling her she couldn't live in a
place her son had visited. For all they knew, he'd already
given Frankie the details. She'd said, "So where am I supposed to go?"

"Somewhere discreet. Do you remember Maltese Rosa?"

"Yeah, the nun." Actually the woman was a tart, but she
was in church often enough to be mistaken for a saint and
could be persuaded to wear a Carmelite habit, for a fee.

George had said, "She's not on the game anymore. She
retired and put her money into property. She should be able
to help you out."

Susan hated to think what she'd end up with.

They were coming down the one-way system on Gower Street, now. George peeled towards Shaftesbury Avenue but told her he didn't want to get stuck in the traffic all day. Did she mind if he dropped her at the next corner, behind St Giles churchyard.

As she got out of the car, he reminded her to take her suitcase. She wanted to know why: "Why don't you keep it? Then when you've spoken to Rosa, you can drop it off at the new flat."

George shrugged. "I just think it's more convenient if you keep it with you."

As she walked towards Cambridge Circus, she wondered why he'd been so iffy. And whether it had anything to do with the amount of cocaine inside the case. She had planned to take a stroll through Soho and get a feeling for the place again. She wanted to know how it would feel to own everything she could see. Hefting the suitcase, she felt more like a bag lady than an heiress.

She took a right off Old Compton Street and started heading up Frith Street. She knew all the streets but very few of the places. George might have bought the leases but he wasn't responsible for everything that went on. All the mobile homos outside the cafés were a definite improvement. Otherwise, the improvements were more ambiguous: no grocers, no tailors, nothing but film companies, trendy clothes shops and, still, the porn shops. Although the bistros outnumbered caffs, so she knew it had to be good real estate.

Around the corner from a club where she once worked a fan-and-feather act, she found the restaurant. The name, *La George*, standing out-and-proud in italics. She tried the door but it was locked. Susan hung her finger on the doorbell, watching through the shopfront window and waiting for the little slap head sat at the bar to move himself. He never did, he lifted his head to look over, mouthed "We're shut", and turned away.

She pushed the bell again. This time he just blanked her. If she held it for an hour, he wasn't going to turn around. She stood in the street, holding her case and feeling impotent. Letting the feeling wilt along her spine.

There was hardly any traffic. Twenty yards away a delivery truck reversed from an alley and blocked the whole street. Its orange warning lights were lip-synched to a synthetic voice, programmed to dalek *danger reversing* over and over, loud enough to be heard over the horns of the cars it was delaying. Susan let the sound play against her nerves for five minutes before she remembered the passage running behind the restaurant. She could get in through the tradesman entrance. Once inside, she'd fuck that little jerk at the bar sideways.

There was a Volvo estate in the alley-way, parked next a pair of fire doors. Susan looked through the car's rear window. On the inside, there was nothing but raw naked flesh on flesh, hunks of animal piled on each other.

The fire doors opened with a bang and a kid dressed in white stepped out, holding a set of car keys in his hand. He asked Susan to excuse him, she was in his way. The first thing she saw when he opened the back of the car was a doggish snout, a torn ear slung at a coquette's angle across its dead eyes. She hadn't seen anything like it since she lived near Spitalfields market in, maybe, 1968 and again in '74.

The kid muttered, "Jesus, I'm supposed to lift that?"

She said, "Is that goat?"

The kid didn't look up but he did answer, "Yeah. Chef's bought five of them."

From inside the kitchen, a low voice with a strong Manchester accent shouted, "All yous, get your arses out there and give the man a hand."

Susan peered around the door and saw a tall Asian boy

in a chef's hat wave his junior cooks towards the van. They came snaking out to the alley, struggling to pass the carcasses hand to hand into the kitchen. The Asian walked over to them, grabbed a goat by its legs and returned inside to slam it down onto the stainless steel work top. He pointed back to the van with a cleaver he'd unhooked from a rack, "There's veg in there, too. Get it all out."

The little cookerboys and girls looked up at him with big eyes. "Yes Chef."

"And when you're done, mince the lamb—they're the likkler ones. Make sure you don't get no brains or nothing in the mix. I'm saving those for something else."

"Yes Chef."

The cleaver thudded into the sheep's belly. The body opened like an unzipped bag.

Susan walked through the doorway, walking up to him saying, "You're the chef?"

The Asian didn't look up, he was an artist with a cleaver and just carried on working through the bodies. He said, "I'm the Chef du jour. The regular guy's done one, so I'm filling in. If you've got a problem with that, I'll tell you what I told them." He lifted his head slightly, nodding to his assistants, they kept their eyes down. "I'm not in the mood for any crap off anyone, less I personally beat it out of them, okay?"

She could believe it. He was elbow deep in blood and the kitchen staff looked completely drained. She kept her voice firm and said: "I'm the boss."

That stopped him for a moment. Not for long. He looked up, caught her eyes and wiped his hands down the front of his white suit. When he held them up, they were still caked red but his smile was wide open.

He said, "Better not shake, eh? But I'm pleased to meet you." He paused, keeping the smile at full power. "That stuff

I just said. I'm sorry about that. I was up all night doing the market and shit. But I was out of line."

Somehow, she liked him. She let him off the hook, telling him he wasn't to know who she was.

"No. I got to apologise. But I tell you, last night was just one fucking thing after another. I guess the pressure got to me."

It wasn't a problem. It wasn't his head she was after.

While he washed at the sink, she told him about the bald kid she saw earlier. The one sat at the front of the restaurant.

He said, "That's Cheb, the maitre d'. I been thinking, he doesn't have the personality for a gig like this. What do you reckon?"

"I agree. I'll go and sack him."

Naz watched her walk ahead of him. She had style. And whatever she was going to do, he didn't want to miss it. He hurried after her, it had been a hell of a night but this just might make up for it.

Cheb was expecting the party decorators to arrive any time but it was a tense wait. Every time the front bell rang, he looked up. But the last time it had only been some woman, standing in the street with a suitcase, probably looking for a hotel or directions or something. He couldn't be doing with that, so he turned back to the television.

Before the party decorating people even started, they were going to have to convince him they could match the visions that were playing across his skull. He had to say, they were getting wild, given an extra boost by the newszak on the TV he'd set up on the bar. Ordinarily, he would never watch a local news programme. He didn't care what was happening anywhere in particular—only what was passing through every city in turn on its way to oblivion. Today was different, the news was speaking to him.

A reporter was walking around what she was pleased to

describe as the site of the apalling incident outside South London's popular rave club the Comecon disco. As she skirted the blue and white police tapes that sealed the area, the cameras zoomed in on the drinks van or focussed on the door of the nightclub. Her voice-over said that the police had appealed for witnesses: anyone who'd seen a group of heavily armed Jamaicans in the vicinity of Wandsworth should come forward.

An interview with the police chief had been promised, right after this break. Cheb turned away from the ads, just in time to see the redhead woman come storming through the kitchen doors. He'd only glanced at her when she'd been hanging on the doorbell. Up close she was a whole lot more forbidding. He knew he'd made a mistake, leaving a woman like her stamping out on the pavement. Naz was following at her shoulder, grinning for the first time in hours and saying, "Do you want to meet the boss?"

Cheb closed his eyes, feeling them swivel beneath the lids like the cylinders in a fruit machine. When he opened up again he was all ready to creep. Since daybreak, he'd ·been telling everyone he was running on superhero confidence but the truth was, it was beginning to swamp him. Even superheroes need to sleep between gigs, just to get their powers in perspective.

It didn't mean he couldn't drag up a piece of diplomacy in an emergency, though.

She said, "Are you Cheb?"

He nodded. Naz, still behind her, was saying, "She's going to sack you. You want me to put in a word?"

Cheb decided he'd go with the pressures of work excuse. It was the truth, however you cut it. When all Hogie could do was roll around the floor, weeping in shame and promising that he'd come good, it was him and Naz that had to run around the market, organise the team of chefs, make sure the party went ahead on time.

The woman was still there: "I didn't hear you?"

He said, "Yes, I'm Cheb."

"The New Age freak?"

Yes, that was him, he guessed.

"Well you look like a dick to me. Fetch me a drink."

There was his superhero confidence—a distant speck disappearing over a tall building. "Yes, ma'am. What do you want?"

"G & T."

As he reached for the optics, a new story started breaking on the telly. A body had been discovered in Grays, Essex, nailed to the floor of a coach parked in a local depot. The newscaster was saying that the identity of the victim wasn't yet known.

Naz stared at the screen. He said, "Nailed?"

Cheb nodded, making sure to avoid his eyes.

Susan looked up, grimaced and flicked the TV off. She said: "That's sick. What the hell's happening to this country?"

His eyes still down, he told her he really didn't know and passed her a drink.

She said, "Now get out, I want to make a call."

Cheb pushed back into the kitchen. Naz was right behind him, hissing into his ear. "You nailed it down?"

"To stop it rolling around, man."

"I don't believe it. You actually hammered nails into it?"

"Fuck, don't hassle me. I reckon I'm hitting a tiredness trough but it's probably just a blip. I should bounce back before the party."

Naz said, "Well, lay off the trips. Better just stick to the whizz."

Maybe not. He thought perhaps it was the whizz that was to blame. He was on his third gram since last evening and it just wasn't doing the trick anymore. He said, "Is there anything we forgot?"

The kitchen staff were working like Lego automaton, the

food getting chopped and parcelled according to the menu Naz was carrying in his head.

"Don't worry Cheb. It's sweet."

"They've not asked about Hogie?"

"I haven't given them time to ask."

Cheb was still worried. "What about Hogie? When he promised to make it up to us, what do you think he might have meant?"

Naz shrugged. He was there when Hogie started making the promises but all he said was, "I don't know, it wasn't my mother he was shagging."

Yeah, well she had to be the only one he missed.

Susan had the idea of calling her hairstylist in Spain. The woman was a friend. Even better she wasn't in the life, she was married to a golf pro whose only handicap was the DTs. Between her salon and his club house, there wasn't much she didn't hear and Susan wanted to know the latest on Frankie.

As the woman answered, she said, "Cassie, it's me."

"Friggin' hell, it's Susan Ball. What's the matter with you, did you watch *Shirley Valentine* on rewind? You're supposed to leave England for the Mediterranean, not the other way around."

Cassie was having a real giggle over that one. Susan had to hold on the line and wait before she could ask about Frankie.

"He's in Manchester, chuck. Hunting you down."

Susan was so pleased to hear it: Callum hadn't told the bastard a thing about her real plans. She could see Frankie now, trudging round Flixton and trying to find her mother's house. She'd like to see his face when he finally remembered she'd been dead almost six years.

Cassie was still on the line: "What about you, love? Are you okay?"

"Just fine, everything's wonderful."

"Where are you staying?"

"I'm between places at the moment. But it looks as if I'm going to have to move into a brothel—don't ask. Listen Cassie, I've got to go. I promise I'll speak to you later."

Before she left, she opened the case and called the chef back. He returned with the little baldie boy, looking sheepish and still calling her Ma'am.

"You two, you're going to be ready for the party, tonight?"

"Should be."

"Yes ma'am."

"And you think it will be a big success."

They nodded.

"Well, just to make sure, dish this out to the guests. Okay."

She put a one kilo bag of cocaine on the countertop, giving it a friendly pat as she did it. "It's cocaine, boys."

The two of them stood there, eyes popping: "Yes ma'am."

SIXTEEN

The London plane was late but only Frankie could get torn up over a fifteen minute delay. No wonder they called him Ballistic. Cardiff offered to buy another round of drinks and left Frankie to kick around the first class lounge on his own.

The previous night, when they arrived in Manchester, Frankie had booked two rooms but didn't even let Cardiff see his. Instead, he sent him straight out to look for his wife. Cardiff had stood in the lobby like a twat, saying, "I don't even know this fucking town. Where am I supposed to look?" Frankie wrote Susan's maiden name on a hotel post-it note and told him to use his initiative. There was no use arguing, Frankie was mad as hell. If he didn't get to a telephone, he'd probably explode. He'd been aggrieved ever since the cab from the airport, when he found out his Spanish mobile wouldn't work in Manchester.

Cardiff spent all night on the job. It was past seven in the morning when he returned, flat-footed and nerves frazzled from the lack of sleep—and more than a mite anxious about telling Frankie there was no trace of Susan anywhere. He was almost relieved, then, to find that Frankie had a new problem. Not only his wife, but his son had disappeared as well. Now there's a double fucker. Frankie told him not to bother unpacking, they were heading back for the airport—London bound, this time around.

Cardiff had no reason, no joy, no feelings nor nothing to be back in Blighty. True, London was better than being stuck up North, but he'd have preferred to stay on the Costa. When he saw the two women sat astride stools in the first class bar he was only trying to make the best of it.

He said, "Watch yerselves, you pair. Make room for a little 'un."

He could tell they didn't think much of what they saw but he kept his end up anyway: "Here, you sisters or what?"

They kind of looked alike, in their late forties and both of them northern birds. He'd met a lot of northerners in Spain. Like he always said, the Costa was a fucking melting pot.

"Can I buy either of you a drink? The name's Sean Doherty." It was the name on his passport but as he stuck out his hand he thought, What the fuck, I'll only confuse myself. "But my mates all call me Cardiff."

They took his hand but immediately said they'd better be going. He hadn't even managed to find out their names. He decided to give it one more spin, trotting around to their side to shout, "Service, por favor. A couple of vodka sodas and whatever the girls are drinking."

Then he turned to them. "Please, ladies. I'm an old fool but there's nothing I wouldn't do for a pair of beauties like you."

He had their names now. They were written on the front of their tickets, face up on the bar. "I hope I got 'em the right way round, not mixed nuffing up or nuffing, ladies. Which of you beauty's Manning and which is Beddoes?"

The smaller one set him straight, saying I'm Mrs Beddoes and this is Mrs Manning. Gloria Manning nodded, that was her.

Cardiff said, "Been anywhere nice, eh? Just back from the old Club Eighteen-to-Thirty, then?"

That always got a giggle in España, asking some old girl if she was down with one of those teeny-bopper package tours. It got a laugh off Mrs Beddoes anyway. She said, "No, worse luck. We're just off for a party in London."

"Party, eh? Can't be bleeding bad. Jet-set lifestyle. I'd be doing alright if I flew down the smoke every time I fancied a knees-up."

Cardiff felt he was moving along smoothly now. Mrs Manning hadn't said much but he never wrote the quiet ones off. That was one of his mottoes. They were always grateful to anyone who could keep up a bit of banter.

Mrs Beddoes said, "My son's friend organised it. He paid for the flight and everything. We're going to the opening night party of a restaurant."

Cardiff said, "Nice. Nice. Sweet. Restaurant, eh? I'll let you into a secret. I like my nosh. What's this gaff called, then?"

"La George."

Cardiff thought that was a fucking funny name, he was ready to make them spell it when the flight announcement came over the tannoy and they were off. He doubted he'd get a chance to speak to them on the plane. He didn't know how they'd managed to sneak into the first class lounge but he was pretty sure they wouldn't be travelling up front with the high rollers. Anyway, now he had their names and destination, he might even take a look in at their party. Always assuming Frankie let him have some time off. You never knew, maybe Frankie would be up for a bit; if he was, he could take his pick. The geezer was single at the moment, after all.

When he got back to the lounge area, Frankie said, "Where've you been, you cunt? We're boarding."

"Yeah, sorry boss. I got pulled off course by a couple of birds. You know me."

"Fucking arsehole. What were you going to do? Slash them up like you did that whore?"

That was below the belt. Cardiff said, "Fair do, Frankie. The cow was my wife."

"You were her pimp."

Cardiff was ready to plead. "Not so fucking loud, eh, Frankie?"

Frankie gave him a shove towards the gate. The final call was flooding through the airport speakers. Cardiff picked up their bags and followed Frankie towards the gate and the transport cop guarding it. When a man was wanted for murder, he could do without that kind of aggravation.

Officially, the woman he killed was only his common-law wife but Cardiff always thought of himself as a family man. That was what he couldn't understand about Frankie. Why did he let his son smuggle six kilos of cocaine into the country. That really was heart-stopping stuff and to do it to your own flesh and blood . . . well, some people would think it was out of order, that was all Cardiff could say. He would never have done that.

Frankie walked ahead of him, setting the pace. Cardiff could not understand why Frankie would want to get into the life again. He had made his fortune. He'd got it fucking taped. Cardiff didn't even want to begin to make sense of it, he had enough trouble struggling through the airport terminal with four heavy bags. If Frankie wanted to sink back into gangster stuff, Cardiff would shut up and tag along. If anyone asked him though, anyone he trusted, what he'd say was: You got to have a fucking screw loose to put your faith in Callum Ball, letting that dickhead put together a monster coke deal.

Ten yards from the departure gates, Cardiff caught sight of Viv and Gloria again. He might have tried hurrying a little, if he could. You never knew, maybe Frankie would be interested. It'd be worth impressing him, showing him that old Cardiff could still pick up the tarts. That way, Frankie might put him on pimping duty. It was better than getting involved in any heavy stuff.

He was surprised to find the girls sat in front on the plane. It turned out they had the right kind of coin after all. All the way to London, he kept them talking. He even helped out with their luggage. Frankie sat there scowling, keeping the stewardesses running but never even looking at either of the two birds.

At Heathrow, Gloria left Viv watching the luggage carousel and went walking down the mall. She was looking for presents but all she found were socks and chocolates. Waiting at a check-out with a tie for her Manny and a pair of tights for Jools, she got caught behind the same obnoxious cockney that had been sat behind her on the flight. His back was turned but she recognised the camel hair coat. When he started waving his hands about, she saw his gold rings. He was passing his time at the check-out desk by playing with his mobile phone.

She heard him say, "Where's my boy? . . . You were the ones supposed to be doing business with him. It's what I'm saying, just get off your arses and find my fucking boy."

Gloria didn't know how long Vivien would be collecting

the luggage. Neither of them had flown first class before. If they had, they would have known about the extra hand luggage allowance and kept their bags by their side. Hogie had insisted on the first class five-star treatment, telling her on the phone she didn't have to worry about anything, he'd put it all on AmEx.

He had sounded weird but it was weird hearing from him at all—it was heart-stopping. He had rung at nine in the morning to say he wanted his party to be a real family affair. Mannie, Jools, Cheb. Everyone's mother. Gloria wouldn't have accepted the too-strange invitation but the next call came from Viv Beddoes. Gloria decided it would look even stranger if Hogie's and Cheb's mums went to the party and she refused. It wasn't until she reached the airport she began wondering where Hogie's mum might be—she definitely wasn't on the flight list.

Frank was still hammering away into his cell phone. Every call he made was about his son. Saying, "Why haven't you seen him? You were his contact, you were supposed to look after him . . . Well find out, then."

There were two cockneys on the flight. This one, Frank, who had terrorised the stewardesses all through the flight and Cardiff, who had terrorised them. He seemed to have disappeared but Gloria supposed he was at the baggage carousel. She had heard Frank tell him to get their cases.

Frank reached the head of the queue and slapped a fist of pesetas onto the counter with a handful of ties. The boy at the till zapped them one by one with his code-gun. Frank carried on talking. Gloria noticed a sign that read: Payment will be accepted in all EC currencies, change will be given in sterling.

Cardiff and Viv Beddoes came wobbling across the concourse together. Everyone's bags were loaded onto the same trolley, but Cardiff had chosen one with a lame wheel. Gloria could hear his voice when they were still only a speck at the end of a long walkway. As they drew closer, he shouted, "Both my Club Eighteen-to-Thirties, together again. How about it, gals?"

Frank had already stomped off towards the car hire stall by the time they rolled up with the trolley. Gloria walked over, nodding towards Frankie's back. "You'll have to put your shoulder into it, if you're going to catch your boss."

She pulled her small case off the trolley. Viv did the same. They left Cardiff to struggle alone, giving him a wave but nothing like a decent goodbye.

Cardiff creaked across the rubberised tiles, trying to keep up. Frankie was well ahead, striding out in his English threads, taken out of the wardrobe and dusted down for this trip back home. It was easy to forget, if you saw someone in swimming trunks and a T-shirt everday, how they used to be. Wearing a Pringle sweater in the evening, sporting golf casuals and Italian moccasins, it had been easy to forget how things used to be. There was something very wrong with Frankie's clothes, today. They were so far out of date, it looked as though he'd finished a ten-stretch and been released into the clothes he'd worn on the day he entered prison. The clothes definitely made him scarier. Cardiff would have preferred to just turn his trolley around, even if he had to push it all the way to Spain.

When an old dear stepped out in front of him, he tried to haul his trolley to a stop but it only sent him spinning to the side. By the time he'd straightened up, both Frankie and the girls were fifty yards ahead.

The women had run up against a queue, stretching so far across the terminal that Cardiff couldn't see where it began or ended. They were caught, struggling to create an opening, standing right by Frankie's elbow. Normally, Frankie would have pushed through without even slowing but he had stopped to wait for Cardiff to catch up.

As he wobbled over, Cardiff said, "Alright ladies, having a spot of bother?"

Frankie looked at Viv and Gloria as if he'd never seen them before. He read the situation and helped out, even giving the pair a wink. All he had to do was put a hand on this old geezer's shoulder and say, "You ain't going nowhere." He got his message across. Fifteen yards worth of people, all of them waiting in a turgid line, just dribbled away.

Frankie ushered the girls through, one of his hands falling on Gloria's shoulder. Viv, always the chattier one, said, "Ta, love."

"You're welcome."

Cardiff saw what was happening, Viv was one of those date-finder types, ready to line her miserable friend up with just about anyone. Frankie was already smiling genially.

Viv Beddoes touched Cardiff on his arm, "Maybe see you at the restaurant, then?" Then she looked over to Frankie to say, "Both of you."

Frankie nodded again, giving them a smile. "You were on the plane, weren't you. I'm sorry if I was a bit ignorant. I was worried about my boy."

Viv gave him a comforting look, "Family problems?"

"Something like that. He's just started working for himself, so I guess I'm being over-protective."

Cardiff couldn't believe it, Frankie was nothing but charm. The story about Callum was going down big with both girls. After the way he acted on the plane, you would have thought they'd have been put right off. Perhaps it was because they were northern birds, they were used to obnoxious men dressed fifteen years out of date. They'd probably been impressed by the tan, as well.

Frankie was jangling his rent-a-car keys in his hand, now. He turned to the women and said, "We're going up West. What about we give you ladies a lift?"

SEVENTEEN

Susan took a look at the fringed lamps, the splashy nylon
bedding and the full range of air fresheners and mail order
perfumes on the dressing-table. George had opened the
window in an attempt to dilute the sugary tart stench with
something breathable. Before the room completely filled
with flies and the noise of fucking above and below, he'd
excused himself and gone looking for the bathroom. If he
found it, she was willing to bet the air was sweeter there
than in this whore's boudoir, courtesy of Maltese Rosa. When
George helped her move in, he'd played it up, laughing that
it was just her style. But he'd made her accept it anyway.

This was how Rosa had invested her life savings: pouring
it into a shaking fuck shack on Manchester Street. George
said she had another three houses spread across Marylebone. It was a good business, the rent was paid by the day,
maid and phone included in the price. Susan told him she
didn't need a maid. What she would have liked was her own
bathroom, rather than a communal lavatory, shared with
another six rooms. That was the only unusual thing about
the place, although it was typical of Rosa. The way she'd
see it, she'd earned her money the hard way and no one
starting the same life could expect it any easier.

The funny thing was, as she got out of the taxi Susan had
thought it seemed okay. It was so close to Marks & Spencer's
head office, she assumed it had to be respectable. Then she
walked inside.

George returned and took a seat on the bed: there was
nowhere else and the bed all but filled the room. He
was already dressed for the evening. Wearing a tuxedo, he
looked imposing; queer yet gravelly, definitely not a queen.
He could have stepped out of *The Godfather*, if it had been
re-made by Pedro Almodovar. He had his primer glass of

cognac in his hand, the bottle close by on the edge of the dressing table. When he opened it, he'd told her it was a moving in present but he was on his third glass and she was still on her first.

She said, "I can't stay here, George. Frankie doesn't know anything about the other place so why don't I move back."

"You can't be certain Callum didn't tell him."

George patted the pockets of his tuxedo until he found his pack of cigarettes. He had been glad to hear Frankie had taken the bait and flown to Manchester. But he wouldn't stay there long once he discovered his boy was missing. He wondered how he'd broach that one with Susan. As he lit a Gauloise, he said, "There's another thing. Apparently Callum's gone walkabout."

"How? I mean how do you know?"

Because he'd seen the body. He didn't say that, though. "It's just a whisper."

Susan didn't seem worried. She just took a cigarette and said, "He'll have gone to a rave or something, somewhere. Now he's probably comatose on some girl's floor, trying to remember where he left his cocaine."

She had the suitcase with her, the five remaining bags inside and the best of her clothes spread out over the bed. She hadn't yet chosen what she'd wear. As she held up a dress in front of her, one-handed with her cigarette in the other, she asked George what he thought.

"Maybe the cream dress."

She held it up, turning to look at herself in the tiny mirror. "I can't tell. I can hardly see myself. How should I dress, you tell me."

He'd already explained they were meeting a few media types at a club first. Just a few magazine editors and food critics that George hoped would help publicise the restaurant.

Susan said, "How do you want me to look, when I'm meeting the press."

George said, "I don't know. But something quiet. Let's keep the focus on the restaurant, not the gangster's wife."

Susan held up a red dress. "I don't know. Maybe if I was famous, it would scare him. I could dazzle him with my celebrity."

George said, "Don't even joke about it. I don't want Frankie turning up at the restaurant."

Susan wasn't listening, she was stretching the red dress across her breasts and stomach. She thought of Frankie, standing dazzled in a pair of headlights or blinded by the Spanish sun. It reminded her of something. She said, "We once took a trip to the desert to visit the set of an old spaghetti western. Frankie was so excited, he bought a video camera before the trip. When we arrived this old gypsy-peasant walked up and told us filming was forbidden unless we paid him. Frankie told him to wait a moment then went back to the car for his shotgun. The old man ran away and we didn't see him again. Frankie stood out in the street, holding his gun and trying to do a Clint while I filmed him. He was saying: 'Have you got a horse for me?' "

"I don't think that was Clint Eastwood. I think it was Charles Bronson."

"If it was, he never said it like Frankie. The only impression he can do is Michael Caine and he hams that. He was standing in the middle of the desert with these two dimensional film sets all around him, waving his gun and shouting out any bits of cowboy films he could think of in this atrocious Harry Palmer accent. He was wearing a Hawaiian shirt and a posing pouch and nothing else. I started laughing. He was already laughing, thinking what a great guy he was, but there must have been something about the way I was laughing because he stopped and began saying What's So Fucking Funny.

"I had my back partly to the sun, because I was working the video camera. When he started shouting at me, I moved. I was nervous. But as I moved, he turned so that he was always facing me. And he was still waving the shotgun. When the sun was directly behind me, he was blinded. His face changed. It wasn't just screwed up because of the sun but really screwed up, you know, like his mind had gone white. I was still videoing him. I've kept the tape and it's a shocker. Something went wrong with him and he spent two, three minutes opening and closing his mouth as though he was choking. Then he turned around and walked quietly back to the car. I was scared to follow him at first but the way he walked, he looked like a beaten dog so I went after him. He didn't really come right for hours, until the evening when he was back in his local."

George said, "Frankie was always more of a night-time person. But weren't we all?"

Susan kept turning the image over and over. Later, in the taxi, she said: "Maybe publicity isn't such a good idea."

George could have wept with relief. "We've got to keep your connection quiet. Let the press focus on the decor and the chef."

He shouldn't have worried so much. He always knew he could do business with Susan. She had hard edges but a soft interior. She nailed him on the accounts but let him know that she trusted him. She would back him, however he chose to run things.

The cab pulled off Oxford Street, turning at Dean Street to plunge into Soho. George had membership of six Soho clubs, which covered just about every eventuality. He might have taken Susan to any of them—a strip joint for old times sake, the Colony Rooms for gin and colour, the casino for a flutter or to one of the heavier bars for a fag hag trip. Tonight they were going to the Sohovian, La La Land for media tarts. He stepped out of the taxi ahead of her and gave the driver his account number while he pointed Susan towards the entrance.

The main bar was done in chrome and leather, scattered with geometric patterns. The windows were covered with a bamboo blind. It would have looked sophisticated, if this was the Costa and it was still 1985. Susan wasn't impressed but followed behind George. He was nodding over to a girl in a corner. Out the side of his mouth he said she was called Annabel and worked on the *Evening Standard*'s gossip column. He thought a girl in the same crowd was something in television and another worked for a broadsheet. He forgot which exactly. He shone them both a small-talking smile. They broke off mid mad social whirl and shouted 'George!'

He signalled that he'd come over and took another periscope look around. A dumpy blonde was waving energetically and hauling herself upright from a low seat. He thought she might be the editor of a newspaper's weekend section or a magazine, something with a foodie column anyway. She joined them as everyone else shifted to make room. George introduced Susan around but didn't mention her connection to the restaurant. The hack Annabel began talking about the chef, saying he was such a Babe, he was just a total Babe.

Another one said, "It's going to be a great success. All my girlfriends, they gave him rave reviews at his last place."

Susan said she hoped so. She had a picture of the tall Asian. He seemed competent, he knew how to use a cleaver anyway.

"You've never tried his food?"

She shook her head, "I've spent the past few years abroad."

Someone said, "Travelling?"

She turned to face the question. "No. Just sitting around. I retired young."

It was an old man, hunched over a whisky paunch,

wearing an ash-face and food-stained tie. Out of everyone in the place, he looked closer to her idea of a journalist. He certainly had the most questions, all of them delivered in a fruity accent she'd long ago learnt to mistrust: *faux* Guards. "You're retired. From what, sweetie?"

George butted in quickly. "Susan was a model."

She nodded. That was right.

"And do you still live abroad?"

"No. I'm staying in a tart's boudoir, over in Marylebone." She shot George a sharp look but he didn't flinch. He just took her arm and steered her round to meet someone new. As he did, he whispered, "Keep away from him."

"Why?"

"Because any minute he's going to work out who you are. He's practically lived in Soho, the past thirty years."

Susan looked over her shoulder. The old guy was still staring at her. She wondered if she recognised him. Now George had reminded her, she certainly knew his circle: a couple of artists, a couple more writers, one old Etonian who'd carried bags for the Kray twins. At least half of them gay and all of them alcoholics.

She said, "He's still staring. Maybe we'd better go."

Along the short walk up Dean Street, Susan tried to keep pace with George but he was lagging too far behind, still schmoozing his pack of girl journalists. She was the first to reach the restaurant and stood for a moment, wondering why the huge window had been blacked out. As she reached for the handle, the door swung away from her. Cheb stood there, erect and alive, smiling in greeting. His face pinkishly flushed to the top of his throbbing crown. His white tuxedo etched with baroque swirls. The cravat at his neck flopped open like an obscene flower, a white goat's tooth, brilliantly bleached, pierced the centre of its rosette. His strides were brown velvet and his high-heeled boots gave him the extra three inches he'd probably always needed. His cocktail hand was crooked at chest height, his ambulatory hand waved her through into the heart of the restaurant.

She went inside.

The restaurant had been re-set, Vegas-style, to cocktail hour. Velvet fringes looped the edges of the ceiling and fell in cascades of flamenco colour to the floor. Warm-oil lights splayed across the walls in liquid swirls. Mirror balls fired pin-spot tracer beams across the swaying crowd. The guests, invited celebrities, journalists and the handful of recognisable London cuisine groupies, were trapped between strangers dressed up as lounge lizard swingers, sashaying to the sounds of brassy Cubana.

George was at her shoulder, staring round with his mouth open. He said, "Who the fuck are these people?"

Cheb said, "They came with the DJ, no extra charge."

George took a beat, then broke into a smile: "Good work, Cheb. Does the DJ take requests?"

Susan was still standing, not sure what to make of it. Cheb gave her another bow saying, "Mrs Ball. Let me mix you up something in a curacao. Do you take it blue or green?"

Susan thought, keep it simple. She said, "Just gin and tonic again." She tacked a please onto the end and gave him a smile.

She decided the bald kid had done well. Though she found the DJ's latest selection disconcerting. She wondered when she last heard Walter Wanderley's Hammond version of "Call Me". She'd never listened to the whole thing with her clothes still in place.

EIGHTEEN

Naz stood between the basted carcasses of goats and mutton and the piles of saffron rice and said, "Everyone get into line. That way, you know you're gonna get yours."

Hogie sat on the surface where they had moulded lamb, parsley and milk into kofta patties, his feet drumming against the steel cupboards below. The boy could not keep his legs still. His laugh was as high as a whipped bitch but more repetitive: eeh eeh eeh, followed by a backwards hiccup like a record spun against its grain. Naz did not know why he felt so wired but he could do without Hogie's agitation.

The cooking crew were forming an orderly queue. Naz said, "That's right. Everyone line up nicely and they get their reward."

He held the palette knife two-handed, at the handle and at the very tip of the blade, chopping the cocaine down to its finest possible particles. He drew the powder into ranks of parallel lines, like ten white bathing beauties spread out on a tin roof.

Naz reasoned with himself. The stress he'd been through, he was entitled to show a few cracked edges. But he knew the only thing bugging him was Hogie. The kid had turned up an hour ago, still unable to speak, but looking unruffled in his chef whites and still capable of cutting a pile of candies into a stack of fancy shapes. It was a suave trick, especially coming from a gimp and Naz was too dog-tired to top it . . . go one better and grab the most respect.

Then Naz looked up at his four juniors, all of them watching his expertise with cocaine and waiting in line for their turn just as he had told them to. He thought: Fuck it, these dicks are impressed by anything. He gave the girl at the head of the queue a tightly rolled twenty, saying "Here, this is something I prepared earlier."

Cheb had been right. He had told Naz it wasn't enough to terrorise the baby cooks, he had to sugar the rod of discipline with the promise of free drugs. It worked, they worked their arses off. They were so excited, they'd be jumping around like kiddies if they weren't so afraid of making fools of themselves in front of him.

Hogie flipped off the worktop and joined the end of the line. He was still giggling. Naz leant back against the warmth of the bread oven and sipped his strawberry yoghurt drink, watching the cocaine being snuffled away. He noticed, when it was Hogie's turn, the banknote was passed over with special respect and the four baby chefs took a step backwards to give him room. They would have looked like soldiers standing to attention if they weren't all sniffling, dabbing at their eyes or rubbing the flutes of their nostrils. It was a case of détente, dual-respect for both him and Hogie. If that's the way it was, it was alright with Naz. He had to admit, Hogie had assembled a good little team. They cooked it up nicely. The proof stood all around them, waiting to be wheeled out and unveiled.

A banquet fit for a prophet, a maharajah, a choir of self-made colonels or a dozen legitimate presidents. A sub-continental feast of superstar dimensions. When the baby chefs had finally got round to reviewing and tasting everything, they knew they had created something special.

Leaning over the coke tray, Hogie was framed by a mountain of coloured flesh and different nan breads. In the polished stainless steel of the worktop, his reflection rose to meet him at the line and kept pace, nose to nose. At the trail's end he snapped upright, throwing back his head to make a straight connection between the nasal passages and bronchial tubes. With the hit, his head dropped forward. Starting at the tips of his fingers, he shook his dangling arms out then, slowly, began raising them up. It looked as though electricity was being pumped into him. His legs began to twitch, slightly sprung at the knees. His centre of gravity focussed on his pelvis. Now Hogie's arms were out in front of him, palms facing outwards and his fingers shivering towards the ceiling.

In a microsecond, Hogie had gone rigid, holding his position then: ba-doom, ba-doom, he shook his hips. Naz thought, Yeah, Elvis.

Hogie about-faced and dropped to his hands in the press-up position. He brought his buttocks up so his body formed a high angle to the floor, then began motoring his legs. He scooted backwards at high speed, keeping his body bent and his frictionless hands slipping smoothly across the floor. His legs were the only moving part and they ripped. Hogie managed two backward circuits of the kitchen before he slipped onto his face. He even managed to slip gracefully, springing upwards as though that was the planned end to the performance.

Naz said, "So is it good stuff?"

It was the first thing Hogie had said all day. "I think I felt something."

Naz grinned back at him. Then he clapped his hands at his team, saying Okay. "Get the food outside."

The baby chefs ran to the edges of the biggest platter, lifting it and beginning walking to the swing doors. As they reached them, Cheb slipped through, excusing himself and avoided crashing into the food. He pointed over to Hogie but spoke to Naz, "Is he sorted?"

"Yeah, I think he's sorted."

Cheb turned to Hogie, "You feel alright?"

Hogie nodded, Uh-huh.

"Sure?"

"Yes. Totally totally sorted. I mean it, I'm fine." He stepped over to Cheb and put a hand behind his head, looking him in the eyes: "Listen, I got to say, you saved me mate. You and Naz, you saved me like Billy Graham. I'm walking in righteousness. I want you to know, I can finish this thing. I can defeat my sins and this cycle of iniquity."

Cheb said, "Yeah? What are we talking about, exactly?"

Hogie never flickered, "I mean I'm going to atone for my sins. What I did to your mams."

Cheb tried to match the sincerity. He put his hands on Hogie's shoulders and brought his head forward, whispering: "Listen, Hogie. No one ever tangoed solo, they must have been willing." Then broke the moment: "So, forget your troubles and meet the people."

Hogie nodded, making for the door. "Yeah, right Cheb. But remember, events are in motion and I'm going to atone. I'm going to beg for forgiveness."

As they watched him leave the kitchen, Cheb turned to Naz and said, "Did that sound like trouble?"

"Fuck knows, he's your friend."

Cheb clicked, "The bastard didn't even compliment me on the suit. How do I look?" He held out his hands, baby-ballerina style and gave a spin.

Naz said, "Sweet."

"Hey, thanks mate. Okay, better get maitre d'ing." He pointed over to the worktop where the kilo bag lay open and said, "Can you get one of your cooker boys to divide it up and start distributing it around the tables."

The DJ called himself Juevo Billions. As the last bars of Sammy Davis Junior's "Rhythm of Life" swung off of the decks, Juevo had his billionaire-style finger primed on the fader button. As he spun the first cued notes of the next record, he nodded over to George Carmichael. George took the signal and stepped to the edge of the makeshift stage. He held his microphone between two fingers and a thumb, his little finger pointing outwards to the heavens as he revved into full croon:

> *In the avenues and alley-ways, where the soul of a man is easy to buy, everybody's wheeling, everybody's dealing, all the lows are living high.*

Susan was impressed. Tony Christie had never caught the pose better. Some of the higher notes slipped out of George's range but he covered well, slyly clipping the difficult words. Susan had heard too many karaoke singers linger masochistically over their shortcomings.

Where George scored big, it was on theatricals. He brought a biblical stoicism to the song. A High Noon seriousness to the line *"Every City's got them"* that she would have sworn was impossible but he delivered with only a trace of camp. When he sang *Can we ever stop them?*, it was a real question. The pay-off, *Some of us are going to try*, rang out with the sorrow of a man who knows he is heading out alone.

She turned back to the bar and asked for a large gin and tonic. George had told her it was a free bar, she had said "It's my money anyway."

He said, "It was somebody's money, but I can't remember whose."

Before Frankie got his hands on it, it had been part of a federal bank's reserves. The nationalised gold of some no-hope country, stolen as it was being transferred to a merchant bank. As she remembered, this fandango republic had agreed to guarantee one of its bad debts with bullion. Susan believed that was the story, although it seemed implausible. She had always suspected their government was insuring its pension fund before the next coup. Anyway, it was a long time ago. Frankie and his boys had taken the money as it was wheeled across a warehouse floor in a secure part of Heathrow airport.

Susan took one look at her G&T and knew she couldn't drink it. The girl behind the bar had absolutely no idea. She slopped so much tonic into the glass that the oily sheen of good gin was lost completely. She handed it back, telling the girl to pour the whole of the drink into a longer glass and stir it up with another two shots of gin.

The girl said, "It might be a free bar, but you're just taking the piss."

The girl was a sour-faced blonde. Susan told her sweetly, "Honey, when I want to take the piss, I'll squeeze it out of you like a sponge. Now, slap the gin in the glass and shut it."

George quickly finished his floor show and joined her at the bar. He'd seen the scowl across the barmaid's face and wanted to explain before things got out of hand: "Mrs Ball is my partner, Jools." Then, introducing her to Susan, said: "And this is Jools Manning, she's a big star on the television."

He only began gushing as he turned back to the girl, "I love *Pony Trek*, I couldn't believe it when Cheb told me you'd offered to look after the bar. I wanted to thank you personally."

Jools scowled, slamming Susan's refreshed gin onto the bar top. "You're his partner, yeah? Well if Hogie tries to take credit for any of the cooking tonight, you can tell him he's a fucking liar. Naz did everything. Hogie was out of his fucking helmet."

Susan watched as Jools clumped back to the shelves and jealously replaced the gin bottle. There was a mirror behind the shelving racks and as Jools tilted to reach out for another bottle her sulky reflection lurched in and out of the frame. As she exited, her image was replaced by another face: standing in the mid-background, deep focus. The face was familiar.

In a moment, Susan recognised the soft blonde curls and ridiculous beard. The same boy that had tracked her through

Harrods and into Harvey Nichols. She held his eyes, nego-
tiated with him via the mirror, waited for him to meet her at
the bar. But he continued to stand there, shifting awkwardly
around a dopey grin. Susan decided, what the hell, she could
make the first move. The voice on the record sang "How'd
You Like To Fly In My Beautiful Balloon?" the Fifth Dimen-
sion version not the Mike Samms hit.

She said, "Do you want to dance?"

Cardiff knew every street in Soho, but recognised less of
the store fronts. He guessed that something like eighty per
cent of Soho had changed hands since his last visit. It was
the little shops he felt sorry for; the old family firms, grocers
and what have you. The brown-wrapper trade was still going
strong, though. To kill time, he stepped inside a few and
looked around. Cardiff liked to have a bit of porn to hand,
for when he felt like reading but didn't want anything with
too many words. In the end, he didn't buy anything. Time
was moving on and, anyway, the gear was nothing like as
strong as it used to be, back in the seventies.

He knew where the La George restaurant was from its
address but didn't know what he'd find on his walk there.

The one thing that hadn't changed were the pubs. Cardiff
checked five different ones to make absolutely sure. When
he reached the door of the La George he had to admit he
was feeling merry. He checked his watch, the dial said nine
and the logo spelt Rolex. Assuming the hands were jerking
round about ten minutes fast as usual, he was still early. He
didn't feel like walking in without Viv and Gloria so he
crossed to the pub on the corner. He could get another pint,
standing in the window he'd see them when they arrived.

Frankie Ball had cried off. He said he had things to do,
people to see. Cardiff had asked if he should stick around
and Frankie said "Nah. You go out with those two old birds."

These two girls, they'd said they were from a place called

Prestwich, which was just in or outside Manchester. Cardiff reckoned if anyone had started talking Manchester to him ten years ago, he would have blanked. Nothing. Once upon a time, he could have boasted that he knew everywhere in the country, so long as it had a North London postcode. In those days, he never came across hillbilly-types but he'd found that living abroad had inflated his capacity for the foreign. There was a big fat bloke who lived on the Costa and sometimes drank in their local, he was from Rochdale. Went by the name of Tetley and was a fucking scary gent in a fight. He knew of at least one famous old villain who'd returned to England after being roughed up by Tetley. Preferring prison to another little talk with the gent.

Cardiff wished he'd asked these women if they'd ever come across Tetley. Rochdale was close to Manchester. For all he knew, they might be related: sister, mother and lover of the sheep-shagging bastard.

The girls arrived in a cab. Viv Beddoes stepped out first. Cardiff could see Gloria trying to pay for the ride through the little window that separated the driver from his backseat customers. He emptied his pint glass and hurried out before she'd finished picking up her spilled change.

Viv looked over, laughing at Cardiff as he waggled over. "Have you been lurking?"

"That's me. A bit of a lurker. How are you, love? And, you too love? Have you got everything?" Cardiff looked around the pavement to see if there were any other loose coins that Gloria had dropped and not found. She was busy trying to close her purse, already stuffed with small change.

Cardiff said, "Give the cabbie a tip, that'll get rid of some coppers."

Viv said, "I already gave him a note. I could have given it him in change but I couldn't tell what he was saying, he talks just like you and your pal. Where is Frankie, anyway?"

Cardiff told her Frankie couldn't come. He'd sent his

regards but he'd got business, you know. Cardiff registered her dig at his accent and wondered whether his impression of a northern accent would go down well. Probably not, the only time he'd tried it he'd got some really funny looks: he found out why when he turned around, the geezer Tetley was stood right behind him.

Viv said, "Shall we go in, then?"

On the inside of the screened doors, Cardiff stopped and took stock. He had to say it, it was a nice gaff. He liked the palm tree effect they'd used for the decor. The music was tasty, too. Cardiff undid another button on his shirt. When Viv turned to look at him, he gave her a wide-eyed nodding grin to let her know he was in a partying mood.

There were a lot of people dancing, quite a few of them sambos but the birds were sexy. Cardiff did notice he was about the oldest person in the room.

Viv said, "That's my son, Jason."

She was pointing at a small kid with a shaved head, wearing a white tux. The kid looked well shocked to see his old mum. Gloria Manning was waving frantically in the direction of the bar. The blonde girl serving the drinks was waving back with a dazed expression on her face.

Cardiff thought, family reunions eh? There's always someone who can't stand seeing their loved ones. He continued to look around the restaurant, pausing when he noticed a bloke who looked to have some grey hair, standing at the far side of the room. That would at least make two old-timers. Cardiff didn't want to feel self-conscious, not when the place suited him so well he could have chosen the decor and picked the tunes himself.

When the grey-haired geezer turned around, Cardiff thought, No. That's what he called a smack in the gob, running into Bum George in a place like this. Cardiff skirted the edge of the room to get a better look at him. The way the big pouf was dressed, he looked to be doing very nicely for himself. Cardiff had heard that George had gone into the laundry business. It wouldn't surprise him, he always thought George was too bright to stick to pimping, especially when he had no interest in the merchandise. It was always a headache, working with women.

Cardiff wondered if George was handling Frankie's finances. What was certain, somebody must be sending Frankie his regular cheques because Frankie was always fucking loaded.

Then he saw Susan Ball. Dancing with someone who looked like Callum Ball, all frocked up in a cook's rig. It was Susan's clothes that had him staring, though. She wore a soft cream dress, slit almost to heaven. A shapely leg unclothed and twisting up to tease her boy's thigh, the two of them clinched in a cheek-nestling tango. Now, what was that about?

All things considered, he reckoned his best bet was to duck out before he was seen and get a report back to Frankie. He began looking for a discreet exit. Bum George was over by the main door, now, working the crowd in a meet-and-greet show and playing queen for a night. Cardiff re-assessed the situation and lighted on the kitchen. There had to be a back way out and this was his best chance, while the chefs were out of the way, serving the punters with shit-eating grins and passing around poppadoms and bhajis.

Actually, that was strange, because the place didn't look like an Indian. There was none of that Paisley wallpaper and no embroidered pictures of elephants. To his mind, they'd have been better with a few canapés, maybe some tasties on sticks. But when he banged up against a long-haired Paki, he played it low-key. All he said was, "Oi, watch it Gungadin."

The murderous look he got fazed him. He was only trying to be pleasant, just wanting to slip softly away into the night but the Paki looked like he was ready to make an issue out of it. Cardiff muttered an apology and put his head down. As he backed into the crowd, the Paki lifted one side of his jacket. Stuck into his waistband: a gun. Cardiff saw it, he was meant to.

He propped himself on a pillar and tried to catch his breath, just pleased the Paki was putting himself back into circulation. The guy was swishing towards the bar, now, his gun so well covered by his tuxedo you wouldn't think it was there. Cardiff watched him lift the bar counter and pass through, smiling at the punters as they queued for snorts of the old nose powder. As they ducked up and down like bobbing birds over water-glasses, rolled notes stuck to their beaks, the Paki smiled above them. He waved a slim hand across the little heaped bowls, gold rings glistening against tan skin as he told everyone to be his guest: there was no shortage nor nothing. Cardiff took one last shufti and looked away again, terrified he might catch the Paki's eyes.

He tried to put it together: Susan Ball, celebratory smooching with her son; Bum George with his name over the door and a Paki enforcer in tow. They were all in it together and, judging by the amount of drugs around, what they were into was Frankie's cocaine.

Cardiff saw a gap in the crowd and rushed for it, pushing through the swing doors into the kitchen. Hoping to make for the doors at the back; unfortunately, the kind where you bang on a horizontal bar and the door is supposed to swing open. Cardiff hated those kind. They were supposed to open so easily a granny with smoke poisoning could get through but Cardiff had never had any luck with them. He ran a morose finger along the bar and wondered how long he would have to stand there, hammering at it and feeling pathetic. When he heard a noise behind him, he still hadn't worked up the nerve to test his strength. He stepped into the shadows, deciding it was better to wait for the coast to clear before he made his getaway.

Cheb finally understood Hogie's idea of atonement. At first the shock of seeing his mum had taken the edge off his hyper drive. He went into white-out, he didn't know what she was doing or why she'd brought Mrs Manning with her. Then the picture came into focus: this was Hogie's act of contrition. Cheb dreaded the possibilities, the kind of scene the boy had in mind, perhaps a tearful confession or something more theatrical. He put on a good-son smile and got ready to sing *Mamee*. Jools and Mannie were following behind, making their way over to their own mother.

Viv said, "Hello pet. Are you surprised? It must have cost Hogie a fortune."

Cheb said, "I think he put it on plastic. It's nice to see you Mam."

He brushed his lips against the skin beneath her high cheek bones, buffing the old dimples that had turned into laughter lines. His mother smoothed her hand across his bald head.

She said, "We met a bloke at the airport, so we brought him along . . ." pausing to look around. "That's funny, he's disappeared. Never mind, he was a bit fat. And a bit old. I was worried that I'd either have to give him the slip or palm him off on Gloria."

Viv had begun swaying her hips to the music. It looked as though it would be a good party. She had thought it would be too mad, dropping everything and flying down to London. Now she was glad she'd done it. There was one thing she couldn't understood, "Why didn't Hogie ask his own mother down?"

Cheb said, "I guess it's just you and Mannie's mum."

Mrs Beddoes looked at Mrs Manning again. Then back at Cheb. Her expression was strange, looking slightly dim but actually faint. Cheb couldn't read it. He waited for it to come into high resolution. When it did, they both knew they understood each other.

She said, "Oh fucking hell. Not Gloria too?"

She took a sidelong look at Gloria Manning. Jools was releasing her mother from a tight embrace. The tears were shining in her eyes before they burst. Then she just started wailing.

"Does everyone in the fucking place know?"

Cheb said, "Everyone who'd care."

"Oh shit."

Gloria Manning was staring helplessly at Jools. Mannie was beside her, shifting around on flat feet and tugging at the sleeves of his jersey with spastic fingers.

Cheb said, "I bet you want a drink."

"Don't you fucking dare leave me."

"I'll be one second. What do you want—gin, whisky?"

"I don't want to be here at all. Where's Hogie? Is the little twat going to make a show of us?"

Cheb pointed to the far side of the room, "He's dancing with the boss."

Cheb's mum squinted through the disco lights, "So who's mother is he with now?"

Cheb shrugged. The second he saw Susan Ball, he'd thought she was Hogie's type.

Viv decided on a drink. "My usual. And keep Hogie away from Gloria. I've always thought she was a bit flakey and I don't want her to do anything stupid."

Cheb went to the bar. There was no one on duty since Jools had left her post but it was still busy. One of the baby chefs had lined little piles of cocaine along the bartop in crème-caramel dishes and the guests were going for it with enthusiasm, passing notes from hand to hand. Cheb turned a forced smile onto them, hoping he didn't look too crazed. They hit him with gigantic beams, all of them too stoned to pick up on the madness. Cheb just waved his arm, said: "Enjoy."

As he got down a bottle of pale ale for his mother, a woman started work on a line. While her head was down, he slipped her credit card into his palm and off the bar. One edge was dusty, Cheb wiped it clean on the side of his leg before he ran it through his machine. He had it safely back on the bar before she'd even lifted her head.

Cheb swiped another four cards through his copying machine while he poured his mother's drink; all the while, grinning like a dick and telling the coke harpies to dig in. He wondered how far he could stretch the rating of the loud-mouth TV exec shouting the odds to his left. If he pushed the envelope with her, she'd have no grounds for complaint. So long as she stuck around, she would have enough material for thirty years of true life docu-dramas: the boy who never had enough mothers . . . it had to be worth paying for.

He took the drink back to his mum. The way things were moving on the home front, he wouldn't get the chance to pirate many of his guest's AmEx and Visas. As he slipped through the crowd, he looked over at Hogie. The guy was oblivious to the problems he'd caused, all trace of his heavy guilt gone, now he was snuggling down with another woman. Susan Ball had her arms in the air, swinging through a louche, loose, breast-enhancing manoeuvre. Then, as a new Hammond intro trembled out of the speaker system, she and Hogie struck out for the kitchen. Cheb hoped they'd stay there. He loved trouble as much as the next chaos-merchant but he couldn't get an angle on this stuff. Better that Hogie kept a low profile.

Hogie was trying to swing to more than the easy-listening sounds of DJ Juevo Billions. He was trying to swing with the new series of events. His mind was wrapped in chemical cotton wool but from somewhere deep beneath the layers, a voice was telling him this was not the right time for a public apology. In the spaces left between dancer's bodies, he could still see Gloria Manning and Viv Beddoes. More than once, they had pointed over and he knew they were talking about him. They were just waiting for him to make his move. But he had decided to go for a postponement, at least. He could be a good boy tomorrow; for now, he wouldn't do anything to risk losing this new woman. Mrs Susan Ball, he loved her name. He loved the way she looked: a dream queen, *déjà vuing* all over the show. He had to have dreamt her up, she was so perfect.

She was also a way better dancer than him, a woman built for lounge-core sophistication. He tried to cha-cha-cha it, to keep to her swaying rhythms but he was out of it. Out of step, out of his depth ... trying to find a way off the dancefloor and lead her into the privacy of the kitchen.

He said, "I gotta say it, you dance divinely."

She smiled. "George Carmichael taught me everything I know."

"Maybe he'd teach me, you think he'd be up for it?"

"He's probably persuadeable, if you ask him sweetly. Where are you taking me?"

He had one hand on that spot where the soft curve of her hip turned to bone, the other behind her back trying to aim her for the swing doors to the kitchen. As he manouevred, he kept stamping the heels of his boots, thinking maybe if he sounded kinda flamenco, she'd think he was still trying to dance.

The wood of the restaurant floor turned to the clatter of tiles. Hogie said, "This is the kitchen ..."

"Suave step."

There was no doubt, she was laughing at him. But he couldn't turn back. He said " ... and I, like, prepare food and stuff in here. But I was feeling ill today so that's why Naz helped."

Both his hands were still in position as he led her round the worktops. Maybe he was hallucinating but the soft cream of her dress seemed to blush in hot-spots, wherever his touch awakened the skin beneath the material.

She said, "I heard you'd been poorly. Are you feeling better now?"

He spooned little doggie looks her way, dropping from bashful eyes. "Actually, I'm feeling kind of weak."

"Really?"

"Oh yeah. And, like, this might be a gross personal intrusion but I fancy you so much I can't breathe. I mean, tell me if I'm seriously misdirected and should take a Louie but . . ."

He wondered: that could work?

That could work. Their lips met. He felt the slight stickness of the surface of her lipstick and then the dissolve, the heat of her breath and the sudden hint of moisture like the sweet syrup of a rum baba, breaking the surface. What he had in his arms; a thrill of perfume, tuned to a frequency somewhere between soft and solid, keeping a space open for him. He felt the folds sweep behind him as he walked inside.

Watching from behind a hot plate rack, Cardiff couldn't believe his eyes. Susan and her boy together, they looked like a shampoo advert: a strawberry blond and a light ash blond, their wavy locks glistening as they kissed under the strip lighting. He thought: Jesus, tell me I missed sexual liberation but I never seen a woman behave like that. Not with her own son. All the time Frankie complained it wasn't natural, the way she mothered their boy, Cardiff never twigged what the geezer really meant. No wonder old Frankie got so weird and twisted about it.

Cardiff tried for a better look. Dropping to his knees, he

took the next ten yards at a crawl until he reached the edge of the counter. The next stretch would leave him exposed. He just hoped that Susan was the type to keep her eyes closed. His chances looked good. She was sat on top of the cooker now, her boy stood in front of her with his danglies bouncing against the gas dials. Cardiff scooted along until he was hidden by a wheelie bin. From here, he had a ringside seat. Christ, he had it in stereo. One time, straight on, as her long dancer's legs encircled her son's waist. And then again, an aerial view as they were reflected in the stainless steel hood of the extractor fan. This was better than he ever could have hoped. Lying there, on the floor, he felt he was flopping into hard-core heaven. It was like a visor had come down in front of his eyes; from this moment on, anything he saw, he saw through porno-goggles, refracted through a long relationship with the video-player and, before that, private cine clubs and their Super-8 extravaganzas.

He had to give the boy top marks: he was some studly operator. The boy was rotating his hips rather than just banging away. He had one hand under mumsy's bottom, keeping her nature-tray rolling against his stiffie. His other hand was slipped under the straps of her dress. He must have undone the zipper at the back because, the slightest pull, the dress just peeled off her shoulders and her boobies popped out in twin points. She was wearing black shiny lingerie that glistened with a wet-look, her white skin rising like froth around the edges. As Cardiff watched them shiver, he was ready to scream: "Haul them out Callum, my son." It was an old habit, cheering on the performers, but he managed to bite his lip in time. He reminded himself: this is for real, it was just too kinky to have been designed as a spectator sport.

What he did do, he switched from her breasts to the boy's reflection in the steel of the hood above them. Just checking for the reaction shot. To him, the expression on the man's

face was the litmus test of what was real and was faked.
He had to say, the boy had a kind of dopey look, more
appropriate to a Walt Disney feature than a true X-cert
experience. And what he realised, in a kind of double-take,
was this wasn't Callum. It was some other boy entirely.
Someone he'd never seen before.

He felt himself deflate. But it was the second disappointment that really finished him off. The boy pulled a packet
of johnnies out of his top pocket and Cardiff realised it
would be all-weather gear from here on in. One thing Cardiff
absolutely hated was not being able to see every ordinance
line on a fellah's todger. Whenever he accidentally bought a
video featuring rubberised action, it just shrivelled him on
the spot. He had his standards and a dick, ideally, had to be
pink with a light marbling of blue and pink veins. Unless it
belonged to a sambo then it should be very black with a
coffee coloured helmet. And, black or white, the sausage
should be bursting out of its skin. There was nothing worse
than watching a teat flopping comically about a guy's bell-
end. No pleasure in looking at a Pepperami through its
wrapper.

Cardiff crawled backwards to the fire doors. He had
thought he was going to see something special and now the
bitter disappointment was too much to bear. He was just
going to leave. The way they were going, they wouldn't even
notice as he slipped out the back. He prayed he could put
a muffler on it.

He braced himself, counted silently and threw his weight
onto the steel bar crossing the doors. There was a click as
the rods pulled free of the casement. Cardiff couldn't believe
it, they opened first time. The force of his thrust sent him
sprawling into the alley-way but at least he was out of the
building.

He ended lying on the paving slabs, looking up at the

Pakistani boy. Cardiff stared back but quickly broke the gaze. He really thought he was a goner.

Cardiff said, "I didn't see anything."

The Paki looked through the open door into the kitchen. He turned back to Cardiff saying, "You gotta've seen something."

"Nothing. Nothing, not me."

"Get yourself some fucking specs, fatman. I can read where she buys her underwear from this distance."

Cardiff closed his eyes and tried to remember a prayer. When he heard the screams, one following another and getting higher, he only knew they weren't for him and that was enough. He wasn't going to open his eyes. Lying there, he felt the brush of cotton across his face as the Paki stepped over him, and then the sound of the fire doors closing. When he opened his eyes, he was on his own.

NINETEEN

Cheb had been standing with his mother when he heard the screams. She pulled him towards the kitchen, saying: "Gloria."

She was wrong. It was Jools who had screamed first, who was still screaming now, all the time getting higher and higher until it seemed every tile in the kitchen would crack. Gloria Manning was only whimpering, her shoulders shaking as she clung to her daughter, the two of them framed between two sides of lamb.

As he cleared the swing doors a step behind his mother, Cheb heard her say to Gloria: "What is it, chuck?" She needn't have asked.

Susan Ball was semi-dressed, stranded on the cooker hobs and trying to palm a pair of panties. Hogie was standing dazed, pressed tight against the stove, the hood of the vent glistening around his head like a halo. He was mumbling No No, helpless to smooth the situation. At least his trousers were buttoned to his waist, although the belt was flapping free. Everyone knew what had happened, only Jools and her mother had actually seen it.

Cheb looked away, catching Naz's eyes as he stepped through the fire doors from the alley-way. He brought a draught of night air with him before he pushed the doors closed and started towards Jools. Halfway across the kitchen floor, he stopped—as though he wanted to reach her but had forgotten the way. She carried on screaming and, only now, Cheb realised Jools's mother was holding her back. She had her hands out-stretched, ready to attack.

Cheb's mother said, "Take us back to the hotel."

He waved a taxi down on Frith Street. Jools was quieter now, she got inside first. Gloria followed, Mannie helping her through the door and then sitting on the pull-down seat, facing the pair of them. Jools and Gloria snuggled sweetly together, their arms intertwined. Cheb's mother squeezed into the remaining space on the backseat.

Cheb faltered for a moment. He'd almost decided to go through with it and take the last pull-down seat when Naz came up behind him. His eyes locked with Jools' through the open taxi door and he stretched out a hand. He said, "I want to come with you."

Cheb tried to step back but his mother said, "No. Don't leave me." Her voice sharp, to the point.

Cheb got in, telling Naz to follow.

"Where?"

Mrs Beddoes said, "The Shaftesbury."

It was a tense squeeze, the five of them together. Jools was taking sobbing half breaths, taking so many she seemed to suck the air out of the cab. Cheb could feel his cravat tighten around his neck, as though the pin was being twisted around. The needle seemed to sharpen, painful jabs spread across his chest. The next time he looked up, the cab was crossing a packed street, slipping between the partyless crowds in Piccadilly Circus. Above them, the giant advertising signs flashed their messages, leaving the brand-names tattooed in neon across the back window—just for a second—then fading again with the movement of the traffic. But Cheb wasn't seeing the crowds or the lights, only the dead space in between.

Like a thumb rubbing away the marks on a piece of plasticine, the movement of the cab caused the crowds to disappear. And like a piece of plasticine that had been over handled, the movement never created smooth new surfaces. The end result was always rank, blackened and greasy, totally deformed out of any kind of shape. Once, in Manilla, Cheb had heard an American sailor describe a prostitute's teeth as a graveyard and the image stayed with him. It wasn't the idea of the dislocated stumps but, more painfully, the gummy mess that encased them. That was like London, too.

They reached the hotel and took the elevator to the fourth floor, walking along a thickly carpeted corridor. Once they were inside the room, Cheb heard himself say, "What now?"

"Tea?"

His mother was bustling around the long dressing table, saying: "I can't find the kettle."

"Room service?"

He saw Mannie prodding at the push-dial of the bedside telephone and, after a moment, saying, "They say it's too late. I'll go down."

Cheb wished he'd thought of that. Mannie just walked to the door, opened it, and he was free.

His mother was saying, "All this fuss, it's not worth it."

No one else said anything. They sat in silence, Jools and

Gloria on a bed, him and his mother on chairs. Sitting like that for upwards of twenty minutes until Cheb began to think that Mannie had just upped and run off. He wouldn't have blamed him.

Finally, a knock at the door.

Gloria Manning sniffled. "He hasn't got a key."

Jools stood up. "I'll get it."

Frankie wasn't actually staying at the Jack Tavern in Holloway but it was a safe bet he'd be there most of the time, from lunch until long past last orders. When Cardiff reached him on his mobile, the background sound of the pub was unmistakeable.

"Frankie? . . . Yeah I got a lead . . . honest . . . let me give you the address."

Cardiff returned to the lobby, ready to sit and wait. He'd seen Viv, Gloria and all their kids arrive. He managed to get the room numbers out of the commissar, just one old pimp to another. Frankie had told him on the phone, fifteen minutes. Until then, Cardiff waited for the sweat to dry on his back and passed the time trying to guess which of the girls around the lobby were brasses and how much they charged per shadey gobble.

When Frankie arrived, prompt to the minute, he wasn't alone. The two guys with him were both young, both hard-faced and bull-necked. They'd just be typical hard men, except they looked to be stoned: Cardiff was going off the way they rolled their eyes and sometimes started giggling. They carried a sports bag each, swinging them from hand to hand like they were off for a kick-about.

Frankie only introduced them as they took the elevator up to the fourth floor.

"These are the guys who were getting that business together with Callum."

One of them said, "We ain't seen him."

Frankie said, "No, they ain't seen the useless cunt." He gave his new lads a look of approval. "We'll sort it out, though."

They walked along a corridor to rooms 424 and 426. The two young geezers stayed put by a firehose while Frankie and Cardiff put their ear to the first door. Frankie whispered, "These boys, I tell you, I wish Callum was more like them. Keen as fucking mustard."

Cardiff looked back over his shoulder. "They're all right then?"

"The fucking business." Frankie looked like he was going on twenty-one again, gee-ed up by having some hard men around him at last.

Cardiff wasn't so sure. The two guys looked to have an attitude problem. They certainly didn't seem overly impressed: either with Frankie or with the situation. They could have been waiting for a bus, the way they just stood around smirking and pulling faces at each other. But Cardiff decided not to say anything, he just walked up the corridor and tried the second door. There was no sound there, either.

"I'll have to knock."

Frankie nodded. Cardiff rapped and waited. In a second, he heard a mumble he was sure was one of the old girls. It was followed by a louder voice that he blamed on Gloria's daughter.

When the door opened, he was staring straight at her: a prosecutor's glare and a sulky face. Frankie pushed him out of the way and walked through, saying: "Hello ladies, fancy going for a night on the town?"

Later, when he was sat up in the lorry's cab, Cardiff said, "I never thought we'd get them out of the room so easily."

Frank was sat in front with the driver. He said, "What'd I say. These two boys are the business. They got imagination."

The lad who'd got in the backseat alongside Cardiff had

lit up a joint. Now he leaned forward, offering it to Frankie between the head-rests. Frankie shook his head but said, "You go on, my son. Enjoy yourself."

The lad passed it on to the driver who took a blast then said, "How was the Browning? It feel alright, Mr Ball?"

Frankie lifted up his gun, an automatic pistol with a long chunky silencer. He said, "Yeah, great. It ain't a Browning though, it's a spic copy. I got one myself back in España. The reason I asked if you could get me the Hi-power, I had this silencer made and it don't fit nothing else."

The lad nodded, still holding onto his dope smoke so that when he spoke he sounded half-choked. "I was going to ask you about that, Mr Ball. It looks the business."

Frankie passed the pistol round so everyone could admire it. For five minutes, everyone was fumbling the joint and the pistol together, tying themselves in knots. When Frankie got his gun back, he said: "Yeah, it does the fucking trick, know what I mean? I tell you, I had a fuck of a job getting one though. In the end, I had to get this Pedro-the-fucking-blacksmith geezer to hand-tool it from the shocks of an old Ford."

The two lads gave him an *Ooh* for his ingenuity. The one driving said, "You know, if you want anything else, we should be able to get it for you, Mr Ball."

Frankie said, "How about that, just like fucking Christmas, eh? And don't call me Mr Ball. Now we're in business together, you gotta start calling me Frankie."

Both lads grinned and nodded, saying Okay, Frankie. After that, the conversation just petered out for the next ten minutes. Finally, Frankie turned back round in his seat and said, "So you were using what? A Beretta?"

The lad nodded. The driver said: "Mine was a Smith & Wesson."

They headed East, Frankie's gun buff chatter joining with the sound of the bodies rolling around the back of the lorry.

Finally, somewhere past Bow, they crossed a bridge and stopped outside a warehouse. The driver swung out of the cab. By the time Cardiff joined him at the back, he had the roller-door up and the other lad was shining a torch into the dark where the three women and the bald kid were lying.

The driver said, "Get cracking." He already had hold of someone's ankles and was hauling them out of the back.

Cardiff got hold of a pair of feet and started dragging what turned out to be Viv Beddoes. In a few seconds, they had them lined against the lorry. All of them wearing long blue snorkel jackets, zipped and buttoned to the neck and the arms dangling free. Inside the coats, their hands were safely cuffed behind their back.

Frankie said, "Get them moving."

Using their guns like cattle prods, Frankie's two lads got them all moving in a line, doing the same duckish waddle they'd used as they walked out through the hotel lobby.

They entered the warehouse, crossing the floor in the semi-dark, following a crack of light that shone through a door in the far wall. The door turned out to be an elevator. One of the lads hauled back the outer door and then the cage door, inside, and they all stepped or waddled in.

The first floor was almost as bare as downstairs. Besides a few broken breeze blocks and an old steel joist, there was nothing but a tattered sofa and an old armchair, which Frankie took. When the prisoners were lined in front of him, he started with his questions. It was soon clear that only the son, Cheb, had any useful information. He confirmed that Susan Ball and George Carmichael were partners in the restaurant.

Cardiff said, "Ask him about the cocaine."

The boy tried to be cute about that: "What cocaine?"

Frankie could be cute, too. He lashed out with a foot and swept the kid's feet away from under him. The boy crashed down, screaming in pain. When he finally twisted around and looked up, he found his mother knelt over him. He had to twist even further before he saw Frankie, standing next to her, pushing a seat cushion to her head with one hand and holding his gun with the other.

Frankie said, "When I blow your mum's head off, no one except her's going to hear more than a pop. 'Course, it'll sound pretty loud to her. What do you think?"

Cheb straightened out pretty quick after that. He gave up Susan immediately, saying she had laid on all the party drugs. He didn't know where she'd got it from but he knew she had more. He'd seen it lying in her case.

He had even more to say, although it was difficult to hear over the sound of the women crying. Frankie passed his gun over to Cardiff, saying: "I can't be doing with this racket. Go on, get rid of them, Cardiff. Take them out, through there." He nodded towards a door, thirty feet away.

Cardiff took the gun, trying not to show any hesitation. He hauled Viv Beddoes back to her feet and got her hopping in the right direction. He looked back, the other two women hadn't moved.

Frankie said, "Go on, follow your Uncle Cardiff." Behind his head, the two other guys lifted their guns and waved them forward. They started waddling after Viv.

The room was a kind of large store cupboard, twenty by twenty. Cardiff stood at the door and shepherded them through. As Gloria Manning passed him, he shot her in the back of the head from a distance of three inches. The impact drove her forward, onto her knees and down to the floor. As she rolled over, he caught sight of the gaping hole where her nose had been. There'd been no more sound than someone whacking a sofa with a baseball bat but she was dead.

He aimed at Jools next. The force of the bullet drove

her back against the far wall, leaving her slumped with her stubby little legs all cock-eyed.

Behind him, he heard Frankie running, shouting, "Jesus Fucking Christ, I meant just take them out of the room. Not fucking take them out and kill them."

Frankie looked from Cardiff to Viv Beddoes. Cardiff paralysed, as though he hadn't got a clue what he'd done. Viv paralysed on the horror, falling backwards and trying to scoot along the floor, still trussed up in the snorkel jacket. Cheb watched her through the door, his eyes locked on her helpless look of shock. He had his mouth wide open: he was just screaming and screaming.

Frankie had to prise every finger open before he could get the Browning copy out of Cardiff's hand. He looked down at Viv Beddoes, just a pair of eyes inside the snorkel's hood, two shimmering discs framed within a white margin. What he could see of her face was pinkish, glistening wet where silent tears covered her cheeks.

Frank said, "What a fucking mess."

Cheb heard another thwacking sound and his mother crumpled down. From thirty five feet, he could see the exit wound that peeled away her throat. Frank Ball had shot her.

Ahead of him, Frankie was saying, "Look what you made me do, Cardiff, you cunt. I tell you what, you're gonna clear this up. And when you dump them, better make it look like a pervert done it. You read enough fucking pornography, you should be good at that."

Mannie stepped out of the bathroom. It was just as empty as the bedroom, nothing in there but a tube of toothpaste, a hairdryer and a big bargain pot of night cream. He shrugged at Naz, standing in the middle of the room with the tea tray in his hands, and said, "I don't get it. They were here half an hour ago."

PART THREE

deepinit

TWENTY

The headline read: TOPLESS MOTHER OF BOTTOMLESS CORPSE. Underneath there was a photograph of Susan, looking much younger and not much less sexy. A tag across the bottom said: Have You Seen This Woman? The paper was offering a £10,000 Reward.

When Hogie spoke to her on the telephone, Susan told him it was a publicity shot, used to advertise her act at the Hula Club in '69. The newspaper had got hold of five different poses; this one showed her knelt on a rug, her hands cupping her naked breasts and a little crown on her head. When he looked it over again, later, Hogie decided it was more of a tiara. After he'd turned to pages five through nine for the full story and the rest of the pictures, he refolded the paper so only her face was visible and stacked it with the others on top of his TV set.

Susan still refused to see him, or even give him an address. All he could do was walk round the flat hugging his mobile. Throughout, he felt as lost and wasted as a whisper of cardamom in a two-can chilli but Susan was only a part of it. Even as he flipped out of the worst bad acid trip any boy had yet experienced to find himself in Susan's arms, something had told him this moment of ecstasy was going to end in flames. The satellite of shame was swinging down, from his loins to the stars, oblivion on toast.

Day One began with the discovery of Viv Beddoes. She was found lying across a Thames Water Authority filter bed in Hornsey. Two hours later, Jools was disinterred from a bottle bank outside Sainsbury's, Islington. No one knew how her killer had got her inside. Gloria Manning lay undisturbed amongst the railway sidings of Willesden Junction for one more day until a trainspotter finally rang the transport police, saying he was puzzled by her naked body. The police suspected all three women were killed at the same time and in the same place but were waiting for conclusive forensic evidence. Rumours of sexual abuse had not yet been dismissed by the detectives involved.

The press had failed to interview either of the two orphan boys. After giving his statement to the police, Mannie moved back to Hogie's flat and the reporters hadn't yet found him. They hadn't found Cheb either and preferred to believe that, like his mother, he was also dead. After another two days with no word, Hogie began to think they were right.

At first, it was Jools who got the most press and airtime. A true star, she'd burned briefly brightly before being extinguished. The soap opera postponed her fictional death out of respect and closed its omnibus edition with a small, printed eulogy to her talent: a line of verse in white on a black screen followed by an EPK of her finest moments. Naz left the room when they ran the clips. He stayed in the bathroom for the rest of that day, sitting on the plastic seat, staring at the flowers on the shower curtain.

It wasn't until the fourth day that the police positively identified the body nailed to the floor of the coach as Callum Ball. That was the morning that the photographs of Susan Ball finally pushed Jools off the front page. Susan called Hogie first around nine am and then again at one-thirty, after she'd bought the lunch-time edition of the *Evening Standard*.

The first thing she said, "He died of a heart attack."

Hogie mumbled uh-huh, he'd bought the paper too. The morning papers agreed that her son was tortured before death and mutilated afterwards but the latest news was that he actually died of heart seizure. It didn't matter to Susan, so she said. She knew who got him killed.

Hogie listened to the soft chokes of her sobs with the receiver crooked between his cheek and shoulder. She wanted him to turn to pages four-through-five and he fumbled the paper open on his lap until he found the picture: a man in his mid-thirties with a sports reporter hair-do and an open-necked shirt. Reading the small print, he learnt it was Frankie Ball, last seen on the steps of the Old Bailey in 1979. A box-out to the side of the main feature claimed that two of the tabloids had men running around the Costa del Sol, both competing to get a more recent picture.

Susan said, "He's not in Spain. He's here."

"Your husband?"

Softly, her voice almost back to normal, now, and only the dried tears causing static on the line: "He's in London. He's been trying to find me."

Hogie said, "Oh."

The *Standard* was trying to link her son's death to a shoot-out at a South London nightclub. Most of the report was speculation, suggesting that he'd got involved in a drugs deal that had gone wrong. No one knew how long Ballistic Frankie had been running drugs into Britain but everyone the paper questioned seemed pretty sure he probably was.

There was just one thing Hogie didn't understand. "So who's Ballistic Frankie?"

"It's a nickname. It's what people used to call my husband."

"Oh. Have you spoken to him yet?"

He heard something rustle at the other end of the line; maybe a head shake or a snort before she told him, No. She had decided to avoid him.

It was the only good news Hogie had heard that week. "So you're, like, separated then?"

"What do you think? He set our son up as a drugs dealer

and got him killed. I'd say the marriage is over." Then a pause before her voice came back on-line with a harder tone. "But it's going to be a messy divorce."

"So, can I come round. I don't like it here, I want to be with you."

Susan wondered what to say this time. She was stood in a hallway, breathing damp wallpaper and shivering because the only telephone was chained to the second floor landing wall. Down a few rickety steps, she could see her own bedroom door standing open. It didn't surprise her when she discovered she had the worst room in the place. Maltese Rosa was happy to help but wasn't going to throw one of her professional tenants out of a more comfortable room. Anyway, the whole building was nothing but a stack of shoebox bedsits. Only the faulty wiring and thumping plumbing was keeping it from collapsing. Susan doubted if Hogie would understood why she was suffering all this on her own. If all she had to do was hide from the paparazzi and psychotic husbands, why did she have to do it by herself?

She said, "Those women who caught us in the kitchen, the ones who screamed at me. They were the ones who were killed, weren't they?"

"Yes. Jools and her mother. And Cheb and his mother, they were there too."

"I'm really so sorry."

Hogie said, "Were they killed by your husband?"

"I don't know. Probably." She didn't know what else to say. And she couldn't decide whether she was being stupid or selfish, keeping Hogie at arm's length. She let the telephone cable twirl out between nervous fingers. "Maybe you should come over."

He was almost unbearably pleased. After she listened to him repeat the address and hang up, she began to think it was for the best. They both needed comforting. And what had she achieved, this past few days. She had spent most of her time answering the phone on over-heated Johns demanding either Correction, Greek or special classes in TV deportment. All she could tell them was this lady was retired, then shout up or down the stairs, asking if anyone wanted some business.

She screwed the tissue she had been holding into a tight damp ball. Diluted traces of mascara were soaked deep into its ply. As she walked into her room, she tossed it on the floor. It landed in a teacup. It didn't matter, every sip of the tea had swelled up in her mouth like cotton wool, she could never have finished it.

She knew, if she thought she would ever be able to kill Frankie, she was dreaming. She had got as far as getting a gun—another favour she owed to Maltese Rosa. At the moment it was hidden under a copy of the *Daily Mail*, among the mess of spray cans and atomisers on the dressing table. Rosa had said it was a woman's piece but when Susan took it out for another look, she still couldn't imagine using it. The grip was mother of pearl or something similar, the rest of it was nickel-plated, stubby-looking and battered. When she laid the pistol down she did it carefully, then she started crying again.

Hogie put the scrap of paper with Susan's address safely in his pocket and started packing his overnight bag. He was just glad to get out of the flat. The last four days, he'd been passing Mannie and Naz in the living-room, around the microwave or in the bathroom and neither of them had anything to say to him. They walked like ghosts, he bumped into things. He wanted to know, still, whether they blamed him. If they ever started, then he would have to start wondering whether he felt guilty. He knew he felt something.

He never did get around to his great act of atonement and, now that was forever impossible, he hadn't tried to tell Mannie the truth about his mother, either. The way Mannie acted, he seemed to want to write it off as just one of those things; you know, like two consenting adults. The only problem with that, they both knew he wasn't an adult: he was fifteen-going-on-sixteen.

Between Hogie and Mannie's old school and the housing estate where Mannie lived, there was a golf club. A screen of trees separated the roofs from the fairway. The day Hogie first got together with Gloria Manning, he'd been lying in a bunker since nine-thirty in the morning, smoking a weak two-skin spliff and holding a bottle of cider. By eleven, the dope was making him queasy, the acid house tape in his walkman was definitely making his head pound. He had no idea whether Mannie had gone into school either but decided to try his house. If he was home, they could chill out together; watch TV and have a cup of tea.

Hogie cut through the trees at the far end of the fairway. At the back of the nearest house was a wire pen with a Rottie dog barking inside. A kid, about ten years old, was beating on the mesh with a cricket stump, making the dog crazy. Hogie knew the boy was being paid to do it by the owner. The man bred certified insane attack dogs.

Hogie walked on, along the line of compact semis. A garden to his left had a single rose tree, the one to the right had a mini van sitting on a pile of bricks. Hogie crossed the road and walked up the passageway to the side of Mannie's house. He never used the front door, always the back.

The kitchen was empty but the door was unlocked. Inside, the breakfast pots beside the sink were dry but frosted with foam. Mrs Manning usually did the dishes before she went to work. If the door was open, then Mannie might still be in bed. Hogie walked through the sitting room and climbed the narrow stairs to Mannie's room. It was the smallest room in the house and if Mannie hadn't kept it reasonably tidy it would have been squalid inside five minutes. The eiderdown was heaped at the end of the bed, off the floor. Mannie wasn't underneath it.

When he heard the bathroom door open, Hogie slipped behind Mannie's door. Across the hall, Mrs Manning stepped out with a towel wrapped like a turban around wet hair. She had another towel tight around her body, running beneath her arm pits. Her breasts were squashed into two half discs, her skin was unnaturally white. She didn't see Hogie. He was peering round the edge of the door and saw every-thing—everything she was showing, everything he could imagine under the towel. She went through a door on her left, into her bedroom. Hogie slipped out of the room and stood, spy style, against the wall. He craned his neck around. Mrs Manning had left her door open a touch.

When she dropped the towel, she had her back to Hogie. She wasn't a fat woman but her bottom was quite big, like a giant milk chocolate Easter egg split into two halves. Hogie wanted to run over, pull those cheeks apart and nose down until they were both giggling.

He got up on his tip toes and crept back to Mannie's room and found Mannie's pistol hidden in its usual place, at the back of the wardrobe, rolled inside a Subbuteo cloth. He pulled back the hammer and flipped out the revolving bit. The six little holes were empty. Hogie opened the card-board box that used to hold the Ajax squad and took out six brassy little bullets. He put them in the gun, snapped the cylinder back and eased the hammer down.

Hogie held the gun to the side of his face as he crept back to Mrs Manning's bedroom, still in secret agent mode. When he pushed the door open, she was stood right in front of him wearing a red satin bra and a blue skirt that covered her from her waist to her knees. The towel turban was still in place. She looked surprised.

She said, "Hogie. What the hell are you playing at."

Hogie felt himself blush through. He knew his legs were about to give way.

She said, "Where did you find that bloody gun?"

He staggered to one side. If he could sit down, then he might be alright. There was a velvet-padded stool pushed underneath her dressing table, he pulled it out with his toe and collapsed onto it. All the while, he made sure that he faced her. He couldn't keep his hand from shaking, the gun was pressed hard against his cheek so that it would remain steady.

"Get out, Hogie."

Hogie's voice came out mid-way between a croak and a bleat, "Take off the skirt Mrs Manning."

"Or what? You're going to shoot me?"

Hogie moved the gun around and pushed it barrel-first into his mouth. If he didn't clasp it two-handed, he might have knocked his teeth out, his hands were shaking so much.

"Don't do that Hogie. Hogie. Put the gun down."

Hogie knew she recognised the gun. She had seen it every ·Wednesday night when her last-but-one boyfriend packed his bag and headed off to his shooting club. She knew he wasn't sucking on a toy. He eased the pistol out of his mouth, just far enough so he could talk. "Take off the skirt or I'll take off my fucking head."

Already, he was beginning to shake less. He knew he could see it through. It even showed in his voice, "I said, take it off."

She held out one hand, soothing as she said, Okay, Okay. She unzipped the skirt at the side, pinching the material together as she did it. The skirt loosed and she shrugged out of it. She was wearing a red panty girdle, a different shade to her bra.

Hogie took the pistol out of his mouth for another brief command. "Open the door of the wardrobe."

She did it. She probably didn't understand at first but as the mirror on the inside of the door swung out she realised that he wanted to see her from all angles.

There was a vinyl clad radio standing on the dressing table. Hogie pushed one of the pre-programmed buttons. He got Piccadilly Gold playing Elvis's "Viva Las Vegas". His soul was already on fire.

"Take off the panties please, Mrs Manning."

She shook her head.

Hogie thumbed back the hammer, it clicked into place and the trigger trembled beneath his finger. Their eyes were locked. He could feel tears pricking in his. Hers were beginning to fill.

She began to roll the elasticated material down, starting at her waist. The panties were so tight, they could only be peeled away. As she bent forward, he caught a flash of black hair reflected in the mirror. Hogie felt his dick swell with a painful tug; a stray pubic hair had caught inside his foreskin. He slipped a finger through his button-down fly and freed himself. His dick edged out beneath his grey denim school jeans.

He had her now but he wasn't sure what to do. She stood holding her panties in her left hand, as though she was saying "Well?" Hogie's eyes were level to her crotch and the tangled mass of her pubic hair.

"Can you come closer."

She hesitated.

Hogie felt the itch of sweat bubbling up on his forehead. "Please do it. Or I'm dead, I mean it."

She began to move.

"Slowly, with both hands on your head."

She put her hands to the top of her turban.

She was right in front of him now, a half-arm's length away. He could just stretch out, a tip of one finger testing the curled springiness of her hair. As he touched her, she flinched backwards. Hogie pushed the gun deeper into his mouth, the sight at the end of the barrel scratched against his palate.

"Closer."

She took half a step closer to him. Near enough now for him to reach out his hand and measure the expanse of her hair to his palm's length. The hair, like her skin still carried the clammy damp of her bath, warm enough to agitate the scent molecules of her soap.

He rested like that for a long while until he felt her shiver. Before she turned absolutely cold, he had to think of something else. When he asked her to get on the bed she just backed away from him in silence until the edge of the bed touched her knees and she fell to the duvet.

Hogie stood. The gun was still firm in his mouth, almost deep enough to make him gag. He undid his belt and popped the buttons one-handed. He hauled his jeans and his undies down together. His dick snagged on the fly-slit at the front of his undies, then sprang out.

Mrs Manning lay where she'd fallen. You couldn't say that her legs were either open or closed.

Hogie pulled the gun out of his mouth again. He said, "Can you . . ." He didn't know how to say it. "Can you, like, put your hands under your bottom and, like, pull the cheeks apart."

"Like in a mucky book?"

Hogie nodded: yeah, that was it.

"Forget it."

A drip of spittle hung off the end of the gun barrel. Hogie jammed the gun back into his mouth, too hard. He felt the roof of his mouth split open and then the flood of warm salty blood. He pulled the gun out and drops of blood fell from the barrel. He felt blood and spit sweep across his chin.

She said, "I'll do this."

She inclined her knees upwards slightly. As she did it, the blackness between her legs began to make sense, to divide into separate defined parts between dark, thick lips.

Hogie hobbled out of his jeans and moved towards the wardrobe. Keeping his eyes on her, he stretched out his free hand and reached into the top shelf drawer where he knew she kept a tube of KY gel folded among her hankies.

As he drew out the gun again, a glob of blood dropped onto his chest and slid to the carpet. He looked from the stain to the tube of lubricating gel, almost apologetically as he said, "I don't know much about this. Will we need this?"

She looked at him in sharp surprise, "How did you know it was there?"

Because he often looked around her room, he knew where she kept everything. He didn't know how to admit it, though. So he said, "I'm in love with you."

"You're not."

"Honest."

He was on his knees on the bed now, hovering above her in the praying position with the gun back in his mouth. When fresh drops of blood fell, they dripped to the fold at the middle of her belly.

Her voice was softer now. "So get rid of the gun."

There was no way he trusted her. He kept the gun in place as he dropped onto one hand, into a press-up position. As he lowered himself onto his elbows, the gun stayed in place. As he probed, first, then surged forward, the gun jolted against his teeth. He carried on pushing.

She wheezed and her hands flew out, gripped him and hung on tight. With her head pinned between his elbows, the cylinder of the pistol grazed the side of his face. He kept the gun in his mouth, he was gagging on it but he kept it inside his mouth.

Holding tight onto Hogie's back, she hauled herself up an inch, twisting her head around until she met his mouth. She pushed her tongue forward, along the metal, and prised open a space wide enough for their lips to meet. The gun barrel ran between their two mouths, greased on blood and both their spit. She tried but failed to persuade him to let the gun go completely and the shards from his chipped teeth gave their kisses a sharp edge.

Thinking it through, he still didn't know if it was a rape story. Perhaps not, if she agreed to sleep with him again; as she did, later. But nothing would have happened between them if it wasn't for that first time and he had certainly used pressure. All he could say, he was only fifteen and threatening to kill yourself was one way of getting a girl to sleep with you.

She did ask him, one time, would he have done it.

He was sure. She nodded. She thought so too, either out of shame or embarrassment or because the thing had gone too far. But for no other reason. That was probably true, too.

TWENTY-ONE

Cheb had a head like a red cabbage. They showed him his reflection each time they walked him to the bathroom and he'd stare at himself in the mirror. He'd been beaten so badly he wouldn't ever have recognised himself. The strangest thing, though, he couldn't feel anything either. He couldn't match this reflection to any corroborative pain so how did he know it was him standing there, swelling and bleeding and dribbling. What he had were disjointed memories.

They told him to talk. Later, they told him to shut up.

Both ways, the beatings always came eventually. What he remembered best was the constant sound of their music. Often, it was so loud he had to struggle to be heard as he tried to interest them in his life story and his personal theories. They were mostly interested in what he knew about Susan Ball and the heap of cocaine she carried with her.

When the music was at its loudest, there were always two of them. Other times, when either Frank Ball or Cardiff were around, the music was nothing but a hum, so soft it might have been an echo, playing over in his head. They worked in shifts, coming to visit him in the windowless room where he now spent all his time, haunting the spot where his mother had been killed. One time, they gave him a chair to sit on, which was nice. True, it soon broke but for a while he was allowed to sit almost at their level as he swatted at their questions. The music was loud that day and they told him not to worry about it. He trusted them by then so when they said they intended to be gentle, he believed it. As one of them said, "Today is Good Cop Day: just call us Cagney and Lacey."

It was Lacey who explained their strategy. "We decided we better go soft on you, Chebby boy. Otherwise we might have another heart attack victim on our hands."

As he said it, Cagney started laughing. Cheb joined in. No, not another fucking coronary case, it was the last thing they needed.

Cagney was the blond one and was kind of skittish. Lacey was more contemplative and tried his best to concentrate whenever Cheb answered their questions.

Another nice thing about Lacey was that he rolled the joints, even holding them to Cheb's mouth. He was grateful for that, there was no other way to smoke while his hands remained cuffed behind his back.

After allowing him a few good tokes, Lacey said, "How's that feel?"

Cheb nodded, it was good.

He looked over to his partner and said, "You remember where we got this stuff, eh?"

Cagney said, "Dalston, mate. I think it's homegrown."

"Could be. What's the best you've ever had?"

Cagney shrugged, "That's the problem. If it's any good, I can't fucking remember."

Lacey had to agree on that. "What about you, Chebbo? What's the best dope you ever had?"

Cheb said, "Vietnamese." Then changed his mind, "Thai."

They both nodded approvingly. Cagney saying, "We got a fucking connoisseur here, what you reckon?"

Lacey nodded. "Yeah, Thai's good. Don't know when I last had any of that shit though. You?"

"Oh yeah. Had some on holiday the other year, it was fucking sweet."

"Thailand?"

"Yeah, Thailand, Goa, Bali. I go for a couple of months every year, do a bit of spliff, bit of opium, get my head together and fly back home."

He reached over to pull the joint out of Cheb's mouth, saying: "Don't start bogarting it, Chebbie boy. You gotta leave some for the rest of us."

Lacey said, "I gotta do that. I mean, I reckon Ibiza's just about had it. It's time I gave India a whirl."

"India's the business. Like I said, Goa. Gets your fucking head sorted. Come back and you're game for anything. Look at Chebbo, here. Proves my fucking point."

They stayed like that for hours that day, just talking, smoking, chilling to the sound of drum and bass. When Lacey started asking questions, Cheb felt so grateful he tried his best to tell them something new. When they asked about Susan Ball he said she was running a psychedelic factory in Shaolin, synthesising phenethylamines which made you wake to the mystery of the ocean and tryptamines which fuelled jet-pack rides around the moon. He told them she was employed by NASA as a consultant. And she wore silver underwear. .

The problem was, sometimes they were on his wavelength. Other times they were different people. Mostly, their attention span was so short, they ended up getting bored. Cagney especially. And then the beating started over again.

Lacey said, "What you say we drag a cooker up here."

Cagney agreed. "Nice one. See how this one takes to a good roasting."

They carried Bic lighters, the smallest disposables. When they lit them under his arse they were really only playing. Cheb hardly felt a thing.

On the days when Frank Ball dropped by, Cagney and Lacey always looked pleased to see him. Even if it was a Bad Cop day, they were nice to Uncle Frank—which was what they'd started calling him. They would even turn their music down if he said it was giving him a headache. And they always overlooked the fact that he was something of an alky and a cry-baby, at least to his face. Apparently his son had just died, which was why they were so understanding. Behind his back, though, they really ripped the piss. In this one respect, Cheb didn't mind their inconsistency. He didn't like their Uncle Frank at all—too drunk or emotional to even begin a conversation, he only ever had the energy to kick the shit out of him.

Uncle Frank called them Sean and Liam instead of Cagney and Lacey. He was so fond of them, it would have turned him inside-out if he knew what they said about him when he wasn't around.

During one of their regular Bad Cop scenarios, Lacey said, "Frankie told me to make sure I gave you one from him. So I guess I should be sucking your dick. But you'll have to make do with this instead."

Cheb saw the curve of the chair leg as it swung through

the air. When it connected, the force began as a tiny, concentrated speck but immediately sucked him up into something
bigger and blacker, like a high speed train moving so fast it
seemed to touch the end of a tunnel a fraction before it hit
the beginning.

After that, the hours collapsed into a series of still frames,
whooshing past but, somehow, still dragging. He saw a big
wet tongue wipe through the air then disappear as his ear
filled with groggy saliva, and through it all Cagney's voice
saying, "Uncle Frankie likes it like that."

Lacey's laugh sluiced around the room. "Does he not
though? Senile fucking bastard."

"Uncle Ballistic."

"Uncle Bollostic." And Lacey's boot came powering into
Cheb's groin.

They talked about Frankie's stupidity, they imitated his
stories about España or his prison reminiscences or they
speculated on what he failed to do to his slaggy wife. Above
all, they talked about his soft cunt son, the boy who dropped
down dead before he talked to them.

Cagney said, "Fair do to him. I can't see Frankie holding
out for as long. He'd have a coronary the second his arse
started burning."

The only person they held in more contempt than Uncle
Frank was little Cardiff. Cheb had to agree with them. Whenever Cardiff came to sit with him, the room would just
shrink into silence. A death quiet, nothing but the jungle
mumble in Cheb's head and the sound of the man falling
apart. He never thought a fat man could rattle. Sometimes
it was so unbearable, Cheb would start speaking of his own
accord. He would begin under his breath, burbling on until
he felt himself hit a possible line and then riding it out. It
didn't always work, sometimes he moved his mouth and
nothing happened. But when he hit a flow, Cardiff would
get up slowly and start slapping him, left and right, about

the head. It didn't hurt. It was just slop, slop, slop and Cheb would swing back into dark tunnels and through them into space.

He opened his eyes. Uncle Frank was staring down at him. Leaning over from the other side were Lacey and Cagney. It was Cagney who was speaking: "Face it, boss. He's fucking tapped."

Frank Ball said, "He's got to know something."

"He's told us Callum was selling drugs at a rave south of the river. At a gaffe called Comecon. Funnily enough, there was some trouble there the other day. The cops say Yardies but I heard it was some Northern Paki outfit."

From outside the room, Cardiff squeaked: "I told you Susan had hooked up with some Pakis."

Frank didn't look around. "What else's he said?"

Only Cheb could see Cagney's smirk. "That Callum was sacrificed by voodoo satanists on a mission from Mars. It's what I was saying Frankie, we've hit him too hard."

Cheb lay between them, gurgling and dribbling.

"Keep at it. Someone's got to pay for what happened to my boy."

Frank turned to leave, then said, "Has he said anything about my wife?"

Lacey looked down at the floor and shrugged—just like Cagney, trying to hide a smirk.

"Well? He must have said something."

"I don't know. Maybe on Cardiff's shift?"

Frank called on Cardiff. Eventually, the fat man came waddling into view and Frank put his question to him, "Has this cunt said anything about my slag of a wife?"

Cheb had said so much, he wondered what he could have left out. She was possessed by juju sex spirits, she sucked on puppy dogs and bit the heads off chickens. She was a priestess, she performed the last rites when Lenin's body was removed from open display and air-freighted to a cloning laboratory in Novosibirsk.

Cardiff shuffled uncomfortably, "He said she's screwing one of George Carmichael's boys. Someone called Hogie."

Cheb couldn't remember saying anything so boring. If he had done, it had been beaten out of his memory. He was beginning to find himself sinking into black spots. When that happened, he no longer remembered anything.

TWENTY-TWO

Frankie told them to leave Cheb for now, "I got another job for you."

He walked out of the interrogation room towards the windows that ran along the first floor of the warehouse. Looking out, he could see water on three sides, if he had eyes in the back of his head he'd be able to see more. The warehouse was an industrial ruin, built on a kink in Bow Creek that had been marooned when a stretch of navigable canal was dug across the bend—what was left was now a river island. When Frankie first saw it, he'd thought it was perfect. It was out of the way and it was quiet. He'd been dead wrong though, it was the noisiest fucking gaffe in the world. It was bad enough when it was just the two boys playing their electronic music. It would be unbearable when their crew had finished setting up their rave sound system on the ground floor of the warehouse.

Just to drive him completely crazy—someone down below started doing a sound check. The windows were steel framed, set into heavy stone ledges, and even they began shaking. What the two boys called drum and bass was rising up through the floor, through solid concrete mind, and was still setting off explosions in his head. And Frankie had a very bad head.

All he could tell himself, it's what Callum would have wanted. It's what Sean and Liam told him often enough: Callum's dream was to run London's biggest raves, mixing the hardest sounds with the more profitable drugs. They were simply following his guiding inspiration.

Liam said, "Getting a bit loud for you, Uncle Frank?"

He shook his head, "Nah, nah. It's alright."

"You want me to tell 'em to tone it down for now?"

He was a good lad. "No, I'll cope, son."

The deal had looked so sweet. When Callum first came to him with it, he was only too happy to help. He'd always wanted something better for his boy than screwing tourists and hanging around spic bars. Now he'd never know if his boy had the balls for the life. Maybe he could have made a go of it. The chances were good, he had enough sense to hook up with a solid crew. Frankie reckoned Sean and Liam were the business.

Sean was standing there, respectfully, a pace behind him. "You said you had a job, Uncle Frank?"

Frank tried to clear his head, that tikka tikka tikka, it kind of got inside you. "Yeah. I just got word from Spain. Susan's staying with this old tart she used to know. I want you to go round there, pick her up. Hopefully, she's got the cocaine so you'll be in business."

"Sweet."

Sean joined in. "Fucking brilliant. Then we'll be able to start paying back on your investment, Uncle Frank."

He told, "No hurry, son. I appreciate what you're doing."

They understood what it meant, too, getting payback for Callum now he'd passed over. Liam said, "God bless him."

Sean said, "Yeah."

Cardiff had crept up from somewhere. Now he coughed

and said, "This tart who's helping Susan. Are we talking about Maltese Rosie? The one who used to work out of D'arblay Street?"

"That's her. Apparently she's running a string of brasses from fuck pads all over the West End."

Cardiff said, "Can I go? You know, have a word, help her decide to give up Susan quietly."

Frank said, "Who the fuck would talk to a slag like you? You stay here with that cunt . . ." he pointed through the far door to where Cheb was lying " . . . I'm using people I actually trust."

Who'd have thought his own mother would have come swinging down on Callum like an angel of fucking wrath. Her problem, all women's problem, was they couldn't let go. Frankie had seen it before. Women chasing the gaga pills with straight gin, out of their fucking boxes the day after their kids lit out. The only difference with Susan, she had to get the menopause like something out of a Stephen King novel. What happened to Callum, that was down to her. He still couldn't believe she'd actually killed him. But Liam and Sean said the poor cunt never showed with the drugs so it must be down to her.

Susan found she couldn't sleep like she used to. By eleven forty-five in the am, she was propped up on her pillows and sliding another dollop of gin into her glass. She followed it with a little tonic for appearance's sake, although Hogie was still fast asleep. She looked down at him, a thin boy stretched across the glossy sheets. He had been sleeping for four hours and she couldn't imagine him waking for a long time yet.

The heat of the room and the nylon weave of the sheets could have been a bad combination. Hogie had managed to slip through without problems, the sheets couldn't chain him, the heat only brought a glisten to his skin. And wherever she was, underneath or above him, he swept her along until she was skimming the surface of the bed with hardly a friction burn. Until he fell asleep, of course.

She took another sip of gin. Because there was no refrigerator, she had no ice. The gin was blood temperature, although her blood was a little hotter. She reached out for a bang of hair that covered Hogie's face, spun it between her fingers and tucked it behind his ear. He had no ear lobes, the curve of the shell just disappeard into his jawline. It was a physiological quirk that was supposed to signify something sexual but she could not remember what. Anyway, he had no loose skin anywhere—except in the obvious, otherwise hidden, areas. Especially in this ball-swinging heat.

She wondered if she was a little drunk.

The sound of a ringing telephone brought her round. She was semi-naked when she swung out of bed but grabbed something lacy and left-over from one of the previous tenants and followed the insistant squeal up a flight of stairs. She didn't even know why she was wasting her time, it would only be another punter following a lead he'd picked up in a Baker Street call box. When she lifted the receiver, she heard nothing but the dial tone. The ringing never quietened. She stood swaying in the hall, unable to work it out. Then she turned on her heels and followed the noise back to the bedroom. She found Hogie's mobile popped in the top of his bag. He was flat on his back, unmoved by the sound. She hauled out the aerial, pushed the receive button and took the call into the corridor.

"Hello."

The voice hummed: "Susan?"

"George. Why are you calling me on Hogie's phone?"

"Just a hunch I had. He is with you, isn't he?"

She didn't want to talk about it.

He came straight back at her in a mocking coo, saying:

"What? You're not going to tell me all about it? Then it must be love."

She didn't know what it was. But if he thought she was going to play a bout of most-salacious neighbour, he could forget it. It wasn't even noon, she was gin drunk and dripping mascara, she was standing in the stairwell of a whorehouse in nothing but a negligee and pom-pom mule slippers. If this was a time for anything, it was a time for privacy.

She shut George up by turning on him, "For fuck's sake George. Leave it. Callum's dead, we're in shit and all you're doing is coming the big puff."

Silence.

Then: "I'm sorry Susan."

She heard her breath out in a whoosh; until then, she hadn't even noticed she was holding it. She said, "No. No. I'm sorry, George."

"Are you alright?"

She was almost crying. So she stopped herself. "No, I'm fine. Over-emotional and a bit broken down. What did you want?"

He said, "Not on the phone, Susan."

"Something bad?"

"Maybe . . . maybe not. Give me thirty minutes, I'll come pick you up."

"And go where?" She hadn't stepped outside the door in days, she wasn't sure she was ready to face the world but he told her not to worry.

"We're just going round to Hogie's flat."

She didn't understand. "But Hogie's still asleep."

A cluck on the end of the phone, "I knew it . . . you've worn him out. You should be more careful, he doesn't come with spares, you know."

"George!"

"Oh I'm sorry, did I puff-out on you again? I didn't mean to do that."

He hung up when he heard her giggle.

Susan re-capped the aerial on the mobile. Walking back to the bedroom, she caught sight of herself in a wardrobe mirror. If she was supposed to be ready in just thirty minutes, she had a hell of a lot of work to do. By the time she heard George Carmichael's voice on the lower landing, hotly denying that he was the guy who'd come for French with Gretel, she was showered, dressed, refreshed. She didn't even feel too drunk.

She leant over the bannister rail and shouted down, "One second, George. I'll be there."

He nodded up at her and escaped out the door, saying: "I'll be safer outside."

Before she left she took another look at Hogie. She meant to write a note. Instead, she stroked the side of his face until he woke.

"Susan. Morning."

He almost struggled to sit up, looking dazed.

She put a hand on his chest, "No. You can go back to sleep. I'm just going out for an hour."

He reached for her and she met his lips. As they released, she said, "Just an hour."

"I'll be here."

She hung over him until his eyes were closed again. As she left, she decided to take his phone. In case she thought how to put it into words.

George met her on the pavement, holding the car door open so she could dive straight in. He cast a look back at the building but she told him she was alone. "You were right about Hogie, he's worn out. Are you sure you can't get spares?"

TWENTY-THREE

Cheb knew the fat freak was sat there, just outside the door. But there was no more contact. Cardiff had run out of questions. If he'd only asked, Cheb would have continued to talk. He had an idea about the East End and all the forgotten rivers it straddled. If he listened he could hear the water and, unmistakeable now, the scampering of feet on the riverbed. It wasn't his imagination this time, this was a thousand little heels clicking together.

He knew that most of London was built on plague pits. He imagined the rivers seeping into the pits and the plague feeding back into the rivers. The clicking of feet had to be the sound of rats, running through the ancient conduits, all the way from the docklands. The rats came with the grain, the free gift in the cereal packets that ran from Sebastapol, from Tyre, from Shanghai. A single rat for every grain, free-loading all the way to Olde London Towne. Imagine, one hundred per cent pure Rattus Rattus faeces mixing in those cargo holds.

Only the facts: 1996, more rats in London than at any other time in the capital's history.

Another: 1996, black rats at last tolerated by their larger brown cousins, cohabiting in a cosy rattus utopia where there's enough food for every rattus to grow biggus and fattus.

Amazing but True: 1996, rattus of either species never stops growing. A five-year-old rat measures a good twelve inches, a fourteen-year-old rat might be the size of a cat. If there were no limits on the growth of ratty communities, a one-hundred-year-old rat could overshadow a jap car and probably out-run it.

What else would you like to know, Cardiff, you fat fuck? Cheb's got all the answers. All you got to do is pump me,

I'll squeal, I'll rat. Come over to your prisoner's cell, he needs your special care, it's latrine time. If I can't empty my head of all this information, let me at least go shit it out my other end.

Cardiff put his head around a door, "What?"

The swollen bruises around Cheb's mouth turned everything into a mumble, "Need Pish."

"Piss? Yeah okay."

Cardiff pulled a knife from his pocket. He made sure Cheb saw it before he walked too close. The knife was thin, more of a shiv with its slim-jim blade and flexi-plastic handle. Cardiff kept the edge tight to Cheb's neck as he uncuffed his hands from the chair and re-cuffed them at his front. Chained like that, the boy could deal with his own fly and answer nature solo. Cardiff hauled him out of the chair and walked him across the floor to the semi-derelict toilets down the stairwell.

Cheb walked slowly, feeling the point of Cardiff's knife hurrying him along but too bruised to take longer steps.

In the bathroom, if he looked to his left, he could make a fresh examination of his face. How were his ears today, still monstrously swollen? Was his nose still flattened, was his smile still missing its teeth? Was his dome still swollen up like Brainiac?

Cheb's shadow swayed across the white porcelain tiles. Cardiff stayed one step behind him. Cheb fumbled at the buttons on his jeans. Cardiff stayed close, knife in hand, only stepping back when Cheb let loose with a powerful jet.

Cheb said, "Do you want a pissing contest? You think you could piss like a fucking horse after someone's beat the shit out of you?"

Cardiff said, "Shut up and get on with it."

He shook his dick, turning around to let Cardiff see it waggle. Cardiff was only two paces away and should never have looked down. When Cheb launched himself head first, he moved like a battering ram. His face was a mess but it was still solid bone. The first lunge caught Cardiff square between the eyes. He carried on butting until the man was on the floor. Even then, he climbed on top of him, head-butting the fat bastard unconscious.

Cardiff occasionally came around, Cheb butted him right back into Dreamland. His head had stopped registering pain. It could be smashed to pieces, it probably was, but he felt nothing and carried on butting whenever Cardiff's eyelids fluttered. He had work to do. It was lucky that Cardiff brought his own knife.

Cardiff woke feeling cold. That was the strongest sensation; he was cold and he was empty. His head was ringing, louder than any other noise around him. He could barely see. Black gauze clouded the long room.

His ears picked out a scratching sound. A multiple scratching. Light returned to the room, oddly dispersed like drapes of a flapping white cloth with dense black sheets in between.

A bent figure crept into resolution. Someone working away with a brush. The unintelligible sounds he'd heard earlier grew captions: the scratching of stiff bristles pushing across a cement floor.

Cold and wet and empty. Cardiff was soaked to the skin. The brushing figure sluiced water across the floor towards a drain. Another black haze floated in front of his eyes, Cardiff tried to wave it away with his hands. He could barely see his hands although he knew they were there, right in front of his face. It was an effort to focus, to keep on focussing. His palm prints flickered into resolution. And the pain began to grow insistent. He felt empty and could only think that the pain was a part of the feeling of emptiness.

A basketcase of old clitches: his stomach had dropped, he was drained, he was gutted. Another dry old dog of a phrase to mix with the pain: he was coming round. He'd been clobbered and that was why he felt drained, why he was belly up.

He smelled the ferrous oxide of blood and the farmyard stench of shit. He'd cacked it. He was empty and he'd cacked his load.

The brushman came over, lisping slightly through fat lips as he said, "You're back from the dead?"

The bald kid, a vivid red blob of a face leering out of his still-dazed b/w vision.

The bald kid said, "I can throw another bucket of water over you. That should perk you up."

There was blood dripping out of the kid's mouth. His face loomed into deep focus. Cardiff saw cuts in his lips, the kid had drained his bruises to keeping the swelling down. An amateur surgeon.

He said, "I'm cold." He was freezing, the fingers he waved in front of his face were chilled insensible.

"You'll get colder. But I could warm you temporarily. There's a space heater on the other floor."

The kid walked off, dragging his brush behind him.

Cardiff tried to move. Another phrase: rooted to the spot. He was sitting down and he couldn't move, neither up nor backwards nor forwards. He couldn't even fall over. He was planted and there was nothing he could do.

He looked at his two white legs, straddling the steel beam he'd just discovered he was sitting on. He wasn't wearing trousers. He fought waves of sickness and reached out to feel for his dick. It was still there, cock and balls. He'd had this sudden crazy thought but his tackle was still there.

The clanking of wheels travelled across the floorway. The kid was wheeling a huge gas cylinder, one of those things that look like the jet propulsion burners that fasten to the underwings of aircraft. He set it up next to Cardiff and walked away.

Cardiff's teeth were buzzing so loudly, he'd thought it was the sound of a drum machine, weaving through the music on the floor below. He was wrong, this was the kind of chattering that could end only in hypothermia.

He wondered if he'd blacked out again.

The kid was setting up a gas bottle, taller than himself, and screwing a brass valve into its top. He began twisiting it around with a spanner.

A click. The whoosh of gas and a blast of hot air like a mother's hug, a warm bed, an oven baking all day long— a thing to make you forget that you were ever cold. When his teeth chattered they sounded a whole lot less bebop.

The kid began speaking. "I want to talk about corn. There's no real alternative. Wheat, for instance, makes for a twisted society: nothing but beer boys and bread heads. Rice just makes you stupid. Can you imagine? Waist-deep in a paddy field, aiming for total inertia, your central nervous system functioning at ground fucking zero? All the greatest civilisations are corn-fed: all of them, Mayan, Aztec, Inca."

The kid was talking slowly, overcoming the ghastly swelling that days of beating had wreaked on his mouth. But the kid was still talking shit. Cardiff tried to concentrate—he felt he had to.

"Corn-fed. I love that phrase, it makes everything sound so tasty. Corn is beautiful. Plant it and it grows so fast you can hear it move. And rice and wheat grains all have to be dehusked but with corn all you do is strip away the outer leaves and you got a fat juicy cob. Barbecue it, boil it, roast or bake it, mash it or dry it out and grind it up for flour. It's got versatility fucking nailed."

The kid sat on the beam next to Cardiff. He stuck his squished red face right up to Cardiff as he said, "How do you like your corn?"

"I don't know."

"You don't know?"

Cardiff tried to wriggle, pain shooted through his empty body, rooted him to his seat. He said, "What's wrong with me?"

"You haven't figured it out yet?"

Cardiff shook his head, the pain drilling him, bewildering him.

The kid said, "Keep working at it, you'll get it. I'll just keep on talking, keeping you informed. The beauty of corn is that it's both reliable and flexible. It grows so fast and in such abundance that every corn-based culture grows at an astronomical rate. One minute, they're cavemen. The next, they're building a city of gold in the middle of a fucking lake. Corn breeds. It speeds up the natural life cycle. You reach puberty early, you reproduce early. You die young."

The kid was grinning and nodding, "It's the perfect fucking food for the perfect fucking society. Listen . . .

"There's no shit about reverence for age, there's no respect for tradition. Everything is pre-programmed, corn produces a society hooked on expansion, reproduction and death. It's built into the technology—

"You have to understand the agriculture technology behind corn. It doesn't need rich soil to grow, all it needs is basic fertilisation. The Mayans lived by the coast, so they'd cast a spell and bury a fish head under every plant. The Incas, they traded guano over the Andes. Either rotting fish or bird shit, they're both perfect, both rich in nitrous-fucking-goodies. But all you really need is blood and shit . . .

"You could kill all your enemies or you could sacrifice your neighbour's family and, hey-presto, you've got another blood-soaked field ripe for cultivation. It doesn't matter that half the society's dead, corn-eaters breed like germs so there's always twice as many babies the next year. That's the secret: blood, shit and sun. The sun beats down on the heads of corn and the heads of the people, it drives them out of their fucking trees. There's blood and there's shit dripping from the bowels of the living and the disembowelled corpses of the dead. The sun at one end of the equation, shit out the other."

Cardiff said, "Disembowelled?"

The kid grinned, "I knew you'd guess it eventually."

Cardiff was sat on a low steel beam, an RSJ propped on concrete slabs. He couldn't move and now he knew: somehow, some-fucking-unearthly-how, he was tied by the arse.

"It's a mesoamerican trick. You're strung down."

The kid was holding his knife.

"It was easier than you'd think: First off, I had to grease your arse and work the knife up there. I got my fist a good five inches inside before I severed the rectum and hauled out your intestines. How many yards of gut do you reckon you had, all curled up inside you? I pulled it out straight and used it to strap you down to this beam. I have got to say, you were absolutely full of shit but there was very little blood involved. Once I'd pulled the intestines out of your arse, they sealed the hole. Even when you were unconscious, the tension pulling on your guts kept you upright, like one of those puppet toys that has a string running from the top of its head and out between its legs. You just sat there, docile, for around two hours."

Cardiff's hand went down to the beam. The touch of slimy like frog skin against the RSJ made him retch, the retching produced a tightening that he felt all the way through his body: like an elastic band wound up inside of him.

"The Mayans would pin people out like this, tied to a heavy log for the vultures to get them. They couldn't think of running. If they tried they'd rip out their own stomachs. I couldn't find a log, I had to use this steel joist but I guess it's an acceptable update."

Cardiff felt himself slipping under again. He was dead.

Cheb caught him and slapped him back to life: "Listen

you fat cunt. You've got one chance and that's fucking slim. If you get swift medical attention, if you get a synthetic intestine, you might live. I'll tell you, you are not going to lose any more blood. You're stoppered-up water-tight, and while that holds you're stable.

"What you have to do, you have to convince your cunt boss Frankie to call for the paramedics. You've got to give him something, strike a deal, so he'll reward you and save your life. You got it?"

Cheb slapped him again.

"You got it?"

The fat freak nodded.

"Tell Frankie that those boys he's so gaga over killed his son."

"Liam and Sean?"

"Whatever they're fucking called. Just tell him."

Out of a sick daze, Cardiff grunted, "If I tell Frankie, he won't save me. He'll kill me himself."

"It's your only hope. Once it's laid out, even he can't be so stupid he won't see it."

Cardiff wasn't so sure. Even the state he was in, he knew it wouldn't help. "He'll still come after Susan and your mate."

"Well that's their problem. Hogie used to diddle my mother so my feelings towards him are a little ambiguous. You just worry about yourself, leave the thinking to me."

Cardiff slipped under again. Cheb gave him his last slap.

"You got it, you fat cunt?"

Cardiff nodded.

TWENTY-FOUR

Cheb stood on the stage of the old loading bay, looking out to the river and feeling the weight of the warehouse above his head. He wondered where he could find some pain-killers although he wasn't sure he was in pain. Talking had been an effort, his lips were so huge he couldn't seem to slip them around the words he wanted to say.

He looked around. It was strange but where he was standing seemed to be hugely busy. Two pantechnicons were parked at the foot of the bay and black T-shirted roadies milled around, wheeling speaker stacks or lighting rigs up the ramp to the warehouse. As they passed by, they looked him over. From their faces, it seemed they'd never seen anything like him before but they didn't get involved. A fat biker-type huffed past, carrying a spotlight in each hand like they were carrier bags. He was the first to speak, asking Cheb if he was "Okay, mate"? Cheb waved the guy away, "You don't worry about me, mate."

He limped down the ramp and slipped between the sides of the lorries. Once round the corner, there were fewer people to stare at him.

When he reached the front of the warehouse, he rested at a window and watched a team of men working a scaffold. The system was four storeys high. Another crew were inflating a giant plastic Sumo wrestler from a gas bottle, holding it steady with guy ropes as it unfolded towards the ceiling.

Cheb shook his cabbaged head. Where was he?

He stumbled out along a cobble road towards a hump-back bridge. At its crest, he looked down to a black slug of water toting garbage debris round a distant curve. Over his shoulder the redbrick warehouses squatted low, dumping over the water. Ahead of him the road staggered like a suicide into a diesel strand of dual carriageway. Cheb walked on past a sign he read as Three Mile Island. He seemed to know the name.

Outside a Tesco superstore. He took the disabled ramp up to the automatic doors. The all-seeing eye recognised him, the doors slid open. The foyer was full of shoppers pushing trollies but their wheels seemed to seize as he passed through. No one said anything but they all stared. An old woman, bent over a tartan bag and trying to fix a broken strap, straightened as he came by. She screamed out loud as his face loomed into her short field of vision. He thought, Yeah, but what do you look like?

Cheb found the pay-phone bracketed next to the cigarette concession. He felt over his pockets and found a credit card no one had thought to take off him. He slipped it over the lip of the appropriate slot and the machine sucked it in.

He got an answering machine. He needed to clutch the wall for support. He kept himself conscious by staring at the LCD screen as the call-charge scrolled upwards.

"Answer, someone answer. Answer, answer, answer."

Someone snatched the phone. Naz: "Cheb, we thought you were dead."

He'd assumed he was dead, too. Was this a beyond-the-grave kind of joke?

"Where are you?"

He didn't know. "Near some kind of warehouse. There's a river, I don't know what else."

"Are you alone?"

"I was with a fat bloke called Cardiff. He's arseing around back there somewhere. To tell you the truth, Naz, I'm feeling a bit weird. Could you pick me up?"

Cheb looked over his shoulder, the girl at the cigarette stall was staring in his direction. He held the telephone receiver out to her, saying, "You, tell this guy the address."

She slipped out of her booth and took the phone from his hand. Cheb felt himself slide down the wall.

George, said "Serious days" and pushed at the door of Hogie's flat. Wind chimes sounded for Susan as she pushed through.

"Frankie is convinced we'll come mob handed."

Susan nodded. She could imagine Frankie farting and sweating and sorting out a pile of weapons. He'd got Callum killed by involving him in his menopausal gangster fantasies and now he was going to see them through to the end. It would be a joke if it wasn't so sick and so dangerous. They had wanted to clip him and now he was tooled up and ready to repel all invaders. They were left with no plan, no hope . . .

She followed George through to the front room and met the boys. Naz she already knew. The next one was called Mannie. She caught both their eyes briefly but it was Cheb she really stared at. He was so beaten he would have been unrecognisable, a match for a spud-boy but nothing human. But it was how Susan had expected someone to look after a stay with Frankie, it's how she felt on the inside.

Cheb looked up. Maybe he had a wry smile, maybe he was dumb or stoned.

Naz said, "It's fucking barbaric. And that's what he looks like after we patched him up . . . before he was a real mess, isn't that right?"

Cheb nodded slowly, trying to get his mouth round a phrase but failing. His lips had disappeared into the black crusted bruises of his swollen face.

Naz said, "But now we know where they are, we go in and kill them."

He was nodding vigorously, staring first at George then at Mannie. Mannie nodded back at him but the boy looked scared to death.

George said, "Just like that?"

Naz kicked a bag at his feet. Susan hadn't noticed it before, now she saw it was full of guns.

George had given her a brief rundown in the car, all the latest information, but she wanted a re-cap. She said, "My husband's teamed up with the people who killed our son?"

Naz nodded, looking over to Cheb for confirmation. The boy's botched head moved slowly, up and down.

George said, "Come on, think this thing through. It's the worst place to try and get him. At a rave."

Naz said, "There's only four of them. There's more of us."

George wasn't having it. Pointing to Cheb, he said, "He says there's four, but look at him. I doubt he can even count to four. What about the bouncers, the security, the road crew. It could be as many as thirty, perhaps more."

"We can do it."

"No we can't. Look at us."

Susan listened to them argue, the three boys and George Carmichael. Naz seemed insane, Cheb was almost dead and Mannie was paralysed with fear . . .

George continued the list, "I'm a fucking accountant, she's a housewife. Hogie's not even here—he's still in fucking bed."

He shrugged over at Susan, like he was sorry for the dig but surely she could see it was stupid. She tried to think of something to say but before she opened her mouth, Mannie had begun speaking.

"I'm up for it. I know how to shoot . . . targets and that." His voice trailed off.

Susan finally said, "George is right. We can't do it tonight."

George offered to drive her back but she told him she preferred to take a cab. She wound a scarf around her head until her face was all but covered. She hoped no newspaper reader would recognise her and claim their reward. Probably no-one would think anything except she was a lunatic, wrapped so tight in this city heat. She spent the journey turning things over. If she could have sent them all in against Frankie, maybe she would have. It might have worked. But there had to be a better way of doing it, a better readied plan—at least one where she wouldn't have to make excuses for Hogie when she kept him at home.

She tried but failed to think of a different scheme. But even as she turned onto Manchester Street, she sensed new disturbances. She was too late.

The door to Maltese Rosa's house was swinging open, outside groups of foreign language students from the local schools were standing, pointing down the hall. And mixed with them, a few brasses wearing their work clothes: basques, baby dolls or school-girl uniforms.

Susan told the driver to stop and wait. She grabbed hold of the nearest tom, "What happened."

"I don't know. I heard shooting." The woman pointed down the road to where other women were peering out of a house window. "I work at one-eighty."

"Is anyone hurt?"

The woman shrugged. "I think the place is empty now."

Susan pushed through the chattering crowd. At the door, she looked down at the scuffled trash across the mat, minicab cards, free pizza deals and home delivered asthma cures. Her eyes travelled up, there was blood on the bannister rail. She walked in.

The door to the lower apartment was broken in but there was no one in the room. She started up the stairs, skirting around the patches of blood. At the halfway landing, she saw the bathroom door was also broken. The floor was swimming in water. There was a stainless steel enema prod attached to the bath taps. Now it was blasting water across the walls, writhing like a robotic snake. Susan looked away, up to the first floor landing. The door to her room was swinging free on its hinges.

The room was torn apart. Her clothes were everywhere, across the floor and bed, and her suitcase lying empty on the floor. Frankie had found the cocaine and Hogie together and took them both . . . it was clear. She pulled the clothes off the bed, the dark and unclean bedsheets still carried an imprint of Hogie's body—and a touch of his warmth. She ran a hand across the sheets to make the bed look decent, straightening out the creases and brushing the stray dust of cocaine onto the floor.

She made it back to the street while the police sirens were still a half street away. As she ran for her taxi, she struggled with her scarf, trying to re-cover her face and soak up the tears she hadn't noticed she was crying. She threw herself inside, saying Camden, and started hammering the buttons on Hogie's mobile phone. One long ring and George's voice floated through the microwaves: "Hello."

"George. Where are you?"

"Susan? I'm still here. Putting Cheb to bed. . . . What's the matter with you? Are you okay?"

How was she? Broken down and homeless and that was the best thing she could say. This was the absolute worse. "He's got Hogie."

"Frankie? How?"

"I don't know. They must have got to Rosa." They both knew that Maltese Rosa would have to be in a very bad way before she'd open her mouth outside a confessional.

He said, "What do we do?"

"Get him back." She paused, felt a bubble burst in the back of her throat. With a mouthful of fresh tears she said, "Please George, please."

TWENTY-FIVE

George Carmichael sat sweating in his overcoat on the hottest summer night of the year. The car air conditioning went off with the ignition and all they could do was leave the window open, watch for movement in the upper storey windows of the warehouse and listen to the music skimming across the water. Spin-drying their minds. When Cheb described the building to him, the first thing he thought was that Frankie had truly lost his mind. Who would hide out above a rave? Looking at it now, it seemed like a fortress. The moat kept them at a distance.

He said, "How's everyone doing?"

Naz spoke from the back seat. "I could feel better. I'll know I'm getting there when I'm stepping over bodies." The shredded nerves rasped alongside his voice, he didn't care who heard it. "We just follow Cheb's plan, it's sweet. One time, a fucking Jihad."

George could have told him: there was no plan. Cheb virtually said as much. Lying there on his bed, beaten to a pulp and breathing through cracked ribs and a gut hernia, he basically said that Hogie was screwed and that was it.

Instead, George said, "Well, we know where Frankie's staying so I guess we've got the element of surprise."

Naz leaned forward again, speaking to the back of George's head. "What kind of gat you want to go with?"

George turned and looked down into the bag Naz was holding open. It was some choice but George hadn't touched any kind of firearm in almost thirty years and hadn't fired one since Boy's Brigade, 1958. "A rifle?"

Naz pulled the bag back onto his knee and started disentangling an assault rifle from the bottom.

George said, "What's that?"

"A to the K."

George thought maybe he recognised it now, it was the Commie-style of rifle, as opposed to the one the good guys carried in news footage and war films.

He took another look at his new partners, Naz in the back and Mannie at the wheel. It just wasn't enough. Worse, only Naz looked as though he'd be any use. The other boy was so nervous that two fistfuls of beta-blockers couldn't stop him shaking. He was sat with his head down, his hair in his eyes, fiddling with a gun in his lap. Maybe they should give him another beta-blocker, perhaps something stronger: Naz seemed to have brought a pharmacy with him, the different drugs neatly wrapped in a chemist's little doggy bag.

George turned round and mouthed, "Is he going to be okay?" His head nodding over to Mannie.

"He'll be fine. If he doesn't stop shaking, I got some Librax that'll bring him down."

George thought he'd need more than that. From the start, the only job he trusted to Mannie was the driving and he wasn't even sure about that after the journey they'd just had. But the boy said he intended to fight. He had an old sporting pistol in his lap and a clutch of bullets in his hand. He kept popping them in and out of the chambers. Naz had been telling him for hours to throw that piece of crap away but he refused. He said it was the only gun he knew how to work.

Naz took up most of the back seat, wrapped in his overcoat and hiding a selection of guns inside it. The coats had been Naz's idea: "When we pull out our pieces, we got to pull them out of something."

George realised he'd never asked Naz how he got into this line of work. An important question like that, it made him wonder whether his interviewing technique needed some management focus. He clearly hadn't asked Cheb enough fancy questions when he hired him for the restaurant.

He tried to think it through again, why was he here? He thought Hogie was a reasonable cook but he wasn't worth dying for . . . in fact, the kid was probably overrated. So maybe the reason was guilt. Susan still didn't know exactly where her son had died or how his body wound up nailed to a coach floor in Essex. If she ever found out, he wanted to have done something to square matters. Although, God willing, he would never have to explain it—he frankly had no idea how the body wound up nailed to the floor of a coach, either.

Naz was ready to leave. Still playing the role of coach and cheerleader, rasping out: "One time, just stick to Cheb's plan."

George could have screamed, what fucking plan? What makes you think there's a fucking plan? Is it anything like Cheb's last plan: how to dispose of a body? Because, from where he was sitting, that was beginning to look really pretty well thought-out and rational. Sat inside a car alongside a psychotic and a terminal depressive, telling himself: yeah just beautiful, but I'm the one that needs his fucking head examining. So why was he here? There was only one reason: he loved Soho and what he'd done to it so much, if he lost it then life wasn't worth living anyway.

Naz was out of the car, saying: "Right, let's infiltrate."

George didn't make him wait. As he stepped out behind Naz he said, "Just one thing, because this might be my last chance to ask. What does Naz stand for? Naseem?"

"No, Nasser."

George had the number of Hogie's mobile but he didn't have Susan's new address. Susan knew, it was a sensible precaution. The only reason she felt bad was that it was her idea rather than his—as though she was posting her vote of no confidence ahead of the election. Now she was sat in a suite in the Conan Doyle Hotel, occupying it in the name of Lee Meriwether. It was imperfect, purposeless, pseudonymously purportive. She felt like one drowned cat and all she could do was wait, alone in her Meriwether drag while she prayed for a quick widowhood. She had gin and TV to entertain her. Gin for the nerves, TV for news reports.

Maltese Rosa Mansif was second lead on the early evening news bulletin. By *News at Ten* she'd been upgraded to the fourth or fifth victim of the presumed serial killer: the experts were divided over whether Callum's heart attack counted as a clean kill or not. The hands on the clock crawled up towards midnight and gathered speed on their downhill run. The gin began to work.

When she caught sight of Hogie, she could not believe it. The DNA of a pure moron surrounded him like a halo as he diced a pound of chicken and grinned out of her TV screen. She jabbed at the remote control button, prodding up the volume. He was stood in a pastel-coloured bay, surrounded by his pots and pans and bowls of spices. The camera followed him to the gas hob and he began to jiggle a frying-pan over a medium flame, saying: "So now you've cut them into cuboids, you got to fire them up with a ton of butter for that all-over tan effect."

Susan scrambled across the room to collect her handbag and Hogie's phone. Clutching it to her ear, she couldn't get the aerial up fast enough. Her fingers knotted together as she dialled and pulled and tried to smooth out the scrap of paper where she'd written George's mobile number. Behind her, Hogie's voice ran on, filling the room.

"What we're doing, we're going for a primo cajun experience. Anyone watching in smell-o-vision, you got to savour the aroma of Mississippi burning."

She heard the presenter begin to thank him and invite him back to her couch for a live, on-air discussion. Susan turned back to the picture, the phone clamped to her ear, and watched as Hogie grinned and loped towards the stuffed velvet sofa. He was still carrying his pan of fried chicken. A headphoned technician had to run over and take it off his hands.

"Yeah, thanks mate."

After five minutes with no reply she clicked off the phone and pressed redial, hoping that when George left, he remembered to pack his mobile. Back on-screen, Hogie was struggling to sit upright on the flop sofa. The presenter was saying how sorry she was to hear about the death of his friends. Hogie was saying, Yeah? The questions ticked on: *How long had he known soap star Julie Manning? Wasn't she staying with him the night she was abducted? How did he feel when he heard the news?*

None of Hogie's answers were too intelligible. He had a fillet of chicken on the end of a fork and was waving it as he spoke. All Susan could make out from his replies, was that the whole thing was doing his head in, you know. He looked no more dazed than usual.

Susan clicked off again, deciding to give George another few minutes. She stood there, helpless, watching as the presenter flicked another page over the top of her pad and began a fresh sheet of questions: *His friend Jason Beddoes had also disappeared? Had Hogie given up all hope?*

Hogie said, "Yeah, I guess. He was my best mate and all."

He was still flicking the chicken chunk, pawing stupidly at every question but he had nothing to say. He'd been ebullient at the stove, he was a fluttering mess on the sofa.

Susan left him hanging, sidelined by the sudden ringing of the mobile phone. She grabbed for it and pressed for an answer: "George?"

The voice at the other end was slurred and swollen, "Nope. The troops have left the barracks."

"Is that Cheb."

"The Cheb Monster, the only brains of this organisation."

"Do you know where Hogie is now?"

"Are you kidding? This is his big chance for TV stardom, he's been looking forward to it all week. There was no way he was going to miss it."

On-screen, the presenter was saying, *And what's your connection with the ex-stripper, Susan Ball? Do you know where she is? Do you know her husband?*

TWENTY-SIX

George kept step with Naz across the hump-backed bridge, over the river and onto the island. Mannie was more erratic, sometimes just ahead, sometimes lagging back but always twitching. George put it down to nerves but it may have been the music. With every step the beats just kept getting louder and louder. They were almost at the doors of the warehouse now and two of the security men had noticed them. Both of them were dressed in black, jogging pants and T-shirts. The shirts had lettering across the front, large enough for George to read without his glasses: *London Rainforest.*

Naz whispered, "We just walk past these guys. Cheb said we should go in the back way."

When one of the security guys shouted, "Invite only", George only nodded, vaguely, pretending that he couldn't hear over the music. Naz wasn't so subtle, shouting back, "Yeah? Is it any good in there, then?"

The two men just stood there, holding their poses and clutching their walkie talkies like a couple of body-builders playing at G-Men: "Invite only."

Naz winked over at George, side-mouthing as they passed by, "Where'd they find these guys?"

George said, "What's this rubbish about an invite?"

"You not heard of the Criminal Justice Bill. Raves are illegal now. This one's probably down as some kind of charity event."

George glanced back over his shoulder at the two security guys, "London Rainforest?"

Naz shrugged, "Well, it doesn't have one yet."

It was hot enough to grow one though. George wondered what the three of them looked like, walking around in over-coats. They would have made an odd threesome anyway, without the accoutrements. He could feel his rifle under-neath his crombie, the magazine digging into his ribs and the strap biting on his shoulder. Naz was wearing an army great coat. Mannie had a plastic mac. He was bouncing ahead of them now, perhaps unnerved by the security team. As they followed him around the corner of the building, the mac flared out and George realised it was an A-line cut, the kid must be wearing his dead sister's clothes.

Naz hissed, calling Mannie back. "Better let me go first."

He had stopped outside a loading bay. A ramp led up to a platform and a pair of heavy warehouse doors. Through the doors, George could see a barrier, guarded by another couple of guys, and beyond the heads of dancers all jacking to the music. He was surprised that they'd left the doors open. On a night like this they would sell twice as many bottles of water if they kept the dancers cooped in the heat. Although he guessed even gangsters didn't want their punters dying on them.

He said, "There must be two thousand people in there."

Naz didn't think so, "More like fifteen hundred." He swung ahead of them and walked up to the security men at their barrier. One guy came to meet him at the top of the ramp, his head bent forwards as he listened to what Naz had to say. After a moment, he looked up and beckoned his partner over. There wasn't a hope of hearing anything above the music but George thought it looked like a negotiation. Naz was giving a pitch to the two men and they listened, occasionally nodding, sometimes putting a finger into the neck of their T-shirts and tugging slightly, as though they were letting off steam. Finally, Naz handed them something and they unclipped their walkie talkies and gave them to Naz. Then they turned and began to walk away.

They'd gone maybe three steps when Naz called them back. They listened again, looked at each other for some kind of mutual confirmation, then nodded and broke into a sprint. George watched as they leapt off the loading bay and headed full tilt for the water edge: amazed as they dived in and started swimming.

When he reached Naz, he said, "What did you do?"

"Paid them."

George couldn't imagine how much he'd need, before he'd do something like that. Naz said, "Most people would do it for a grand."

George looked out to the water, he couldn't even see their heads anymore. "Won't the money get wet."

"I also said I'd shoot them if they didn't."

Mannie was ahead of them again, already half way over the barrier. George was a step behind, wondering how he was going to climb with the weight of his crombie coat, not to mention the rifle and the two spare carbines. He didn't need to think about it, Naz put a hand on his shoulder and told him to wait. A moment later, he'd pulled Mannie back over the barrier, saying: "We don't get ahead of ourselves, bud."

It suited George. His first full sight of the warehouse just stopped him dead. Now he stood back on the loading bay, hands resting on the barrier and his nose pressed against the wall of heat, sweat and noise-studded light.

There was no dancefloor, just rough poured cement scudded with sweat puddles. Along the back wall, the speaker stacks rose up like two sides of a triumphal arch, topped with an enormous lighting rig. Stuck up there, the rig looked like a battery position, blazing laser fire into the crowd below. And underneath, at the very centre of the arch, there was the DJ standing at his decks. The guy should have been dwarfed but the arch gave him a kind of grandeur: like Caesar or Stalin. Except this crowd was no disciplined mob—it was a giant insect culture brought out of a microscope, an alien swarm on wings.

George didn't know what he'd expected. He'd kind of quit the club scene lately but in the eighties he would occasionally let himself be dragged to places like Heaven or The Fridge. He knew about house music and even quite liked it. To him, it was nothing other than Boy's Town, Hi-NRG disco stripped to its essentials. Maybe he'd thought a rave would be something like that: up, up-lifting, up-for-it, up in the air hand-waving with everyone glamming it. But this was something else entirely. It wasn't even house music. This was, according to a word he'd heard but never quite believed, the Jungle. And he hadn't seen anything like it for thirty-five years.

Back in the early sixties, he couldn't get enough of the mod clubs round Soho. This scene recalled the frugging amphetamine dancing of the R&B boys: times-ed by about five in size and intensity. The dancers had the same look: the mad staring eyes, the gallons of sweat running off their faces and washing their heads away to grinning skulls. Ecstasy was an amphetamine. He could only half remember the formula but liked the sound of it when he first heard it: 2, 3, 4 Metadioxymetamphetamine. Something like that. The numbers at the beginning made it sound like an R&B track, the count-in followed by the blurring rush of the words. George had dropped an E on a few occasions but each time in private loving company. He could see now, he'd missed half the experience. But coming on it like this, it was a toxic shock. He couldn't even control his breathing. It was speeding up, threatening to match the 200 beats per minute of the noise around him.

He turned away from the barrier, mumbling "Time for a cig?" Naz nodded, Okay.

He searched through three pockets before he found his pack of cigarettes. He pulled out two Gauloises, ripped off the filters and stuck them in his ears, glad he'd switched from filter-free a few years back. He turned one of the cigarettes around, put it in his mouth and passed the other to Naz who said, "Thanks, bud. Any time now."

The cigarette was lit, George just couldn't suck the smoke down his throat fast enough.

"A fucking Jihad. You up for it, bud?"

He finally got it out. "This is crazy. We can't go through with it."

Naz slapped him on the shoulder and said, "Don't even think about it."

George looked straight at him. "Why the fuck are you so calm?" His voice sounded steady but that was nothing but hopelessness.

"Like Cheb said, we just stick to the plan and it's sorted."

He had nothing left. But he tried to read Naz: What was sorted?

Naz put an arm round George's shoulder, like he understood how the man must be feeling. He said, "I'm not stupid. I'm not gonna walk in a place and just get killed. But Cheb's got it sorted out. He's spread dissension among the enemy. Now that Frank Ball knows who really killed his son, we don't have a worry."

George didn't believe a word of it.

Cardiff was nothing but a wet patch on the floor, smelling

of disinfectant. Frankie had told his boys to wrap the rest of him in plastic sheets and bundle him away. Half an hour later, they were clanking back in the elevator, as cheerful as when they left. Liam saying, "He sleeps with the fishes, Uncle Frankie."

Frankie gave them a grin. "Nice work boys."

They dumped him in the river, like he told them. They'd done a good job swabbing Cardiff's mess off the floor, too. But they'd had no luck tracking Susan, despite what they'd done to her Malteser friend.

The two boys were taking it easy, now, sat on the joist where they'd found Cardiff, just smoking and gassing about their holidays. Frankie had to hand it to them, they had stronger stomachs than most of the men he'd worked with over the years. Because it was a fact, Cardiff was a mess when they found him. If his time ever came, Frankie only hoped there'd be a true geezer around to put him out of his misery, like he'd done for Cardiff. The guy had gibbered and pleaded but, deep down, he had to know it was for the best. The state he was in, what else could he do? What you got if you ain't got a colon? It was over in a second, bang, and he'd put one right between the cunt's eyes.

He took another swig, drinking to Cardiff. Here's to you, son. You weren't much but you took a bullet without running. Not that you could run far with an RSJ stuck to your ring.

Across the room, Sean was saying, "Katmandu."

"Du what?"

"Katmandu, guy. You wanna try that."

"Yeah? I been fancying a bit of that. Get my head sorted."

Frankie watched them, separated by twenty yards of compound floor and by the half-drained brandy bottle in his hand. Separated by how many years? He wouldn't have said it was possible but they'd been talking about dope and holidays for around four hours. The way things stood, he almost began missing Cardiff. No, what he really missed was peace and quiet.

When the music started, Frankie considered sending one of the boys out for earplugs. But he'd rode it out, just continued squinting out of the window and gritting his teeth. A few hours ago the queue was so long it started at the far side of the river and snaked over the bridge to the warehouse doors. It was gone now. A few minutes back, he'd seen three tramps walk by, the clowns wrapped up in overcoats in this weather but he guessed if that's all they owned, then that's what they had to wear. Now the only people left down by the dock were the hired security. They stood in a circle, recognisable by their black T-shirts. He knew the logo across the front read *London Rainforest*, but only because Sean and Liam were wearing the exact same shirts. That was just one of the new ideas that Liam had to explain to him. Something to do with the law, the advantages of a charitable status and the importance of a corporate identity: so the punters knew they were getting quality. "Caring enviroment, quality sounds and quality gear."

They'd told him there were around fifteen hundred people down there, all of them dancing, drugged to the sockets. At twenty quid a head, not counting what they spent on drugs, that was serious coin. He couldn't fault the business, only the fucking industrial health.

Liam was asking whether Katmandu was that place the Beatles went to chill out? Sean seemed to think it was.

Liam said, "I tell you what, someone who's been given a hard time. That Yoko fucking Ono."

"Yeah?"

"Too fucking right. Everyone giving her this, giving her that, saying she's the tart what broke up the Beatles. But I tell you, I'd give her one."

"Yoko Ono?"

"Yeah. I'd give her one. And another thing, I reckon she's

a good singer. I mean, she's not your Aretha fucking Franklin but she gives it some stick. There's this track on *Some Time in New York City*, that tears your fucking heart out."

"I heard that one, guy. It's a shocker."

Yeah, they were a cheerful pair. They were wrong about Yoko Ono though. It was McCartney who finished the Beatles.

TWENTY-SEVEN

The programme was over. Hogie was back in the hospitality suite, standing at the centre of the bar and trying to entertain as many people as he could. A girl beside him was doing her best to decorate his arm but he liked to wave his hands when he spoke and she kept slipping off. With the pressure off for a week, the room was packed—not just with the guests and their people, but also technicians, researchers, friends, whoever. It was a wrap, it was a party.

Hogie's one aim, as he was trying to explain, was choosing a drink. He was mainly complicated by the range of optics on offer but a subsidiary distraction was the fact he knew the barman. They'd worked together in a Four Seasons hotel out West but the big surprise was that the guy still seemed to like him. He asked why Hogie didn't just have the usual.

"I don't know. What did my usual used to be?"

"Cider and brandy."

"Shit man, you'll blow my cover. They still think I'm a fucking gourmet."

The girl on his arm was a skinny media chick, looking extra bright in the strip-lit party room. She was asking, "Did you really turn up to that Liverpool show off your face."

He told her, "Yeah. But I was straight this time." It was a bare-faced lie and she seemed to appreciate it.

Looking at the bottles above the bar he remembered Susan drank gin. He thought he could go for that but before he said anything the show's producer swept up behind him shouting, Hello Genius.

They double kissed for about the fifth time since they'd got off air and she ordered a round of beers. "Is that alright?"

Hogie said, "Uh-huh. Sweet."

She was dragging some of the other guests around with her. Not, thank Christ, the geek TV shrink. But all the other ones: a pop star who Hogie believed was Scandinavian and a comedian who might as well have been.

"Hogie's got a new restaurant and it's just fantastic. I was at the opening. Fabulous."

"Yeah?" Hogie sucked at his beer. "I thought it was a bit fucked up, you know?"

A few beers down the line, Hogie remembered he was carrying Susan's cocaine. He had doubts about the security of the house she was staying in, so he'd taken it for safe-keeping. Now he broke open a bag, tipped it into a saucer and started laying out a few modest lines on the bar. Everyone ahead formed a queue. All of them panting round, asking if they could have a blast. He stood there, saying Sure, giving it big smiles all around and listening as the comedian repeated, word-for-word, the exact spiel he'd used on the show. Hogie began to suspect the producer had deliberately dumped the guy on him. She was quick enough to disappear on another circuit of the room. He could hear her still, lapping up compliments everywhere she went. Apparently the show was a great success. She'd got a scoop, an exclusive post-murder interview and she could expect to be in all the papers in the morning.

Everyone was getting louder, wilder. Different strangers were constantly coming up to him, asking him personal questions about Jools. The comedian was head down in a plate of his cocaine, cracking on about the quality gear in a frankly schizoid accent. The pop star was throwing a sulk, a cameraman had asked him to sing "Fernando" and when the guy claimed not to know the words had insisted on reminding him. Over in the far corner, the producer was screeching about her night at the restaurant's opening party, telling everyone she was actually there the very night the people got killed. She admitted it, she was getting so fucking hot, she swore she had a news antennae. If you wanted to confirm her brilliance, you just better get into line.

There was nothing louder than the producer. Not until the screaming started at the door. But this was another woman entirely. Her voice, reaching higher and higher, battling it out with a security guy. She was saying, "I'm his Aunt fucking Susan and I need to see him."

When Susan finally broke through the door and pushed towards the bar, Hogie didn't stand a chance. He never even saw the punch, just took it in the head and slapped forward, bouncing off the bar top. It was then that Susan noticed he'd laid out a little bowl of cocaine. She thought, Jesus, no phone call or note but he managed to remember that.

He shook his head clear, giving her a goofy smile. "Susan?"

"What the hell are you doing here, Hogie."

You could have pushed a knitting needle through his ear, it would have come out the other side as clean as it went in. He stood there and said, "I've been on TV. It was a contractual obligation, you know?" He nodded his head at a thin girl stood next to him. "She'll explain it. She's a researcher here."

The girl was staring at Susan, recognition clicking through. The only thing in Hogie's eyes was dizzyness.

Susan said, "You've got coke hanging out of your nose."

He wiped the residue away with the inside of his wrist and handed her a rolled tenner. She looked down at it. She might have slapped it out of his hand but she didn't. She elbowed the researcher and the comedian out of the way and picked up the whole saucer.

"So where's the rest?"

Hogie pulled his satchel off the floor and showed her the neat rows of plastic bags, all perched together on top, only one of them ripped open and spilling its white powder. She took them all, emptying the saucer into the open one as she transferred them to her handbag. The grains of cocaine that stuck to the edges of the saucer she wiped away with her finger and made a pass under her nose. Her eyes didn't water, she didn't even blink. When she looked up at Hogie, her final, nose-clearing, sniff came out as a snarl. "We're going."

Hogie nodded, Okay. He had a coat and a couple of carrier bags at his feet. He fumbled them together, saying: "Maybe I should say goodbye to the producer, you know, out of courtesy."

She didn't think so. She hurried him along by driving the edge of her handbag into his head and keeping it up all the way to the elevator lobby. Behind her, she could hear the researcher shouting, "I'm sure that's her. Susan Ball. The mother."

Then another woman's voice, much louder, screaming: "Get on the fucking phone, then. Get a crew after her."

The voices faded as the elevator doors slid closed. Just fourteen storeys to the mezzanine. Susan used the time constructively, letting the cold of the air conditioning drill through her until her spine was frozen rigid. Hogie just carried on swaying. He didn't even lose his stupid smile.

It was all-action in the lobby. Susan grabbed hold of Hogie's arm and steered him around the big wraparound desk. She tuned out the noise of the receptionists and the guards, even though they were pointing directly at her. Their mouths moving, saying It's Her, but the actual words lost in the blank fuzz of the TV screens that lined the entrance hall. Susan didn't pause. She dragged Hogie into the revolving doors and spun him inside. Outside lay the jacked-up piazza that overhung the Thames. They were almost there. But as the doors finished their revolution, the flash bulbs started popping.

She still had one hand on Hogie. She flung the other to her eyes. Shielded, she saw the pack of photographers scampering towards her. Most of them were shouting her name, some were trying variations: like *Suzie* . . . *Sue* . . . *Suzie Ball*. A voice to her left, louder than a megaphone, yelled *Piss Flaps*. She turned to see a huge fat man in mid-lumber, holding a camera to his eye. He got a perfect, full-on. expression: a look of shocked surprise soaking across her face. She glanced at Hogie, the surprise was there as well. She got a better grip of his arm, if she hadn't dragged him through the paparazzi dogs, he would have stayed rooted. She hissed, "Keep your fucking head down."

They ran ahead of the pack, down the ramp to where the car was waiting, lit by the sickly pearls of the street lamps. Hogie seemed only to recognise it as she pushed him into the passenger seat.

"Is this mine?"

Susan nodded, pointing towards the backseat, "Cheb gave me the keys."

Cheb stayed huddled to the corner, invisible until the interior light came on with the open door. As Susan pulled away from the kerb, he kept well back, out of range of the photographers that crowded to the windows. Even when she broke free of the scrum and pointed the car at a ramp leading up to the Bullring, he kept still. If anything he looked worse than when she picked him and the car up in Camden, worse than he had all day. His eyes were set into bulbs the colour of ripe eggplants, splitting at the centre. He had pricked his lips to reduce the swelling once he realised she could barely understand a word he said. Looking at him in the rear-view mirror, Susan could see the blood trickling at the corner of his mouth. But he was moving and that was a miracle. She'd asked him earlier, How are you coping? She soon found out; the boy had his pockets full of prescription drugs: assival and morphine and the syringes to go with them. Like he said, Drugs weren't just for fun. When she asked how he'd got them he'd told her Naz had seen him right: "He looks like a Paki gangster to you. When he goes into a chemists, he comes on like an Indian doctor."

Hogie was up on his knees, now, facing backwards in his seat so he could stare at Cheb. He choked when he first saw the state of him. All he could say when he found his voice was: "Oh fuck, fuck Cheb. Fuck."

Susan never once took her eyes off the road. She told Hogie to get down and do the same. He caught the edge in her voice and turned to drop into his seat and turned his eyes on her, all puppyish and pleading. Be Nice.

"I said, Look straight ahead."

He flinched away, fixing on the bridge and the city rising up beyond. "Don't even breathe."

Cheb rose up for the first time, looming out of the dark to club Hogie once across the head with the butt of a gun. Hogie slumped. With one hand on the recliner lever and the other fisting a wad of his long hair, Cheb dropped the seat and pulled Hogie out flat.

She asked, "Is the bastard unconscious?"

Cheb shook his head, "Not yet but he soon will be."

Susan turned and saw the outline of the hypodermic syringe. Cheb was holding it clamped between his teeth, like a dog with a bone. Keeping his hands free as he pinned Hogie's neck to the headrest with one arm and used the other to pull up the sleeve of his chef's smock and slap up a vein. She said, "Do you want me to slow down."

"Better not. Keep ahead of those reporters." Cheb had found his vein. Susan flinched, wishing she hadn't turned at just the moment the needle disappeared into Hogie's arm. As Cheb pushed on the plunger she heard him say, "Motherfucker."

"He really slept with your mother, too?"

"Yeah. And I don't think he even liked her very much."

"I'm sorry."

"I'm just jealous." He said it with a grin, turning his head so she caught it framed in her rear-view mirror. He was almost where he wanted to be, a true-life monster. His face all the colours of shadows: green, purple, black and blue. He had his knife in his hand now. She couldn't look in the mirror without seeing the glint of the blade, flashing in the dark as he got to work on Hogie's face.

She asked, "Did he tell her he would kill himself, too?"

Cheb had told her all about Hogie's career on the drive to the TV station, all the details of the tricks and blackmail he liked to use. She was just confirming the facts, she'd already passed sentence.

"Of course he did. Why, what did he tell you?"

Susan refocussed, staring deeper into the rear-view until Cheb disappeared and all she had were the headlights of the traffic behind her. She'd left the press pack stranded on the South Bank but now there was some kind of van on her tail. It had a weird aerial on its roof and she saw glimpses of it as she hit every turning through the city.

She said, "We'd better hurry and get him over to Frankie."

TWENTY-EIGHT

Frankie took another pull from his duty-free brandy. His boys were still talking, even tapping their feet to the music below. Judging from the herby smell and the fresh clouds of smoke, they were passing round another spliff. Frankie took a look at his watch and read the dial as four. He'd been planning to sleep and let the youngsters keep an eye out for trouble. The deafening fucking music below had kicked that idea toothless.

Looking out of the window again, he thought he saw something beyond the river. Night blind and brandy tight, he couldn't be sure. He narrowed his eyes and the blur resolved into a car—a late arrival for the rave below.

The car parked on the mainland and a couple began staggering towards the bridge. The pair had moved several yards before he realised they were holding someone between them, a slumped figure barely moving its feet.

He shouted his boys over, pointing as he said, "What they up to?"

Liam ambled across, looked and shrugged. "There's a geezer out there, he's out of his tree already. No way the cunt's getting past security."

The three of them slowed as they reached the crown of the bridge. The one on the dope seemed to be convulsing. His friends dragged him over to the side wall. Frankie got the running commentary off the boys: the guy was heaving up his guts. His pals were holding onto his arms and coma guy was doubled up, retching into the shadows below the parapet. Stranded there, the two helpers were lit up by the moon: one with reddish blonde hair, scattering moonlight; one of them bald, soaking up the light until his head was a chunk of moon rock.

Liam said, "You know what Frankie, I reckon it's your wife."

Frankie sloshed towards the window, staggering sideways and slamming hard against another window. Even with his face to the glass, he couldn't make out a thing. "You sure?"

"She's in every fucking newspaper."

The group were moving along now, out onto the cobble-stones of the island. Frankie said, "Who's she got with her? Is it Pakis?"

Sean was just behind him, saying, "I don't think so. I only see three of them."

The group kept moving, drawing closer to the side of the warehouse until they dropped out of sight. Frankie stood on tip toes, trying to look down as he shouted: "Where'd they go?"

Liam was rooting through a sports bag. When he came up he was holding an automatic rifle diagonal to his chest. He started running close to the windows, sometimes hopping as he tried to look straight down. "I see them." He tried to get into a sniper's position, hugging the wall.

Frankie lurched, the brandy swinging left-right in his stomach. "Gimme that bag."

Sean skimmed it over. Frankie tried to stop it with his foot but fumbled, moving too fucking slow. It slid right past him. If there was anything out there, he'd missed it. If he could ever have seen it.

Now Sean was shouting, "Here, what's that?"

A truck had stopped at the edge of the water. Dim shadows gathering in front of it, half-lit in the pool of its headlights. As a second truck came crawling towards them, the shadows resolved into a group of men and women. They broke their circle to give the second van room to pull alongside.

Frankie said, "Get me that fucking bag."

Sean had it held out for him, all ready, and Frankie

fumbled inside. He recognised the thick cylinder of the flare as his hand closed around it. "Open the window."

The windows were sealed. Liam came running back and hammered out a square pane with the butt of his rifle. Frankie popped the strip from the top of the flare and tossed it in an arc to the river below. The water lit up red, the tow path flickered as though a dim orange bulb was swinging over it.

"You see anything? Is it Pakis?"

Sean wasn't sure. The group had disappeared behind their trucks as the flare burst on them.

Liam said, "I think they scooted."

"They're taking cover you cunts." He swung a kick at the boy as he staggered for the bag again. This time he was going for a sawn-off. As always, it felt so right in his hand. Big but short, built for surgical thuggery.

He began filling his pockets with cartridges. Liam had popped another pane and was stood at a window with his rifle stuck through the hole, aiming down and ready to squeeze.

Frankie trotted towards him. "It's Pakis, innit? Am I right?"

"I'm not sure." The kid was freaking on him, you could hear it in his voice. Frankie accelerated to a run, as ready to slap his face as look outside.

The three of them were lined together at the window, trying to focus on the far side of the bridge, when the light came on. It was so powerful, coming from the water's edge, it threw them all into silhouette. Frankie turned, blinded, staring at the sharp outline of Liam standing next to him. He didn't know what was outside, he almost expected helicopters or tanks, even siege engines.

"Well, who the fuck do you think it is?"

Liam faltered, "I think . . . I think it's the television news."

There was a third TV van joining the two already in

position on the quay side. Another broadcast crew, setting up more banks of lights. When they threw the switches, they flared white, swaying on spindly stands. Every one of them aimed at the side of the warehouse. At their feet, camera crews and lone photographers were fanning out across the bridge.

Frankie said, "Who brings the fucking media to a gang war?"

Liam was screaming next to him, "This isn't a fucking photo op. We gotta get the fuck out of here."

"No." Frankie wasn't having any of it. "We stick it out."

Hogie staggered forward, flecks of vomit coating his face, nausea bucketting inside his chest. His brain never stopped spinning, picking up static as it turned. The lights kaleidoscoping off the water. The ticking of a million off-beat clocks. He blanked again.

His sight returned in blotches. First his feet, one boot zooming into focus and whiteing out, then the other. Trying to lift his head he caught lumpy chunks of melody, bite-size pieces that were heading straight for him until they shrieked and swerved. The sound of a needle dragged across its groove and bunny-hopping into another beat. There was never a moment's silence but Hogie could still feel an empty space growing in his head. He could feel it, his own brain a swollen lump of emptiness, spinning inside its jelly.

He was dud-boy, pushing at the edges of a huge soft crowd. The hands keeping him upright held him just feet from the swaying mass. Still-life dancers, caught in a strobe, appeared ahead of him, their bodies creating rippling wakes as they slid away again. He felt the heat tightening the skin across his skull. He felt the shared sweat fill the building with pearl beads and tasted the spray as the waves broke over him. And through it all, the music washing by, holding everything together in soft suspension. Until he hit another hole and started slip-sliding away. Another black spot to fall into.

He came round. He was lying face down on a concrete ramp. Two hands cupped either side of his face, lifting it gently as he lifted his own eyes. It was Cheb, crouching down to connect with him. Hogie focussed on the baldness of his head and the spiral of colours bouncing off it, turning the reds into UV slide-shows and the blues into warm-oil paisleys. Hogie tried to look further. Maybe he saw speaker stacks, dancer's podiums, a flying Sumo wrestler twenty feet tall. Susan Ball floating in a blush haze. But there was still a problem with his head. The hurt inside, the stinging on the outside.

Cheb's voice at his ear, "Don't say anything, you don't need to know anything."

"Cheb, is that you?"

He wasn't sure. Did it sound like Cheb? Did Cheb sound so crazed?

"Just keep quiet."

"What's happening, Cheb?"

"This is it. The grand sacrifice, the willing victim, the way out of this mess. So keep it shut."

Hogie tried again to lift his head. He saw, in Cheb's hand, a slim-jim knife blade, a glinty twinkle winking on its sharpened edge. Cheb touched the blade to Hogie's lips, stressing a *shush* sound. Then another head appeared on the scene, lowering itself slowly until it was almost cheek-to-cheek with the Cheb monster.

Hogie recognised the voice of George Carmichael, "My God Cheb, is that Hogie? What have you done to his face?"

TWENTY-NINE

Cheb said, "I customised him."

George crouched there, between Cheb's battered head and Hogie's raw melon, and said, "You shaved him?"

"Yeah. My own mother couldn't tell us apart."

It wasn't a very smooth shave: parts of Hogie's head shone, others carried a buff of blond fuzz, smaller sections were grazed red. But it was thorough enough, Hogie was bald from crown to chin, hair and beard both gone. Cheb leered down at his handiwork, still holding the knife he'd used to do it, the long shiv blade like a scalpel in his hands.

A blast of dry ice sprang up from under the barrier, sucked out of the huge steaming warehouse by the colder night air. Hogie seemed to smoulder at the edges, Cheb just smoked. When George Carmichael felt his eyes turn spongy, he stood up.

They were all here: Susan looking anxiously into the crackling blurr of dancers; Naz holding a walkie-talkie to his ear and trying to make sense of the static; Mannie, loose and flitty, flapping around in his A-line mac; and Cheb and Hogie; both bald, and both, in their different ways, practically senseless.

Cheb joined Naz at the barrier and asked for an up-date.

Naz put down his walkie-talkie and told him what he'd heard. "The bouncers are going mad. They've seen the TV crews and they're worried they'll appear on the breakfast news."

Cheb said, "So what are they doing? Running out?"

Naz nodded, Uh-huh. "So what now?"

"We split up. Two teams: you, Carmichael and Mannie; me, Hogie and her." He nodded to Susan who was now crouched over the unconscious Hogie.

George didn't understand anything. "Two teams? To do what? What the fuck is happening?"

Cheb said, "It's all over. You go and grab some glory with Naz, go hold the media at bay."

Susan was hauling on one of Hogie's arms, trying to drag him towards the barrier. Cheb took the other arm and between them they hauled him upright, rolled him over the barrier top and let him drop to the other side. As she swung a leg over to join him, George touched hold of Susan's shoulder. She shook him off with a grim face.

"Leave it, George. We're going up alone."

"Going where?"

Naz was on the move, heading back towards the main forecourt at the front of the warehouse. Before he disappeared, he called for Mannie and George to follow him.

Susan waved him away. "Go on, George. We can deal with Frankie." She and Cheb were fully over the barrier now, struggling to support Hogie's dead weight as they launched into the crowd.

"Deal with him how?"

"By making sacrifices. It's over George, you go on."

It was the last thing she said. The last thing he heard before the crowd swallowed her. Then George was left there, between the waterfront and a sea of dancers. He shrugged and turned, loping down the ramp until he picked up speed. Mannie was ahead of him, already at the corner of the warehouse. George followed him, pounding down onto the cobbles, all the time wondering why? Why the blazes? Why the blaze of light? And as he rounded the edge of the warehouse, he saw Naz in triumphant silhouette. Standing there, swaying in his great coat.

Naz dominated the forecourt. The whole yard was lit up like a stage, the light coming low over the river to throw shadows at his back. Behind him, the last of the security team were running for the far side of the island. Ahead of him, the cameramen were shouldering heavy-duty video cams across the bridge while strings of mike dykes followed on, pointing their equipment like hairy bazookas. All they could see of him was a lone gunslinger, made gigantic by his own shadow. Naz took a few giant zigzagging steps, partly to feel the way his overcoat swung, unbuttoned. Partly to get the mood right in his own mind.

He had already decided he was going to use a Smith & Wesson, a combat magnum with a barrel over eight inches long. He thought it was a joke gun when he first saw it, among the crop he took from the Comecon. But it suited this scene. He would have liked to wear it at the side, so he could thumb back his coat and quickdraw. But he didn't have a holster so it had to go at the front, nestled above his belt buckle. The cameramen were within fifty yards now, almost close enough for him to appear in focus but still a looming shadow.

It was one of those moments. Naz began striding towards the lights and the action. He kept his steps long-legged, slow. He felt his coat lift in the breeze, swinging from the vents like synchronised tails. The TV cameras had him in their sights, the press photographers were sparking around them. Naz shook his trigger hand out to relax it, brought it up to rest lightly on the butt of the magnum. Then drew. His hand out straight, the pistol so steady it pointed like the finger of judgement.

The news crews began ducking, weaving. The press cameramen hit the floor. One of them launched off the bridge and slapped down into the water.

Naz lifted the gun two degrees, the barrel sight aimed dead at one of the light stands. His first shot hit the exact bulb he aimed for. It was all so smooth, the gun was a marksman pistol with virtually no recoil. Naz had underestimated it. He saw now, it was a suave piece: guaranteed winner gat-of-the-month award. He adjusted and fired at another stand, taking out the centre bulb in a battery of nine. When he levelled off the gun and pointed to the crews, they began to get the idea he could hit them whenever he chose and started rising off the cobbles to pull a rapid retreat. As long as they stayed on the far side of the bridge, off his island kingdom, they could film all they wanted. He imagined how he must look, framed against the bleak brick of the mills, rising high above the water: the easterner, Clint Asia. He shot out another bulb, just out of devilry, then threw some poses out into the hail of flashes: the gun crossed at his chest; then hanging loose from his dangling hand; then pointing to the moon above him as dust rose off the cobbles.

Looking out from his window, high above the scene, Frankie said, "What the fuck's that about?"

He turned to Liam. The boy's mouth was open, his head shaking. He didn't know either. If he had a best guess, he didn't come out with it. The elavator had begun screeching, hauling its cage from the warehouse below, and the sound sent him sprinting from the window to take an offensive position. As the elevator juddered into place, he was right in front of its steel doors. His assault rifle was shouldered and aimed, he was ready for the opening attack.

Frankie nodded his approval as he sneered his way over. He carried his shotgun crooked open in his arms with the cartridges suckered in their holes. A few paces from the elevator, he snapped it shut and took his position next to Liam. The two of them armed and dangerous, the first thing anyone would see as they stepped out of the elevator. Frankie had to say, he liked the set-up.

He called for Sean and pointed him at the doors. "Go open it, we got you covered, son."

Sean walked over to the heavy outer door, grabbed the handle and started hauling it back. The light inside the cage threw out a beam that grew fatter and fatter with every inch, making a path of light for Liam and Frankie as they stood shoulder to shoulder, guns facing the elevator like a two-man firing squad.

Frankie looked at Liam, noting the concentration in the boy's eyes as he held his rifle steady on the widening gap. He wondered whether to say something, a neat epithet, but he couldn't think of anything so just swung his shotgun to the side, tight into the boy's ribs, pulled the trigger and sent the boy into a bloody sprawl.

Sean looked up, a glimmer of shock as he saw his partner jerk sideways. Then Frankie swung the barrel onto him and blasted him where he stood.

Cheb and Susan heard the shots from inside the elevator, but saw nothing. The outer door was only a quarter open. They stood and looked at each other and because they heard nothing else, Susan nodded at the door.

"You'd better open it?"

Cheb nodded. When he let go of Hogie's arm he expected him to stagger, if not fall. But Hogie only sagged slightly and stayed upright.

Cheb pulled back the inner cage door and got ready to haul on the outer one. The morphine was still holding him together but he felt the weight of the heavy door. Maybe the strain would be too much, he'd just void his bowels and lose his cool and his togetherness in one.

He was convinced he knew how the scene would play. It was a teaser: the sliding door would uncover Hogie first and then Susan. As he stepped out of the shadow of the door, he would form the last of the trio. And Frankie would stand there, confused, staring at Susan as she stood perfectly framed between twin bald heads.

Frank grinned. Looked up at the tall guy and down to the dwarf and said, "Fuck me, two baldies."

He was calm, standing with his legs slightly apart and his

shotgun open, carefully plugging the smoking chambers with two new cartridges.

Susan made the first move, stepping out of the cage as she said, "I think we should talk."

He nodded, maybe they should. He wasn't hostile, just guarded.

She told him, "I've got most of the cocaine that went missing."

She took another step forward, holding her handbag open for her husband to see. Four bags of cocaine, still heat-sealed in polythene covered bricks and nearly all of them pristine. The seriously depleted bag was now bandaged with sellotape.

Frankie twitched a little smile. "I want you back."

She said, "I know. It's been a mess." She looked at the bodies sprawled on the floor, the fuckers who'd tortured Callum to death. Frankie had evened the score there.

She said, "I brought the boy I've been sleeping with."

"You brought this Hogie geezer?"

She nodded. Frankie snapped his shotgun up but held it loosely. He had one hand on the shortened barrel, the other on the stock and trigger but he wasn't aiming. "So where is he?"

Cheb walked forward. When he was thirty inches from the barrel-end he said, "I am Hogie."

Frankie stared down at him, "You?" Back to Susan, "Him?"

Susan nodded.

"The sick fuck who killed Cardiff?"

She shrugged, "I've got strange taste."

Frankie took a short pace forward, his shotgun no more than two inches from the boy. All but chest to chest with the baldie dwarf as he looked him over. He didn't believe it. His eyes wandered up, over to Hogie and then, slowly, all the way back down to Cheb.

"Cardiff described the geezer. He said he had blonde hair,

something like Callum." He locked his eyes onto Cheb's. "Why'd you shave it off?"

Cheb said, "She liked the feel of the skin between her legs."

"No way. I don't fucking believe this."

Cheb yelled, "I am Hogie and I claim my destiny."

Frankie's finger never left the trigger. As he squeezed, Cheb's hand flashed upwards. As the first bullet thumped into him, he had the shiv blade hooked deep behind Frankie's chest bone. He pushed again before the second bullet pounded him and he lost his grip. Frankie hardly seemed to notice. He stepped backwards as Cheb buckled and fell forwards. The only sign Frankie had been stabbed was the blue plastic tip of the shiv, poking half an inch out of his shirt. When the blood began trickling out, it was only a speck against the material.

All the while, he was staring at Hogie who had staggered forward a pace and was now trying to open his mouth. Slowly, dopily, the words came out: "No. I am Hogie."

Frankie lifted an eyebrow, just a slight query. He seemed more distracted than anything. He let his gun swing, one-handed, to his side and rubbed his stomach with the other. He looked almost thoughtful as he stroked his hand upwards until his fingertips settled on the exposed blue stub of the shiv. He twisted it between his thumb and forefinger, as though it were another nipple sent to puzzle him. But even as Susan looked for a sign that he understood what was happening, the beetroot red of his face, the Spanish sun and the damage of high blood pressure, drained away. He was dying.

He dropped the shotgun and sank to his knees. Susan turned around and took Hogie's hands; he was wobbling, too.

"What's happened?"

She told him, "It was Cheb's idea."

When Cheb explained it to her, he had talked about the sun, about the Incas and Aztecs and blood and death and other things. But mostly, he ranted about sacrifice. He was an Olympic psychotic but he had a plan and wouldn't do a thing unless she agreed to go through with it: right up to the moment of sacrifice when he would die with Hogie's sins on his mind.

She said, "Don't worry. He had a rational explanation."

She couldn't put it into words but she knew she understood. She had already sacrificed so much. Her son was dead and forgotten and, now, so was her husband. And all she had to show for it was Hogie. Who wasn't worth a damn but was the reason she had gone through with it and was the only thing she wanted. So there was another sacrifice.

It was understandable that she had wanted him to suffer a little first. And, whether he realised it or not, at the last moment he had been willing to die for her.

THIRTY

Travelling first class inter-city to Manchester, a man had room to spread. Naz had taken up the whole of the table with his newspapers. He skidded one of the large-sized Sundays round one-eighty degrees so Mannie could look at the photograph.

Mannie said, "I've seen it." He'd even read the copy inside.

"Yeah, but what do you think?"

He looked it over again, a shot of Naz in a telephoto blur, straddling his own shadow with his legs spread like he was getting it every night. If you looked carefully, you could even see two figures running around in the background; headless chickens, one with grey hair wearing a crombie overcoat, the other wearing his sister's mac.

Naz tapped it, confidentially. "That's the one."

But he was on the front of every other paper too so he had plenty to choose from if he changed his mind.

The pictures of Naz had thrown the whole story off-centre. Mannie hadn't yet read one report that made sense of the whole massacre, or the deaths before it. It had been easier to hype Naz's image than to dig for the truth.

Naz didn't agree. They'd argued about it for the best part of two hundred miles until Naz finally said, "Look, I know it don't mean shit to you. You lost your whole family and that's it. But getting my photo up there, it puts me on the same level as Jools. And that makes me feel better every time I remember the way I felt about her."

So it wasn't just an overnight, mismatched thrill. Told right, it stood as an epic of love. And there were quite a few of them, just waiting to be told.